Note to Self

by

Andrew Milner

Note to Self
©Copyright 2018 Andrew Milner
(Republished 2020)

ISBN: 9781986146210

This is a work of fiction. Names, characters, places and incidents are used fictitiously and any resemblance to persons living or dead, business establishments, events, locations or areas, is entirely coincidental.

© All rights reserved, including the right to reproduce this book, or portions thereof in any form. No part of this text may be reproduced, transmitted, downloaded, decompiled, reverse engineered or stored in any form or introduced into any information storage and retrieval system, in any form or by any means, whether electronic or mechanical without the express written permissions of the author.

Published by: **www.andrewmilnerbooks.com**
All rights reserved.
ISBN:

ANDREW MILNER BOOKS

Chapter One

When I see the films where the boy gets the girl, it makes me sick. Is that really how life works? I know there are obviously some happy endings but life sucks really, most of the time and for most people. I was the product of a long happy marriage, my parents were married for sixty years, can you believe that, bloody sixty years? 'It was different in our day' they'd say, but in all those years I never heard them argue. They always seemed happy and right up until the day my dad died, they held hands and told each other 'I love you' every day. Bless them both. I think Mum is really struggling to cope since my dad died, you must do if you've been together all that time; almost everything they did was centered on the other.

Both my grandmas were friends and were in hospital at the same time as there was only a day between the births. Mum and Dad grew up together on the same street, went to the same schools and even worked together at the same company. Right from the minute they were born they were together and destined to spend the rest of their lives as one. When Dad retired in 1998 he played a lot of golf and Mum would walk round the golf course while he played and although she never liked the sport she just loved being with him. I think the term soul mates was invented for them. At parties they sat together, if Dad went off to talk to someone the first thing he would do would be to bring Mum in on the conversation or introduce her to people and she would do the same to him. He would drop her off at the WI meetings and pick her up afterwards and would pop in and say hello to all the other ladies. None of the other husbands were like that. My dad was a true gentleman right up until the second he died. When he got poorly and I went to visit him in hospital, all he was bothered about was that I would take care of Mum. 'Make sure she's looked after; ring her every day and take her shopping, you know she doesn't like being on her own.' I should have written everything down as I can't remember half of what he said I had to do but I'm sure as long as I look after her he'll be okay with that. I'm sure Mum will tell me if there is anything she wants, she's not lost the plot yet and has a better memory than me sometimes, I think every so often she just feels lost, yet other times she seems really independent. It's only been a year and two months since he died so it's all still new and still raw.

I went round last week and she was sat in the quiet crying, no TV on, no radio on just sat staring at the picture of them both above the fireplace. Real nice picture it is. My ex took it at their golden anniversary party and we had it framed for their joint seventieth birthdays. I don't suppose it helps when it's there looking at her every time she's in the room but it means so much to her and it is a lovely picture. They're sat side by side with Dad on the right as you look at it wearing his favourite black suit and Mum wearing a lovely red suit top with the gold earrings that he bought her for their anniversary. She has a diamond necklace to go with it now after last year's anniversary made all the more poignant because he died not long after. He was a lovely man and loved her to bits although on the odd occasion when he did get frustrated with her he would retreat to his shed and hammer some wood. I think it's real sweet to see old couples still holding hands after all those years but with Mum and Dad it wasn't to steady themselves, it was love. Good old fashioned love. They don't make it like that anymore, not for me anyway. I suppose I loved my ex in the beginning but the last five years were just one big plod on.

Mum and Dad got married on Valentine's Day in 1953. My dad said life was hard but happy as the country was still recovering from the war but the feeling of togetherness was still the essence of the community. Everyone knew everyone else and you could leave your doors unlocked. Mum still says that now. 'In my day we didn't have to lock things and everyone is getting VD now.' She makes me laugh because the connection between crime and VD isn't that obvious for me, she quite clearly means CCTV. I remember Dad saying that they had sweets at the reception at the church hall because sweet rationing had finished the week before and both of my granddads clubbed together to buy every guest a toffee apple and a stick of liquorice. Can you imagine going for eight years from the end of the war without proper access to sweets? I'm not sure I'd survive without jelly beans. I wonder if narcotics anonymous will help me with my jelly bean addiction 'cos I can easily do two packets in a day. Have you the seen the amount of calories? Eight hundred calories for a standard packet of jelly beans, no wonder the husband left me, it's because I'm fat. I should have seen it coming though. The warning signs were all there telling me the blinking obvious, but I chose to ignore it. I just bought a bigger size when my clothes were too tight. I think I was more upset about having to buy bigger sizes than I was when he left. A man can be replaced but my lovely nice flat tummy figure can't. Well, I say a man can be replaced, a chance would be a fine thing at the moment, I wouldn't be that fussy but nothing is happening on that front, I think if the chance came by I wouldn't know what to do and secondly I'd be scared in case it's healed up. I have to say that I couldn't imagine ever having sex again. It's a while since I was last physical with him and I think then it was more an accident than intended. I wonder if people can do things like that in their sleep. I mean it's one thing to sleep walk but to have sleep sex is another. I can't say I enjoyed it whether he knew about it or not, it didn't leave me feeling like the earth had moved – put it that way. And when I say nice flat tummy figure I use the flat word fairly loosely. It's not too bad but maybe not actually flat.

I love looking at the wedding picture of Mum and Dad and I love black and white photographs too. I think it was 'the knob' that got me interested in photography so these days I try not to appreciate it as it validates his completely pointless presence in my life. I did rip hundreds of his prize possession photos up when he left though; I knew it would be better than ripping up his clothes. His clothes were only fit for ripping up anyway, even a charity shop would have looked at me with a 'what the hell' expression, in fact I'd have been too embarrassed to take them in. I would have had to wait until midnight and then dress completely in black before going to the charity shop for fear that I would be recognised or that my number plate would have been picked up on CCTV. Newspaper headline – 'Frenzy as fat frump leaves antique fashion at charity shop'. The outfits on Mum and Dad's wedding picture were much more stylish than his clothes and they're from the fifties. Mum wore a white V neck dress and a huge white silk flower in her hair on the left side and Dad wore his RAF uniform as he had just finished his national service. You can't tell on the photo but Mum's bouquet was pink and white orchids mixed with gardenias. She still loves orchids now. 'I've got a lot of memories to take with me,' she says. Sometimes I come to see her and she just sits at the window looking into the garden. She says when it's sunny she can see my dad out doing the garden and she watches him as he pulls weeds and prunes things and then he looks back and sees her and waves to her. She waves back. I think it's lovely that her memories of him are so strong that she can literally see him. Oh god, I'm off again, I try not to cry but I think I cry not only 'cos I miss my dad so much but I think it's more that I cry because I want to feel how she feels. I did love the knob in the beginning I know I did, but it seems a lifetime away that I can remember feeling anything for him other than the hate and anger that I feel now. I suppose if he was still here I would be content and just plod my way through life as is expected.

I married him and just thought that was it. You don't expect to be approaching fifty feeling like this. I'm not suggesting all my friends are happily married by any stretch of the imagination but you reach the point where your life is just plain old comfortable and you get on with it. I didn't miss him when he was at work, I didn't ring him at lunchtime to say I loved him and I didn't plan my life around him. Well, you don't do you? You don't plan your weekends and days off together, you just do your own thing but on a night you sit down and watch TV together and wake up next to that familiar feeling every morning. That's what I miss, the routine, the familiarity and even the contempt at times. I say that, but we never did agree much on the telly choice either really, I like my soaps, which he doesn't, although he watches them and will ask, 'who's he married to, who they talking about, is that the one who was in the shop earlier?' and then when I say 'I thought you didn't like soaps,' he'd say he was just being polite and taking an interest. Taking an interest, cheeky sod, he didn't want me to take an interest when he was fraternising with Lucy Loose-lips. And then there's the rubbish that he watches, he calls them documentaries but the world's biggest boobs isn't a documentary in my opinion. I've always thought my boobs were pretty ample and for my age they look fine, but her boobs blasted mine into oblivion. Bloody documentary my arse, it's a freak show. I think the only thing we ever agreed on was *You've been Framed*, and as I look back I can only imagine that was because he used to love laughing at other people's misfortune but if you ever laughed at him he'd kick off. If he ever hit his finger with the hammer it was like the end of the world and if you so much as dared to crack a smile in the effort to keep the laugh locked away he'd see red. There was this one time when he was putting up a four-hook coat hanger in the downstairs toilet and with all relatively new houses the walls are paper thin. He spent ages measuring it up, distance from the ceiling and distance from the floor, distance from one side and distance from the other side. He put the pencil marks on the wall and double checked the measurements again, and then put the rawlplugs in. He tightened the coat hanger to the wall, put the coats on it then stood back and admired his work. Within five minutes the bang ruined his pat on the back cup of tea and when he opened the toilet door the coats on the floor gave him the indication that something had gone wrong. He was left with these two tennis ball sized holes in the wall where the hanger had ripped itself away from the wall. He went ballistic and ended up hitting the wall with his hand causing a further hole, then started ranting in the kitchen about the shit quality of the house, which I'd like to point out was his choice, and then whilst still involved in a swearing rant he knocked the hammer off the side of the table that he hadn't put away despite a request from me to do so which had been clearly ignored, as per usual, which then dropped onto his foot. I thought he was going to punch me because all I could see through the tears of laughter was a red faced snorting pile of anger. Got to be one of the highlights, that. Consequently, I have two patches of poorly filled holes in the downstairs toilet which he said he would sort out, although the coats on the hanger which was properly fitted by a proper workman hides them as this one has stayed on the wall, and a crack in the floor tile in the kitchen.

Note to self – Get the job done properly first time round. Further note to self –Don't expect a knob to do a good job.

Chapter Two

I felt a spring in my step not experienced for many years because of the newly arrived sunshine. Confidence in abundant measures swept over me that morning as I pushed the quilt off with my legs and flung myself head first into the day. Stepping over the quilt on the floor, I pulled back the blind and peered out into the garden and because the sun was shining the garden looked nice. I could hear the birds chirping away and the gentle hum of summer quietly floating by. It seemed much later than the 08:00 displayed in red square digital numbers on my bedside clock, and knowing that time was on my side made it a more enjoyable waking up experience. It was a complete contrast to the frantic minutes to spare routine of normal days and I have to say I much preferred it this way.

Note to self – I must get up earlier more often.

As the flow from the shower head covered me in warm water I rid myself completely of the summer night time sweat and I felt clean, even the nooks and crannies were cleaned out. My whole body felt alive as I turned the shower off and stepped naked from the cubicle onto the newly bought soft and fluffy bath mat. I hadn't intended to buy a new bath and toilet mat but Marks and Spencer had a sale on and any girl knows that a sign saying 'sale' means that you just have to buy something, anything; wanting it is just a bonus. So there I am laden with matching mats, two new towels and one of those containers for your toothbrush. Quite why I would buy a container for one solitary toothbrush is completely beyond me and I refer only to my previous statement about the sign that changes from 'sale' to 'buy me' right in front of any good pair of female eyes. The kitchen scales, new hand whisk and the small green frying pan that I got from Lakeland are a little bit more needed than wanted but I suppose I could have lived without them. Tossing the old ones into the bin I couldn't help but think that they had a bit more life in them yet.

I threw myself backwards onto the bed not quite dry but safe in the knowledge that the quilt, which was hurriedly thrown back onto the bed, would pick up any excess water from my back. I caught sight of myself in the mirror on the dresser and although not tilted towards the bed for any reason, I thought that I actually looked okay. Maybe it's because I can't see my tummy properly as I'm lying flat but my boobs haven't disappeared under my arm pits just yet which is always a bonus. I know on my sixtieth they will. I'll be able to make them touch each other round the back but I suppose by then I won't really care, no-one will see them. Actually no-one sees them now which is annoying because I have quite nice breasts. I suppose I might as well do my not-so-regular lump check on them seeing as I'm lying here naked. Palm of hand on the side I think it was, and roll it around to cover the entire breast. It feels kinda weird doing this. If Patrick next door could see me now he'd have a heart attack. I thought he'd died last summer when he caught sight of me in the garden topless. Well, I say topless it was more open dressing gown instead of topless, not that I realised or indeed intended it but he got a right eye full. I was mortified but looking back it was quite amusing. He tried so hard not to look but gave up and had a right good old stare at them. Mind you, it was nice that a man took an interest in them, 'cos the knob didn't. I could walk naked through a bedroom and he wouldn't even notice. Too busy thinking of Lucy Loose-pants I think. I mean, what's she got that I haven't except a size ten figure, long blonde hair, nipples as big as my doorbell, legs up to her arse and a pout that would make any trout jealous, and I should know I've seen the pictures!

As if she really fancies him. God knows why she's with him, it certainly isn't for his money, charm, personality, looks or a big you know what, he hasn't got any of those and I can't see any woman finding him attractive, but good luck to her. I think I feel more sorry for her 'cos she will realise what a mistake she's made and he will end up looking like a right timmy all on his own after she dumps him. Then he will realise that he made a mistake. His mistake was obviously leaving me. Who else would put up with him picking his teeth and eating the bit of food from his finger, and who else would put up with him picking his nose and rolling it around in his fingers before launching it across the room, and I'm damn sure that he doesn't fart under the duvet when he's in bed with her. I mean, she's young and pretty and I can't imagine what she thinks when he's sprawled out on the bed in his horrible white Y-front pants that look like a nappy. I'd love to know what goes through her head when she sees it 'cos she can't think phwoar! It's making me sick thinking about it. I mean Brad Pitt can sprawl around wearing whatever he wants letting his bits hang out but he can pull it off, or better still, I can pull him off. He's so fit. If I thought for a second that she really fancied him I'd probably feel better about it but I think he chucked away our marriage 'cos his head gets turned too easy. He's always been the same but I never thought for a second he would do it. Can't blame him I suppose, he's a bloke, they all think with their bits and it's the only thing about him that's small enough to represent the size of his brain. I can see her looking fabulous in her silky undies and bra, 'cos he likes silk, I know that 'cos he always asked me to wear silk knickers for him, and there he is laying on the bed with his things hanging out the side of his pants, she must wonder what she's doing. I'm not against sex and sometimes I quite liked it but when you've got an overweight pig grunting down your ear it's a bit of a turn off. I can hear him saying it now, the same thing he said every week.

"You never want to do it anymore."

I remember one time I said to him. "Look in the mirror and you'll know why." He was like a spoilt child, he went on a diet and started running which lasted about three days, then he stopped 'cos he was sick one night after having a lager and a kebab for tea before going running. Of course I exaggerate how bad he was, he wasn't really that bad, not all of the time anyway.

I am getting used to living on my own, I love having the bed to myself, I never really did like sleeping with him that much and sometimes I would wait for him to go to sleep and go into the spare room. When he asked me in the morning why I was in there I would come up with some cock and bull story about not feeling well, or his snoring woke me up or Jasper, that's the dog, wouldn't settle but all reasons were because me being the caring wife, I didn't want to disturb him. That would mostly happen on a weekend because we both had work through the week but I would know on a weekend he would wake up feeling frisky. Two things that he would do regularly. He would either just try his luck and just start groping me thinking I would feel the same way or cuddle into me with his 'thingy' out. Either way, a big turn off for me. And even when I did relent and think 'oh go on then' the morning breath would kill it stone dead for me, he'd never think to go clean his teeth. Then he'd get upset 'cos I didn't want to kiss him. I have to say although lonely, it is much nicer on my own.

We did actually get on and he wasn't all bad I suppose. I mean before he started sleeping with luscious Lucy things were okay and I wasn't always frigid. I think it's the same in most relationships to be honest where the bloke is always up for a bit of sex and the lady is just too busy or too tired. We girls use sex to our advantage and know what to do to play him like a fiddle. We can get him to do most things with just a promise of sex. I remember once him begging me for sex for about three weeks and I just didn't want to do it and he got really insecure and nasty about it. 'You don't love me anymore,' and 'I'll find someone who will do it,' although at the time I didn't believe the latter, more fool me. Note to self – don't always disbelieve. Anyway, one night I fancied it and to try and prove a point he said no. Calm as you like I walked away, got undressed and put my nightie on. I went back down walked in the room provocatively making it obvious I didn't have anything on underneath. Within three minutes he was like a panting dog at my side. They're so easy to control and manipulate. I bet she doesn't have to do anything to manipulate him, he'll be doing his panting dog routine all too readily for her. Bit false for my liking but when your judgement is clouded by a slightly late mid-life crisis… but I can see why his head was turned. When I went through his phone and found THOSE pictures I just knew. That's how I know her nipples are big enough to hang a coat on. Beautiful round areola, gorgeous natural boobs but the most perfectly large, sticky out, calculated nipples. I zoomed in on one of the pictures 'cos I was strangely curious to know if the erect look was manufactured, as in she'd played with them to get them like that for the benefit of the picture or if it was just their normal look. I never really thought much about my boobs until that picture made me self conscious about my body, but I'm okay now because through my jealous insecurity I studied every inch of my body. Apart from a flabby tummy which most women my age and many a lot younger have, except Lucy Lovejoy, and a bit of cellulite on my thighs which most women my age and many a lot younger have, except yeh you guessed it, HER! I don't think I look too bad. A few wrinkles on my forehead, a few on my boobs and some on my tummy aren't too bad for someone still in their late forties, well, very late forties in actual fact, but still forties all the same. I'm not sure how I feel about the big five-o, but I don't suppose I can do a lot about it. I certainly won't be embracing it like Madonna did prancing around in lyrca sex clothes but neither will it spare me.

Chapter Three

As I have already said, and although denial doesn't blot it out, I am approaching fifty. I will have been living and breathing this God forsaken air on this planet for fifty years. Fifty bloody years! And what do I have to show for it? Nothing. Well I say nothing; I have more than most so I don't want to sound ungrateful. I'm pretty fit, health wise, although Patrick next door would take the other meaning of me being fit, I have my beautiful amazing daughter, I still have my mum and I have some good friends and some not so good – sorry Sally, but calling me Emmy just doesn't make the grade as far as I'm concerned. I think I look okay for my age, my hair is in good nick, my teeth and boobs are my own and I have not had a fight with gravity as I have let things go south if they so wished. I like my eyes as green is my favourite colour, and I think I look fine without make-up if I decide not to wear any. But the other day I went to Morrison's and not for the first time in my life – although certainly the first time in Morrison's – I felt underdressed. There were girls in there, I say girls, I'm talking about twenty-year-olds who had enough slap on to make-up a whole modelling agency. It was plastered on, proper thick it was. Perhaps they got a plasterer who was skimming the walls in houses down their street to trowel it on for them. I could have licked my finger and written my name on their foreheads. Some of them looked like they'd been Tango'd they were so orange. And what's this thing about plucking eye brows and drawing them back on? If you want eye brows don't bloody pluck them. Don't even get me started on the clothes. One girl wore a white blouse with a black bra underneath but her cleavage was pushed up through the gap of the blouse which was unbuttoned to her belly button. She'd completed this ensemble with a grey blue denim skirt that looked more like a belt and these black leather boots. Her hair was long, blonde curly and draped over her shoulders. This poor old bloke walked into a display table full of packets of donuts which were promptly dispatched all over the floor. His eyes just about rolled on the floor with the donuts. She just walked off with her neat arse wiggling as though she hadn't noticed the pandemonium that she had just caused. All the blokes stared apart from the ones who were with their wives, but even they pretended to stop to look at something on the shelf when in reality they were checking her out. I honestly didn't know whether to be disgusted or jealous. I'm not sure how I would have looked in a short, no, extra short denim skirt and a top which would only cover my boobs if I buttoned it up. I would never put on make-up to go to the shops as I don't see the point, maybe if I go out on a night and get dressed up then yes, but not to go to Morrison's, no offence to Mr. Morrison intended.

Later at work, the image came back to me of the girl who wore far too much make-up, but the way she dressed with such confidence wouldn't leave my mind. Note to self – Try new things. I started to browse shopping sites and by the end of my shift had clocked up a 'try to forget about quickly' total of £225. I knew that I could always send them back so didn't feel at all bad about it although shopping in work time is not the best use of my time at work when my things to do tray had to be moved as it was blocking my view to the computer. I did wonder though which shops Lucy Loose-draws would go to. I had a vision of the knob coming round one night and I answer the door dressed in beautiful silky knickers and bra that she would buy to wear for him, and then I watch as his eyes follow my lovely flat tummy down to the forbidden fruit where he knows he wants to go but I won't let him. Okay, I threw the flat tummy part in for effect, but to see his face would make my revenge all the sweeter. In fact I haven't ever thought of revenge until now. Not sure I can really be bothered by it as my life is much better off without him, why would I want him to realise what he's lost 'cos he might want to come back, and that ain't ever gonna happen.

So, that night I was late home from work as I called in to see if Kirsty the beautician, who works and owns Kirsty's on Trafalgar Place, had a spare appointment and also because she did and I filled it. My nails are now pink with black shapes and designs apart from my thumbs which are black with pink shapes and designs. They look fantastic, or did until I got in the car and chipped one of them on the gear stick. But the thing that I find hard to accept is that I have now become a victim of plucked eye brows. I say plucked, Kirsty says shaped but either way the tweezers removed some of my eye brows which in my opinion is plucking. She said I could highlight the shape with the brow pencil that matches my hair and she just happened to have one on sale. And that 'sale' word again made the item jump into my bag. She knows me so well and we've only just met. Anyway I walked out of her shop with new nails, new eye brows and a professionally applied face, not to mention the brow pencil on sale. It wasn't until I came out of Kirsty's that I started taking more of an interest in people and what they were wearing. I say people, I actually mean women, girls, ladies and some of the models out on the street like the ones I had seen in Morrison's, and which was my reason for being at Kirsty's in the first place. I wonder if they know the girl in Morrison's from the other day 'cos it looks like some of them went to the same fashion school and the same beautician, although I suddenly realise how attractive they look rather than trashy and trampy. Yes, some have way too much make-up on but some have just got the balance right. I noticed a couple of men walked past me and smile. My first thought was that I have something stuck on my face. I only had a complimentary cup of tea at Kirsty's so it can't be anything that I've eaten and forgotten to put in my mouth with the rest of it. I could feel myself becoming really self conscious not helped by the fact that more men smiled at me. I haven't gone red in years, well not since the piece of toilet paper in the back of my cozzie in Majorca but although that was some years ago the embarrassment still shows its ugly head now and again.

I caught sight of myself in Greggs window and actually thought that I looked good and maybe it was that fact alone that made men smile at me, typically I look for the negative. Note to self – Think positive. I did think positive once after seeing the pictures on his phone, I quite positively thought that I'd be able to ram the whole phone up his arse but opted for throwing it against the wall instead. The sight of his arms flapping around, jumping up and down and telling ME that I was being unreasonable still makes me want to hit the bastard. ME, unreasonable after seeing the naked body of a girl half my age (nearly) on my husband's phone, I'd love to show him what unreasonable is but ramming the phone up his arse still doesn't come into the unreasonable category in my opinion.

On arriving home the absence of the neighbour in his garden made me slightly wish he had been there. I don't fancy Patrick at all, not remotely my type and definitely over the upper age limit of 58 that I have now set for myself as I have had to start thinking what sort of man I would go out with. I know that Patrick would give me another ego boost about how good I feel after the one received today and the one that I have given myself. All those years that I went through both marriage and childbirth never really giving much thought for how I looked now seemed like a world away and at nearly fifty I have started to feel inadequate amongst other women. I'm not entirely sure though that during childbirth even the most vain woman could be bothered with doing her hair and make-up and false eye lashes as it contrasts completely with the sight of lying there with legs akimbo grunting like a pig and showing off your glory to any young doctor who happens to be walking through at that time. Midwife would be a good job for the knob looking at semi-naked women all day, mind you I bet half of the women going in to give birth wouldn't be that nice, and even the fit ones don't look so good covered in blood and placentas. Even the knob has standards and I'm not sure Lucy Lickylips would look great in a position of childbirth and I would love to see how the girl in Morrison's would cope with broken waters and baby poo.

I can remember arriving at hospital after my waters broke and being shown into the delivery suite which looked as nice as you would expect for a torture chamber where you know the worst pain you'll ever experience in your life is awaiting you. I put my bag down and the knob went off to find a drinks machine which was probably his way of going off to eye up the nurses as when he came back he said he'd been talking to a lovely nurse. I thought he meant nice person when in reality he obviously meant nice looking. I found some blood on the floor under the bed, not a lot but splatters so I told the midwife when she came to check on me and she said they hadn't used that room for years. Marvellous, I thought, not only am I in a torture chamber, it's a bloody old fashioned torture chamber too. What a lucky girl I am.

I wonder how many numbers he came back with after his trip to the drinks machine. Thinking back I don't remember him returning with a drink, however maybe I am being unfair as I wasn't in a fit state to check. I remember saying that the baby was nearing its third birthday he'd been gone that long. He said he got lost looking for the machine in his usual monotone lying cheating dirty git kind of way. Anyway, I don't want to talk about him at the moment because I am about to peel potatoes with a very sharp knife and it may be too tempting to go round to hers and peel him in half. I will however refrain and count to 10, and if that doesn't work I'll keep counting. I wonder how far I will get if I count until I am completely calm. They probably haven't even invented a number that high yet. I will do my best and stay calm because the last time I made sausage and mash for my tea I could see his face in my mash and his manhood was the sausage. I realised I was being too generous so to be more lifelike I cut the sausage in half.

Pushing the food around my plate I actually wonder if I'm looking for some sort of sign, I can't see his face and try as I might to place peas into the mash it just isn't happening and as I stare at the sausage I actually wish it was his thingy although I'm not entirely sure now that I've calmed down a bit if I would touch it or stab it. I opt for the latter only because it has been places that I really don't even want to know about like Lucy Loose-labia. Scraping the wasted food into the bin I realise two things, firstly my new look has not made me feel any better as I have nowhere to go and secondly Jasper could have eaten the sausages that I have just disgorged into the bin. My thoughts then ask if it is right to give the dog a sausage that I have recently likened to my ex's penis, I choose not to answer that for fear of having extreme images in my head. I have had my moments of viewing porn in my youth but at nearly fifty, to bring animals into the equation is too far.

Note to self – Act your age.

Chapter Four

I don't know if I should put make-up on or not to be honest, I don't want people to think I'm on the pull. A drink with a friend and a spot of lunch doesn't warrant a lot of slap, although maybe a bit of lippy to hide my newly discovered lip wrinkles may help. I've never really noticed the wrinkles on my top lip before. I suppose I could put some foundation on with a bit of lipstick and hide them that way, but then again if I'm not on the pull why do I want to hide things like that and if I got lucky, or even extremely lucky and some Brad Pitt lookalike snogged my face into next week, the slather would end up washing it away which would make my wrinkles show regardless. Oh to hell with it, no foundation then, just the lippy. I'm not getting dressed up though; I have a pair of black trousers which I'll wear with that new top I got from Matalan last week. Luckily I managed to cut the label out without any trouble 'cos I know she'll check. I think she looks for the size to prove to herself that she's slimmer than me but I'm not convinced she is. There's not much in it I'm sure but since she met her chap she's in the comfort zone where a few pounds goes on because you stop making the effort to lose weight. I know exactly what'll happen. She will walk in…

"Oh, Emmy, I love the top dear, wherever did you get it from; I must see," and then she'll proceed to go round the back and look for the label, whilst clocking my size. Well it won't work this time 'cos there isn't a label. She shops at Harvey Nichols because she can and buys the best and most expensive of everything but I can't and I don't think she understands it. I once went with her to Harvey Nichols. We'd decided to have a day out in Leeds because sometimes living there you go to York or Manchester just for somewhere different but Leeds is the best shopping place ever. She bought a pair of knickers for £36 from there and a Colette charcoal jersey and lace chemise which cost £65. My whole knickers drawer doesn't even cost £36. The chemise was a present for Moneybags Marcus. I love it how she buys a present for him but it's for her. The only benefit he will get is to look at it, touch it, take it off and get a his wicked way. And then we went for a cup of tea. I thought she was paying, well she did, but only for herself. I was left paying £19.50 for a smoked salmon and cucumber sandwich and a cuppa.

"What sort of tea would you like?" the young thing serving asked me. On catching sight of the price list on the wall behind her I wanted to say something completely different to what I did.

"For that price I want gold plated tea," was on the tip of my tongue, but instead I followed suit.

"Darjeeling please dear." I don't know why 'cos it was horrible. It didn't even taste different with my little finger sticking out like how Sally seems to drink but give me a Tetley teabag any time. I felt cheated for the rest of the day, wasting nearly £20 on that stuff and a three fingered sandwich which was as small as his, well I won't say it. And I hate being called Emmy, that's something else that winds me up about her. I'm not sure why I stay friends with her to be honest 'cos my tolerance of her is very low sometimes. It's okay as long as it's a Costa every couple of weeks or so, I can't really cope with her for long lengths of time. That day in Leeds I'd had enough by Harvey Nics time.

I look okay, the mirror wouldn't lie to me would it? Right, what time is it? I really must stop talking to myself, people will think I'm going mad, well they would if anyone was here, but as it's me and Jasper it doesn't matter, she doesn't seem to care that much, she just thinks I'm talking to her and wags her tail now and again.

"Be good. Mummy's just popping out. You be a good little darling won't you. Mummy loves you, I do. Yes I do." That look that she gives me says it all. First the look says 'why do you talk to me in that patronising voice' and the second 'I still don't know why you called me Jasper as I'm a girl.'

"Bye bye, Mummy won't be long." Because, Jasper, you are all I have left that's why and as you're my baby I will milk it for all it's worth. As I pull the door closed, I can hear her running back down the hall. She'll probably enjoy the peace, although I'm not that noisy. Maybe she doesn't like Barry Manilow. I usually have *Copacabana* or *Bermuda Triangle* playing when I'm getting ready or the Bee Gee's *Night Fever* although it's Thursday so wouldn't be right today and I'm not exactly going out as in going out although I suppose I am sort of going out.

These Carmelo shoes are a nightmare, I don't wear them often 'cos they catch the back of my heel but as I paid £100 from Moda in Pelle for them I like to give them an outing now and again, for that sort of money the pain is worth it. Again I didn't intend to buy them, but they had a magic sticker on them, 30% OFF. Even though I was looking at a Gemmabag as I need another, this caught my attention. And the bag was on at £139.95 so I actually saved money. My mum nearly had a heart attack when I told her.

"You silly bugger," she said, "paying £140 for a bag." That made me feel better 'cos she obviously misheard and it did seem a lot for a bag so paying less for shoes was a good idea. Despite not really wanting shoes, I'm wearing them now so I obviously did need them really after all and I still have my Fiorelli Olivia bag as well as my old Gemmabag so I clearly didn't need a new bag as much as I thought.

I can see Jasper perching on the chair arm as I pull out of the drive and there's Patrick who's pretending not to look but I'll wave anyway 'cos he probably is. He's not looked me in the eye since last year, mind you, dirty old bugger would rather look at something else. Well he's had his one and only chance and I can't see me flashing off to him again. I suppose looking back it is amusing but if I had chosen to flash my boobs at anyone it wouldn't have been Patrick, maybe Owen and Joe the twins at No.43 might have been further up the list than Patrick. Still can't work out why they live at home at their age, they must be in their thirties and still live with their mum and dad. Owen drives a BMW 3 series and Joe drives a Jag yet I have never seen either of them with a girl, I think I have just inadvertently answered my own question. The dad is a strange one though, I've seen him at night wandering round the streets, he reminds me of a tramp as he wears these wellies that seem to be cut a bit shorter than they're supposed to be and a zipped up mac. Even when it's summer he wears his mac. I always thought he was just a bit eccentric but Julie next door but one thinks he's a perv. I had never thought of that until she said it but now she has, every time I see him I expect him to flash his goolies at me.

I always get here before Sally and I'm sure she thinks that as she is better than me she should arrive after and keep me waiting. I wouldn't be surprised if she didn't park around the corner and wait for me to go in and sit at the table like a lonely plonker so that people would think I'd been stood up or something and then she could make her dramatic entrance as the patron saint and saviour of all lonely and desperate nomads.

I decide instantly the second the smell of food hits me that I want to stay for lunch. We didn't plan it but I hope that Sally hasn't eaten. I do love Frankie & Benny's although Sally thinks it's a bit beneath her. The waiter smiles at me because either he remembers me from before or I look hideous without make-up and he can see my lip wrinkles through the lipstick. It's a nice smile but one that I can't work out if it's friendly or sympathetic. He's very nice but I am now so aware that I try and hide my face as I speak to him not realising until after he's shown me to my table, a table for two in the corner, that my actions would have come across as a schoolgirl 'I've got a crush embarrassment'. I don't of course as he is way too young but he is very nice nevertheless. His hair is short and black and I can see his hairy chest through the first couple of buttons on his white shirt which are very sexily not done up. He has a real nice tight arse which is shown off in his tight black trousers, Oh my god what's happening to me!

"Emmy darling." I knew it, she can't help herself. I'm

sure her voice tries to reach levels of poshness never reached before. I remember her when she had nothing and after a series of relationships with men of class she was going to ballet and top restaurants and hotels. I don't want jealousy to get involved in this conversation so I will leave it there.

"Hi," I say nice and calm and, common. Well, I think I sound common but maybe I don't. I try and form my words properly after years of correction from my grandma when I was a child but I will never live up to the standard set by Sally.

"Emmy, I love that top dear, wherever did you get it from?" As predicted she stands at the side of me and pulls the collar out. Ha! my plan worked.

"Oh this old thing? I can't remember."

This is now the bit where I sit and listen to her and what she has done since I last saw her. There will be tales of money spent and places visited, not your run of the mill places but galleries and museums in London where Marcus has taken her. I love things like that but can't just take off and go due to finances but for her it is not a problem. Note to self – Retrain as a human resources manager so that I too can meet a rich banker. Scrap that, I would just end up with a wanker. Mind you at the moment I would be quite happy with a rich wanker, I would just like to be treated like a princess if only for a short time. I can't remember exactly where she told me she met Marcus, she has definitely told me but I would have gone into standby mode. But it was somehow through work and even though I work at the same place I haven't yet met any rich men. Maybe my time will come, who knows?

I have no idea what she's on about as I am still watching the waiter. Well I'm not quite sure why they are called waiters at Frankie & Benny's but for the purpose of my fantasy which is evolving inside my head as she witters on, I'm calling him a waiter. I'm not entirely ignorant and I do catch the odd sentence as it finds its way across the table to break my gazing at him, but spending ten thousand pounds to get the living room decorated and the weekend trip to Paris coming up in a few weeks is not as impressive to me as his cute tight arse.

Suddenly a thought enters my head. I have realised maybe not for the first time but certainly the first time in this category, how much fun it is to be single. If I wanted, or if it was offered to me on a plate which it won't be 'cos he is a stallion, I could leave 'Miss full-of-myself Landers' and fly off into the Italian sunset with the waiter. I say Italian only because of his dark looks, his black hair and short side burns but because of that, the stallion fantasy sticks and will be enjoyed for some time to come. Sally returns to the table after giving the order to another waiter who walked past as she doesn't like waiting once she's ready to order and I wait with bated breath to see if my waiter will be the waiter to bring our food. We should have ordered straightaway as it seems to be getting busy but if we had she would not have had enough time to bore me to death about her life for as long as she has already done so. It's hardly surprising that nobody has attended to our table when every time they have come up Sally tells them we're not ready to order and then when she's ready she chases another waiter half way round the restaurant. I know what I want but I'm not sure he will be on the menu. Just once it would be nice for her to ask about me. Mind you, what could I say? 'Yes still single, yes still looking for Mr Right. No there's still no action in that department. Yes he's still with the young beautiful sexy Lucy Lick-me-all-over, or slag as I prefer.' Maybe talking about Sally is slightly more interesting after all. Although I would quite happily turn the conversation to the waiter.

I can see him standing by the till which, if I time it right with a toilet visit, I will walk right past him. With my decision made I nearly fall over the chair next to me in a rush to get out. Have you ever tried to walk so casually past a guy? It's like you over compensate which I can feel myself doing. I feel like I'm on a cat walk with a hand on my hip and the feet crossing over each other at the front. I'm not of course but that's how it feels. I feel as though he's watching my every step looking me up and down. I can feel his eyes burning into my clothes to see my naked body. God it's getting hot in here. I slow down in a teasing manner playing with him as I walk past running my tongue along my top lip highlighting my red lipstick that I want to smear all over his mouth. I walk close almost brushing past him giving him a taste of what it would be like to touch me.

I get inside the toilet and I feel the door open after me. I hold it open thinking a lady is following me in, but it's him. He doesn't say a word but holds me, cuddling me close, brushing my hair with his face. He kisses my neck and rubs my shoulders and I can feel myself melting in his presence. He rips my clothes off in one pull and makes love to me there and then. Well, it's not like that at all really but how nice would that be? Maybe I would change the toilet for a nice hotel somewhere but as I am desperate according to my friends, maybe a toilet would be okay just this once. Anyway I walk past him and clock his name badge for my own information, and continue to the toilet without him looking at me once. When I come out, he is nowhere to be seen. It looks like Kevin has gone and when I sit down I see him in the car park getting into a car driven by a girl with long dark hair and sunglasses. They kiss and drive off. My first sexual encounter for a long time, even if he knew nothing about it, comes to an end. I resign myself to the fact that I must now listen to Sally.

Note to self – I really must get out more.

Chapter Five

I sometimes feel that I am getting old before my time. I know as much as I try to avoid the subject I am nearly fifty yet I suppose I don't help myself sometimes. Today I have brought Mum to the church hall for the knit and natter session. I truly cannot believe that I am here. I have a complete sinking feeling as I walk in, Mother on one arm and a bag of wool on the other. I feel as though it is me who should be coming to classes like this now with my rapidly approaching countdown to old age. Knit and natter, I think stitching and bitching is a much more suitable title. These ladies really don't hold back. I said I may as well wait for Mum as by the time I get into town to do some tea time shopping it would be time to pick her up with the traffic being busy. They sit in a circle, like a witches' coven and do far more bitching than stitching. I smile as they continue their annihilation of people oblivious to the fact that they have an alien in their midst. I don't know their names other than Elsie as she is my mum's friend or should I say I didn't know them but after listening to them I'm beginning to feel like part of the gang. There is one lady amusingly called Phyllis who has blue hair and clearly qualifies for the blue rinse brigade. I say amusingly called Phyllis as she reminds me of Phyllis who was in Coronation Street and had a thing for Percy Sugden. More bizarrely than that, the caretaker at the Church hall is called Percy. The one with the large gold earrings who looks like she would be more suited to a caravan at a fair rather than a church hall either has a speech impediment, a very strange accent or she's just plain naughty because he calls him Pervy.

"Ere, Pervy. Can you get me a chair so I can sit there?" And good old Pervy, err Percy, just does what he's asked without a word. Obviously he's been married far too long which has made him into a robot who just obeys women. They must all be deaf 'cos no-one seems to notice her calling him Pervy but I find it amusing, although I try to keep my laugh to a minimum which is actually quite hard otherwise I'll be noticed. I can hear their conversation now in my head.

"What you laughing at?"

"Nothing." I would say trying to sound as innocent as possible.

"What's she laughing at?"

"What did she say?"

"What is who laughing at?"

"What did you say?"

"What did who say?"

"What's she laughing at?" So to avoid all that, I pretend to yawn, sneeze and tie my shoe laces (despite not having laces) cough or just sit red faced stifling the laugh as I'm already doing. They settle into a fine routine of knit one, pearl one, bitch about someone, knit one, pearl one, bitch about someone else. Mum is just as bad. She doesn't go out much since Dad died but she doesn't really need to go out much. Coming here once a week she gets enough gossip to last a lifetime.

Old Betty, who I now know had her cataracts done last month was finally able to see clear enough to catch her husband Old Jack touching up the barmaid in the legion last Sunday. Betty never goes to the Legion 'cos

Jack never invites her but as it was Stan's birthday on Sunday and as she was feeling much better with her new vision, she went. Obviously Jack forgot that she could see and had his hands all over the barmaid. Betty went off on one and slapped Old Jack across his face and poured his pint over the barmaid. I will re-tell this story from now on as I now feel that I personally know the people involved. I obviously do not, but I feel after an hour of stitching and bitching I not only know them but live my life with them. I actually wouldn't mind meeting Betty, we could share stories on men being complete dicks.

Then there was Moira who went out in her car last week. She goes to the town centre once a week to do her chores. She always parks in the car park behind the swimming pool and walks through the park. She could see some little ones playing on the swings and there was a couple on the roundabout. There's an old shop in the park that gets really busy in summer. She walks out of the gate and goes past the library. At this point I'm sat on the edge of my chair and can hardly move with the anticipation of what's going to happen. Then she said she walks down past the bus station to the bank and then calls at the fruit and veg shop to get a carrot for tea to go with a chicken breast and the frozen peas in the freezer. I am now on the verge of shouting at her. 'Please tell me, I can't take the anticipation.' Obviously the story isn't as interesting to Phyllis 'cos she's nodded off, dropping a stitch as she went. She could actually be dead and no-one would know. Anyway to cut a long story short which I have managed to sit through without bursting, the story of her going into town didn't really matter as that wasn't the point of her rabbiting on for so long. The actual story was that on her way home her mobile phone rang and not wanting to answer it whilst driving she waited until she had passed the Army barracks and turned right because she can pull into the golf club car park to answer it. She did say that she can go home that way but it just takes a little bit longer. Anyway the phone call was from her daughter so she rang her back. After all the detail about going into town and which shops she went even correcting herself at one point because she got two shops in the wrong order I felt somewhat cheated because she didn't tell me what her daughter Natalie rung her for. I felt that for her to leave out this detail wasn't fair and left the story incomplete in some way. Whilst in the car park she noticed a car in the far corner and thought her neighbour Sydney must be playing golf as it was his car. She pulled alongside and saw a plastic tube coming from the passenger's side. She saw Sydney's wife Anne squeezing out poor old Sydney's colostomy bag with the words 'He needs to go.' Well at this point I nearly vomited and jumped up from my chair causing poor old Phyllis to wake up at supersonic speed with a potential heart attack. Mum practically choked on her tea coughing until she almost vomited, and Pervy Percy gasped for breath choking as though he had just consumed the contacts of the bag in question.

Phyllis recovered with the use of her inhaler, which she nearly emptied into her lungs in one go, causing her to be a bit hyper which made Percy concerned for her. He started fussing around her trying to wipe her head with his hanky 'cos he thought she was sweating. This off-white hanky had clearly been in his pocket for some time due to the big yellow crusty patches on it which made me retch for the second time in a short space. Phyllis was hitting him to try and get him away from her, my mum was too busy talking to notice anything and Moira who had just about come up for air after her riveting story-telling looked like she had seen something worse than poor old Sydney's colostomy bag being emptied and joined me in the choir of heavenly retching.

By the time we put the chairs to the side for Percy to stack up in the cupboard I was so traumatised I was already planning on booking a hair appointment, nail appointment or liposuction or just about anything for this time next week, anything would do just to get me out of coming here again. I don't want to get old but the thought of spending time here every week with colostomy bags and three week old snot-filled hankies just makes me want to find the nearest bridge and accidently fall off it. Mum really wanted to go out for tea after but as I feel sick I could not eat nor do I have the slightest appetite to attend to. Forget diets and exercise, I would tell any woman how to shed a few pounds, it's called knit and natter at the church hall courtesy of Pervy Percy and his cronies Phyllis and Moira. I will never eat again.

My mum's idea of shopping is a stark contrast to mine. Mine involves spending money or rather, larger amounts than her. Her idea is to walk around the pound shop picking up item after item saying things like, 'that's good for a quid,' or 'I can't believe that's a pound.' The reason why it's in the pound shop is because firstly it is a pound and secondly it's crap; plain and simple. Two packets of digestives with a packet of rich tea in the middle, is a pound. If I took her half a mile up the road there is a Morrison's where she could get the Morrison's value ones cheaper than buying from the pound shop and they'll be much better quality. It's come to a poor and sorry state of affairs when I am encouraging my mother to scrape the bottom of the social ladder and buy value food. I have to admit, I would not personally buy the value ones but they're okay for Mum to dunk in her tea and then spend ten minutes with a table spoon fishing them out. She'd make a good gnome sitting in the garden fishing all day with the amount of practice that she gets from dunking rich teas. After much consideration I think I will be okay sitting with a coffee whilst Mum tucks into her favourite pea and ham soup with a bread roll so we go to Morrison's as we pass it on the way. As we walk down the back of the checkouts and get closer to the restaurant part, the smell of food hits me. It actually smells nice so it wasn't the thought of eating it that made me sick. As soon as the lady put the bowl of soup on the table and I saw the colour and texture of it the retching started. It reminded me of a cross between Percy's crusty handkerchief and old Sydney's colostomy bag all mixed together and served with a buttered bread bun. The knit and natter entertainment was just way too much excitement and out it came. As it came from my mouth it was thick, orangey pink and copious in the amount. It went down my front, down my mum's front, all over the table in her soup and some even splattered on a snotty nosed kid who had the misfortune to be sat behind Mum. It stank so much it dampened down the smell of food which was a positive if you think I had just emptied my stomach and lost my appetite in one go. It made my mum want to go home and clean up which was good although the staff didn't see anything good in any of it. The manager had to get a cleaner to clean it up and someone else came to pacify the mother with the sick-covered child. I'm sure a few free meals would have covered it along with the payment to cover the laundry bill. The cleaner was wearing the same coloured t-shirt as the rest of the staff so my assumption was that she wasn't a cleaner at all, but just someone who had annoyed the manager enough for her to warrant a punishment like that. It was my sick and I'm not even sure that I would have liked to have cleaned it up. Once I had put mine and Mum's jackets in the boot of the car inside the black bin liner that the knob used to keep his dog walking coat in I sat in the car pondering the thought that at the very least I maybe should have offered to clean it up myself. My guilt was short lived because by the time I set off I felt sick again. Mum didn't say anything but I know if I'd have been the victim of a sick attack I would be furious.

Arriving at Mum's house the washing machine was loaded up and any mum's answer to make you feel better was delivered into my hand. As the steam rose from my cup of tea the evening's stitching and bitching session seemed a lifetime away and I knew that Jasper would be expecting me home soon as she knew I was never out for long, a sign of my sad life perhaps?

Note to self – I must be more interesting.

Chapter Six

So I have the task of taking Mum to line dancing tonight. I said before that she doesn't get out much and maybe that was a lie as she doesn't seem to be in at the moment. It's a far cry from her sitting in the window seeing Dad in the garden waving to her; I think if I asked her at this precise moment she would not even be able to remember what her windows look like, glass obviously, but the design: whether it is a split into four or not. I'm not complaining as I'm pleased that she's getting out more but it just seems all a bit sudden. There is the thought that maybe she has just realised that life is too short and you can sit moping around if you so wish but life will not wait for any man or woman and with this in mind she is seizing the day. Not sure of her choice though as line dancing and stitching and bitching are now encroaching on my life and they're hardly lifestyle choices that I would make for myself. I will, however, keep them in reserve and if I ever get too bored with myself I may pull them out to use as a plan B option. Next week I will do the taxiing but will try my damnedest to stay out of the actual room. I am sure that the vomit that followed stitching and bitching would not be a weekly occurrence for me and I'm sure stories of colostomy bags can only be told once without losing their effect.

Once again and for the second day running Jasper has had a short walk so that I can be at Mum's on time. Although slightly later in the day than last time I arrive bang on time which surprises me more than it seemed to have surprised her. I have never been one for punctuality which I'm sure came in very handy when the knob was screwing Lucy Lockjaw to the floor when he should have been doing DIY, or Doing It in Y-fronts which would have been a more suitable name for his version of DIY. In fact he should have been doing anything BUT screwing her. He was my husband, it's just a shame he forgot that part. If I had been due home at 3 o'clock he knew that I wouldn't get there until half past which would give him more time to finish off, not that he needed that long. Thirty seconds would have been more than enough. I try and rack my brains thinking at any point if there were signs that he was playing away and maybe that I was so wrapped up in my plodding along little existence that I wouldn't have noticed even if they had been doing it under my nose. I can't think of any but in the process of thinking if there were any signs I seem to be blaming myself, something which I promised myself I would not do.

Why do women always blame themselves when their husbands go off with someone else? I have been through all the excuses with him.

"You never want to have sex."

"You're always too tired for sex."

"You never come near me."

"I can't ever touch you without you pulling away."

"You never cuddle me."

"You're frigid."

"You never look good for me anymore."

"I was stressed out with work and you weren't there for me."

"You don't understand me."

"You never want to go out on a night anymore."

"I can't help it that other women find me attractive."

"You don't do anything to keep me at home." I could go through each point as I did with him but I can't see how that would help now. Most of them are pathetic male attempts to justify that it's okay sleeping with a tart behind your wife's back, but I can't help it if other women find me attractive is the biggest piss take of all. Firstly, you are not attractive; it is not a compliment when some tart has sex with you. Stressed out with work is another joke. Not only did I have to run around after my dad when he was alive and now my mum, I have in the past run around after your dad when he had his by-pass op and when your mum wanted to go to the hospital every day and sometimes even twice and then when she fell down those steps at the church fete, I was the one taking her to the doctors', not you and then on top of working myself you expected your bloody tea on the table when you got home from taking pointless photographs of half naked tarts, or models as you called them. Stress? You don't have a bloody clue, pal.

He never hit me, not even once did he raise a finger to me, I would have knocked him into next week had he done so, but he did as much damage to me without physical violence. I can't imagine why these women put up with being hit all the time. Those men that hit women are bullies; the knob was just a dick. I have now realised that I am better off without him but would sometimes just love a cuddle or a meal out. Eating out with Sally is not even close although I must go back to Frankie & Benny's again to see if that waiter is there. My mind still spares a thought for him and my fantasies are still based around him.

And so it is the waiter who takes up the space in my thoughts as I drive quietly pondering to the line dancing session. Mum is full of tales about Gloria down the street and how she has just had her varicose veins done, like I really need to know that, and how she had to have her dog put down last week because it had an anal sac disorder, a wart problem and mouth cancer.

"Poor little Benjy," Mum said about a million times on the way to the community centre. More like poor bloody vet having to play about with an anal sac disorder. Once again my mum has ruined my appetite by introducing me to old people's conversations when I am way too young. I still have a functioning stomach and properly functioning bowels unlike her and her cronies where it seems to be one short tube with no control. Mind you, the amount of prune juice she drinks it's hardly surprising she has no trouble ridding herself of her stomach contents. When I pick her up and take her out or if we are out or eating in a cafe or similar food based property her words of 'I need to pop to the loo' conjure all sorts of thoughts that I really don't need. As I approach fifty and take stock of my life and look towards the future I have realised that I have nothing to look forward to. I face a future of stitching and bitching, colostomy bags and dogs with anal sac disease. This wasn't part of the plan.

I sit in the car outside the community centre listening to the music seeping through the opened side door. I haven't heard *Achy Breaky Heart* for years and it brings back unwanted memories of the knob trying to dance at Pat and Tony's wedding anniversary. He did know how to make people laugh and I can see why people liked him. To remember him line dancing to this song makes me smile. He had no idea how to line dance but his attempts were cheered on by both the sober people and the drunken idiots. The latter group was the one that he fit into perfectly. There is something wet going down the inside of my nose as I see him with his thumbs clasped into his jeans pockets waddling like a duck to the newly invented line dancing for beginners. I haven't cried for some time but I cannot help but let this solitary tear make its way down my face pointing out that it's blatantly clear to me that I still have some way to go in my recovery. We did have some happy times and I will let the tear and the smile mark that occasion but I cannot dwell. He's gone and I'm still hurting.

I get out of the car and light up a cigarette. I class myself as a non smoker as I don't smoke every day. I stopped about eleven years ago and don't particularly miss it but I do enjoy the occasional secret cig. Not many know and Jasper doesn't seem likely to tell anyone as the only time I have one is when she and I have a walk. She has on a couple of occasions given me a disapproving look but whether that is more because I take her for the walk round the back of the cricket ground where no-one will see me smoke or not is open to discussion. She likes to go through the fields at the top of the park near to the stables but some of my friends have horses stabled up there so I may get seen. Funny how I worry about getting caught smoking even though I'm forty-nine.

I look through the door to watch the old biddies and laugh when I see a handful of ladies and one gent strutting their stuff. I say strutting, it's more like watching a group of zombies learning how to walk. Their suppleness isn't great – not that I can talk 'cos mine isn't either, but at least I can bend my knees. The sight would be complete if they put their arms straight out and made a groaning noise. The moves to the beat seem more accidental than natural rhythm and with her clicky hips my mum and her backing dancers finish the dance at different times. It almost makes me want to smoke another cigarette just to carry on watching. Then it's toilet time for some as half of them can't go for an hour without a wee and the other half need a cup of tea. They all pay £1 a week for the pleasure of being part of the class but don't have to pay for the hall as Joyce, one of the members, is on the committee of the community hall and gets free usage leaving me appalled and disgusted that there is even corruption in the lowest form of committee led government. I jest of course but for the £1 you get a cup of tea and a biscuit. It's hard to know how the community centre says afloat as Mum says that last week the line dancers had cakes and buns afterwards because the baking club, of which Joyce is also a member, had been in and left some for them. I assume that the baking club are treated the same as the line dancers and also get the hall free. This attitude flies in the face of the cuts that every other sector has to apply to its business and I am hard pressed to see how, if the NHS followed Joyce's business plan, it would survive beyond a day although a free colostomy bag exchange programme would be useful for people like Sydney. I say that but I am not entirely sure how the whole colostomy bag thing works as I have not had many dealings with them before. I hope I never do either or certainly not beyond the knit and natter session as the thought of pulling into a golf club car park or a lay-by somewhere to squeeze out every last bit of shit doesn't fill me with joyous thoughts. I would imagine though now that my thoughts have turned to colostomy bags that it would be a very good way to see if someone really loved you or not if they were prepared to take hold of a bag of stale and somewhat smelly shite and empty it out for you so that you could refill it. If they do then they pass the test, if they don't then they aren't worth bothering about. The hour passes much quicker than the stitching and bitching one did but somehow it didn't seem half as much fun. Ideally carrying clean colostomy bags would be better but I assume it may be difficult to plan your bowel movements for a whole day.

Mum has a corn on her little toe on her left foot which has gotten much worse through the line dancing session of today and which also exhausts the topic of conversation for the journey home. I can't say that I am that interested in her corn but as my face gets close to it to apply the small round cushioned pad that sits around it to offer comfort as promised on the box, I know I love my mum dearly and a corn on her toe is one thing but she better not ever weigh up my love for her by means of the colostomy bag test.

Chapter Seven

I would do anything for Beth. Anything at all, even empty the contents of a colostomy bag, although I'm sure she wouldn't expect me to. She would probably be more mortified than I would be to do such a thing but as long as she knows I would do it if need be. Although I'm hardly likely to tell her, otherwise she would have me sectioned. Can you imagine that conversation?

"Hi Darling it's me."

"Hi, Mum, everything okay?"

"Yes darling, I just wanted you to know that I would be prepared to empty your colostomy bag for you."

"But I don't have one."

"I know, but if you did have one I would be prepared to empty it for you."

"Okay that's nice, Mum, thank you."

"My pleasure. Bye."

"Bye, Mum."

Could you imagine her face, thinking her old mum had finally gone doo-lally tap, although I would stop at asking her if she would do it for me. I'm not even sure that I would ask her to come with me to the knit and natter group that I would automatically be entitled to join when I reach that certain age. I wonder if you get an invitation through the post when you reach 70 like the telegram from the Queen when you get to 100. I don't think I would want to be 100, I guess it would be okay if you retain your faculties and mobility and bowel control but to sit and vegetate in front of a TV isn't my idea of fun. It's great if you can get up and walk to the kitchen for another pack of Doritos or peanuts and then go back to the vegetation with the new supplies but if not I think I'd rather pass. Many a night me and Jasper curl up on the sofa with a pack of Chilli Doritos, she loves them although drinks half a bowl of water afterwards. She makes me laugh. When I feel sad it's like she knows and gives me a look that says 'it's okay, Mummy, I'm here.' Well I say that's what it says, it's probably more like 'feed me' but for my own comfort I will stick to the first one. Funnily enough, the word doo-lally always stays in my mind because I remember Dad telling me when I was young that it came from a British army camp in India where the soldiers were so bored they literally went mad. The camp was called Deolali. Always wondered if that was true or not but something which I remember all these years later. I must Google it. Google is God's own website and the source of all knowledge. If it isn't on Google, it either doesn't exist or it isn't worth knowing.

Beth has lived away from home for two years and I miss her loads. We talk every few days 'cos she works hard, bless her. She lives in Deira in Dubai working for Emirates Airlines. She loves it, jetting all over the world, not that I'm jealous. Well maybe a bit but I wouldn't fit into the category of beautiful which she and all her colleagues are in. She hasn't spoken to her dad since he left me from what she says so that makes me feel happy 'cos she's on my side. Not that it's about sides but when it comes to point scoring which inevitably happens with break ups, it's nice when the child has your back. She has a lovely apartment which she shares with two other girls and although I've not seen it yet I am saving up to go and see her. She was due to come back last month on the Manchester flight but then they asked if she wanted the Sydney to Las Vegas flight instead, so no contest. I do get regular updates about the sex life of Saskia, one of her flat mates who is from the Czech Republic. She likes airline pilots and is quite open about her shenanigans. I've learnt a bit about things that I never knew. I always thought spit-roast was to do with food but my eyes have been well and truly opened up along with my imagination to tell you the truth, but now that I know these things, I do kind of see how it gets its name. I'm not a prude by any stretch but activities in the sexual department are for two people in my opinion, not more and most certainly not an odd number. Sally is a bit of a lively one and now she's seeing Moneybags Marcus she's getting plenty. She had been on her own for about a month before she met him but moaned for three of those weeks that it was healing up, horrible thought I know, but that's Sally. One minute she's as posh as they come the next she's got a mouth like a sewer. She has always been one of those who think they're better than anyone else but that's just her, I guess. It does my head in but I put up with it. We have arranged to go back to Frankie & Benny's again next week, well she wanted to go somewhere else but I opted to go back to see if the Italian is there. He clearly isn't Italian but it's better for my fantasy if I call him it. If he is there I am going to give him my number. I may need a drink to give me the courage to do it but I am determined that this is the next step forward in my life. I have been hurt, I have been at the bottom but now is the time for the climb up and if I can get a quickie on the way then who I am to complain. My words, what's happened to me? That's not me talking. I sometimes feel that someone has taken over my brain. Another bonus of going to Frankie & Benny's is that if I end up paying for myself, I can afford it. Going to Tilly's where she usually goes is an absolute fortune and at least I know I can afford Frankie's.

Beth doesn't have a boyfriend at the moment. She was seeing a lovely guy before she went but decided to call it off as it wouldn't have worked with him being here and her in Dubai. They speak now and again but as he is always begging her to take him back and I think she finds it uncomfortable. She gets plenty of attention 'cos she's a stunner just like her mother and I know he doesn't like that. Note to self – A compliment given by one's self is still a compliment, just take it. She's real good is Beth and doesn't invite any attention but with her long brown hair she can't avoid it. Blokes home in on her. She's too friendly and talkative and she smiles at everyone, that's probably why she's good at her job. She looks fab and she likes people, she's got a gorgeous smile and pure white teeth. People make me laugh how they think they're in with a chance with someone who is clearly way out of their league and I think that's the case with our Beth. I have probably just contradicted myself there in a way as I fall into that category with the Italian. Here I am planning to give him my number and go on a date with him, but he is so way out of the league that I play in. It has to be said that when the knob was putting his dangly thing into places that I don't need to know about with Lucy Loose-bits he took himself into a much higher league than he had been in for the last twenty years and I certainly couldn't hold myself up against her. Maybe if it went on a one-nighter and I pulled out all the stops and made a real effort I could have got a draw but would have definitely got thrashed in the replay. Anyway she is welcome to him because I know one day that she will wake up and smell the coffee and realise the thing next to her is made with sour milk. Whilst I'm on the subject of likening football to sex and the thing that keeps me going is that the Italian who is premier league will maybe at some point get a cup game away against a non-league side (me), and whilst the score is quite often 5 or 6-0, it is about the taking part and my god will I enjoy the taking part. He could smash me for a 10-0 victory but I'd enjoy every single second. Once again my thoughts have been taken over by Sally's type of thoughts although the very idea does appeal to me, I cannot lie, I think I'm going to look forward to my next meal.

    EastEnders always entertains me. It's much more lifelike than Corrie although I love them both and also have a touch of Emmerdale thrown in too. I realised how all my favourite men in each soap are so different. We had this conversation at work the other day and I opted for Steve McDonald in Corrie 'cos his personality is lovely and you'd have a real good laugh with him, David in Emmerdale for obvious reasons and looking like David Beckham helps but in EastEnders I'd be torn between the cheeky chappy Alfie and Max. I think Max would be too much like the knob with his womanising ways although Alfie has had his moments too, but Max would know how to make a woman happy, before running off with her mate it has to be said. Lisa in admin likes Phil Mitchell. She says she likes to feel safe with a man. I'm not sure they've invented such a thing yet as a man who can pull the wool over your eyes that much that you actually feel safe with him. Bizarre though how we all go for different things. Some men wouldn't look twice at Lucy 'look at me aren't I gorgeous' with her nice hair, cleavage, fabulous figure and, who am I kidding, of course they would. And standing next to me they're even more likely to. I'm 49, she's 25. I'm flabby, frumpy and downright jealous of that cow. Not 'cos she's got him but because I want to be pretty and I'm not but she is. She could have any bloke, why did she chose him?

It seems strange that I should be thinking of him and he's just texted me. I haven't thought of him properly for a while other than in a very negative way and I suppose in that way I have thought about him loads but he's just asked me if I can meet him for a coffee in town. Not sure why I would want to meet him for a coffee but he's asked. I will ignore the text for a bit which will buy me some time as to what to reply. I know if I go I will want to slap his face and if I don't go I will wonder what he wants. Now starts the battle of should I, shouldn't I? It is a battle of wills between the camps in my head. Enter the fat man in the suit with the microphone dangling from the ceiling. 'In the blue corner, fighting with a strong influence of curiosity is 'you should go'. And in the red corner, fighting under 'a leopard never changes its spots and it's safer not to go is 'don't go'. After my head has been punched several times and feeling like a punch drunk heavyweight boxer I still have no idea what to do. I have forwarded the text to my two best friends, Sally who I have a low tolerance for but is still one of my best friends, and Dawn who is on holiday at the moment but can at least offer me a bit of advice via text. I have other friends as well and more than two which I'd like to make clear otherwise that makes me sound like a bit of a Billy no-mates. The fact that neither of them are here when I need them is completely irrelevant. At work we have a small clique who sit and gossip at lunchtime and share our experiences and laugh at things, usually it is me that shares my experiences and they all laugh at me. They were fairly supportive when the knob went off with her but as with all workplaces there's always one who gives you a dig in the ribs. That person at my work is Sally.

"Well you can't blame him; look at the state of you." The supportive, cruel and damning words that still hit the nerve now. That's why I have a low tolerance of her sometimes. Everyone else, well most of them, told her she was being a bit harsh and the other couple found it funny. Funny that someone can be as blunt as to say what everyone else is thinking. I have since shed the few pounds that she pointed to when her finger dug into my stomach and at the moment I am beginning to think I look fine. As previously said, my boobs are nice and apart from the bit of sagging and flab here and there, I think I look okay. You have to remember that I am approaching rather too quickly for my liking the big five-0, and along with that daunting feeing I have to compete with a model half my age. Sally seems to have the magic touch that attracts men, which by some is called being easy. It's worked for her and she seems happy enough. Oh, where is my rich man to give me a credit card for my birthday?

Chapter Eight

As is usually the case now, I have come to see Mum again. I try and get here as often as I can and watch as she sits in her chair occasionally glancing out into the garden. I wonder if Dad is waving or if her newly found independence has blotted him out. I see her look at the picture on the wall and realise that despite the new groups and the acquaintances that she's met, he is never far from her mind. This makes me smile. I'm happy that she remembers him and I'm happy that he still plays a strong part in her life but I'm sad too because I miss him like mad, he was such a presence in my life and I relied on him heavily for love and guidance. Mum gave me love too and plenty of it but a girl needs her dad's love no matter how old she is. As I drive away from her house and see her waving from the window I feel a real sense of loss tonight. In six crap months last year I lost the two men in my life. One chose to leave and one didn't. If I could have had the choice I would have kept my dad. I am grateful that after the knob left my dad was there to support me through it and despite his many years he would have ripped off the knob's head and displayed it on the church railings. That is if the church still had railings as they had been taken for a different purpose during the war which at the time was much more important than displaying the heads of cheating lying husbands.

Dad was my hero. I am no different to any other girl who worships her dad. A dad is the only man in a girl's life who is steadfast, loyal and strong. I remember a day when I had sufficiently dealt with what had happened with my marriage that I could talk about it and although they witnessed the moment of me seeing the evidence on his phone, I discussed everything about it with them. I remember one day at their house discussing it and my mum said that I must have done something wrong to make him look elsewhere whereas my dad just put down his newspaper, took his glasses from the end of his nose and quietly, without a word, he got up. The folded newspaper landed on the small square coffee table placed strategically between their chairs and he came and hugged me. He held me so tight that I felt safe. I cried into his shoulder and he stroked my hair. Mum was not very good at finding the right things to say but I didn't expect her to blame me. Dad told her to shut up as he let me into a little secret. In his soft whisper into my ear he confessed that he never liked the little prick in all the years I had been with him. He always had a way to make me smile even when my heart had been ripped out and torn in two. Forever the hero. That night he drove me back to my empty house as I couldn't drive for crying and sat up with me all night in the same way he did on the day that it happened. He sat in the chair and I sat on the floor with my back against the chair with his legs at either side of me. He talked to me and comforted me for hours. When I finally fell asleep somehow he managed to lift me onto the sofa and put a blanket over me. I will never know how he did it as I'm not a little girl anymore other than he's my dad and he has special powers. That night the bond between my dad and me was cemented forever and ever amen. I had worshipped the very ground that he walked on all my life and in one act of selfless understanding, he showed me why I loved him so much. My parents have been so opposite ends of the scales in my life. My mum was organised, tidy and led by routine whereas my dad was fun, spontaneous and loving, always having time for a cuddle. He would throw me up in the air and catch me, bringing me tight into him for a cuddle before I ascended into the skies once again. I'm not for one second suggesting my mum wasn't loving because she was. She always had time to spend with us and on rainy days would get out the big thick book called '101 things to do on a rainy day' and we would make finger puppets, bracelets and princess crowns until teatime. I loved teatime 'cos Dad would come home from work. I never knew as a child what my dad did for a job other than he wore a shirt and tie. When I got a bit older the title of draughtsman was mentioned but I was not remotely impressed by that. Had he played chess all day I would have been more impressed because anyone can play draughts, even me. Not until I was much older did I realise it had nothing to do with the board game. Charlotte didn't seem as close to Dad as I was which suited me because I liked to have him all to myself. She would go to Mum for the cuddles but I liked to feel safe. That night when the knob had left, my dad made me feel safe just like he had back then. When he first became ill, the knob was nowhere to be seen and I had to face the prospect of losing my dad for the first time, and face it alone. I could not speak of my fears to Mum because she had to deal with it too. Remember they had been married for 60 years and she also loved him. We had to be strong for each other and for him but the problem was that he was the strong one not us. We needed him to tell us it would be okay not the other way round and we weren't as good at it as he was. When I told him it would be okay I didn't even believe myself so why would he believe me? Nonetheless the very first hospital visit was awful. Mum and I had sat in the car park for over half an hour finishing our tears and then composing ourselves so that when we saw him we could be strong for him and not appear weak. As we stepped onto the ward and approached his bed I couldn't even see for the tears. My big strong dad looked old and frail, his posture had crumbled as the cancer had spread. He still smiled though and his eyes burst into life when he saw me. At that point I knew for sure that I was his favourite. Charlotte had pursued a career in journalism which had taken her around the world many times over but had forgotten the simple and basic things in life, like her family. I haven't spoken to her for a couple of years now but every now and again I think I must send her a text or email. I haven't yet but the thought is there. We do that a lot, promise to keep in touch with people and then don't. We are just so busy in our own little lives. Even so I really should make the effort with Charlotte, she's my sister and we used to be fairly close, she doesn't even bother with Mum that much. She sends the occasional letter but she's busy and we understand that. She came home for Dad's funeral but left pretty much as soon as he got put in the ground. Always looking for the next big story she is. Shame she couldn't lay Dad to rest first but there you go. Good job Mum and I were there for him.

What a day that was. I hate funerals at the best of times but that day we could feel his presence the whole day. It started first, thing absolutely pissing it down. Mum was in a flap and I couldn't stop crying. I was so close to my dad as I've already explained. Mum had bought this black hat to wear with her black dress and she put it on the back of the chair. I was sat in the kitchen having a cup of tea whilst Mum ironed her dress and this black thing shot past us. I thought it was a cat before realising that Mum didn't have a cat. We then realised that Jasper had got Mum's hat. Could we bugger get it out of her mouth. Anyway she chewed it until there was hardly anything left. Well there was a brief outline shape of a hat which reminded me of Oliver Hardy when the top gets cut off of his bowler hat and when he puts it back on his head it goes through the hole. Mum obviously didn't put it on her head but that's what it would have looked like. She started screaming at Jasper who looked up to see what the fuss was about as she chewed another piece of it. So then Mum's in a flap panicking about not having a hat to wear when the smell of burning tells her that something is wrong. The iron shaped burn in the front of her dress gives her the clear indication that she cannot wear the dress either. I started laughing as it solved the problem of the dress with no hat. After about five minutes of being slumped against the fridge she saw the funny side. The only other dress that she could wear was white, so she stood in the kitchen doorway dressed in a white dress which strangely looked similar to her wedding dress. Mum has this thing about the lead mourners at a funeral should wear a hat which is usually black, but as Jasper had other ideas her black hat was not an option. The only other solution and although a bit of a contrast, she pulled it off. A white dress with a pink hat. Dad would have laughed his head off. It caused a few raised eye brows at the church I can tell you but my dad liked a laugh and she gave him one. The sun shone at the graveside when his coffin was lowered into the hole and just as I looked up to the sky to say goodbye a single white dove flew past. I have never had such a strong message from anyone that I was being watched. At that point a smile came over my face that stayed with me for days. My dad had just told me that he was with me, still thinking about me, just as he had done so when the knob left me and he came to comfort me when I needed him most. I needed him then and he was there. No-one else mentioned the dove which made it all the more special for me as it was a private message from him to me. Mum looked fabulous in her white dress and despite the pink hat he would have been proud to have been stood by her side. Unfortunately due to circumstances he couldn't stand next to her but he sure was there.

Back at the house, Mum played a great hostess and because she was busy she seemed fine. Big smiles and loads of sandwiches which the WI had helped make kept her mind away from the real reason that everyone was in her house. Then right at the end when the first people were about to leave I saw her looking around. I knew that she was looking for my dad so that she could call him to come and say goodbye as she always would have done, they had a ritual or routine when you went to their house visiting where they would both greet you or wave you off together. On arrival at their house your coat would always be put on their bed and when it was time to go, one of them would get the coat and then together they would follow you outside put their arms around each other and wave as you drove away. No matter what the weather was like that is how it was. But as people left from the funeral, Mum went outside to wave people off, and I took the place of my dad. I could feel her fingers digging into my back as her arm went around me. That was the first sign that my mum was about to crumble. As the last of the people left, she broke down, closely followed by me. I was angry that Charlotte had left early because she should have shared our grief. She should have hurt like we were hurting, he was her dad as well and yet I was taking on all of the child grief and I had no-one to share that with. I had to support Mum, and Charlotte should have supported me. She didn't even come back to the house and still, even now, I cannot forgive her for that. Beth didn't make it as her flight home had been cancelled due to engine trouble, she had a good excuse but found the time to send me a lovely message on my voicemail that I got when I woke up. It was very thoughtful and I played it to Mum who took huge comfort from it too. She's a good girl and clearly takes after her mum.

Chapter Nine

Mum thinks I should go and see the knob and hear what he has to say. I didn't get a text back from Dawn and Sally thinks I should shove the coffee up his arse. Not sure how I would do that as the cups at Costa Coffee are very wide. I suppose that would work to get maximum pain. I have also wondered if he has asked me to meet him in Costa because it will be busy and I won't scream and shout at him. It's funny when you are in a situation like that the people around you are blotted out and it doesn't really stop the red mist descending like it does. I try not to make a scene but when I lose it, it's easier to let it out than to count to ten. I think in this case I'd still be counting to 100 by which time my head would have exploded.

Full of the same curiosity that killed the cat I set off into town. I have plenty of time to get there just in case I decide to talk myself out of it. I can't imagine being face to face with him for the first time since that day. Picking up his phone because of these suspicions that I had didn't prepare me for what I found. He worked long hours but then he always did and he was always smelling of ladies' perfume due to the environment of his studio but something didn't seem right. He started being cagey about where he had been working. He wasn't always in the studio and when I asked him where he had been he seemed to be unsure in his answers. I had never suspected a thing before but now I started to have thoughts. Those thoughts turned into suspicions and the suspicions turned into the truth.

It was a Sunday and I remember in the morning watching Ski Sunday because I had seen it advertised a few days before and I remember saying to him that I used to watch it all the time with Dad when I was a little girl. So I recorded it and we watched it as live but about fifteen minutes after it started because my mum had rung me. They were coming to dinner and she was wanting to confirm a time and see if I needed anything bringing. I told her to either buy a sherry trifle or to make one 'cos she makes a lovely trifle but the last few times I'd asked her to make one she'd been too busy. I'm not sure why though 'cos she's bloody retired. She's constantly saying 'I don't know how I used to have time for work, I'm never in,' which makes it worse when I ask her to do something for me. During Ski Sunday I had seen him looking at his phone which was at the side of his leg and almost hidden down the side of the sofa. He kept glancing down, I could see through the corner of my eye but once I'd noticed him looking I was watching for it. Then he would get up to make a cup of tea then he'd say he needed more milk and then more sugar and then he needed a wee, it was like any excuse to get up. This went on throughout Ski Sunday and then I started preparing dinner so I stopped noticing. He seemed edgy. I even remember him saying that Jack, one of the lads from the suppliers of his work equipment, had asked him if he wanted a pint at the local. He doesn't even like Jack. Well he's not called Jack he's called Adrian but they call him Jack 'cos Jackson is his surname and they can't call him Jacko 'cos they've already got a Jacko and they've also got an Adrian too so he's called Jack. He's always saying that he hates going to the suppliers when Jack's there 'cos he doesn't like him and will often go on a Friday morning as Jack doesn't work Fridays: he works Saturdays instead and has his daughter on a Thursday night. You've got to have a good memory to be a good liar and he quite clearly hasn't got a good memory. He doesn't even go to the pub that he mentioned going to which was another thing that didn't seem right. We were aiming to have dinner at about five thirty and all this time his phone had been glued to his hand. He said the texts were about work when I asked him but I definitely at this point thought it was lies and I didn't believe him. Just before dinner my parents and the knob had been watching cricket and I had been in the kitchen. Every time I looked through to the living room Mum and Dad were so much engrossed in the TV they might as well have been sat at Headingly. He was merrily texting away unaware that he had been spotted. At the table there was no sight of the phone. My mum for some bizarre reason always has a runny nose at the dinner table so I said I'd go get her tissues out of her bag as I hadn't sat down to eat; I was just finishing up dishing out. She always has a packet somewhere nearby and I always remember as a kid her turning around to the sideboard and getting her hanky out of the top drawer the minute she sat down at the table. It became just a part of meal times although why she never got it out before she sat down I will never know. The funniest thing of all was that after a few years my dad started and would joke about her giving him her nose. The funniest thing turned into the most vulgar thing when they started having a shared hanky and would clearly pass it between themselves whilst eating. One would eat whilst the other had a blow and then they would swap. Urrgghh, parents, you can't pick them.

As I reached into my mum's bag to get her paper hankies for them to share I heard a buzz and knew instantly what it would be. My phone hardly ever makes a sound but it does not vibrate. I'm not even sure I would know how to make it vibrate anyway and my mum and dad are unaware that phones can be used anywhere other than in the house, or they were at that point, my mum has since discovered mobile phones and texts quite a bit. I say she texts, well she does text but the space between words has somewhat kept its presence a secret from her and instead she puts a full stop. It makes reading a text from her like trying to crack a Second World War code. Although programmes about Bletchley Park are extremely interesting, I don't want to be in one and she writes it like a letter without punctuation which I find highly annoying.

dear.emily.are.you.coming.over.today.if.so.i.will.make. you.a.cheese.and.ham.sandwich.tell.me.what.time.and.i. will.make.it.for.when.you.come.can.we.go.to.the.shop.too.as.i.need.milk.or.can.you.get.
some.on.the.way.i.will.see.you.later.love.mum.

That was the last text from my mum on my phone and as you can see some degree of basic education is needed to decipher it. Dad wasn't as bad in one sense as he knew where the space key was but he just never checked his phone.

"Dad, I texted you this morning to see how you went on at the doctors'. I've been so worried and you never replied," I said one particularly stressful day after waiting hours to hear from him. The drawer opened and the words 'oh I forgot to put it on,' were paired with the beep of the on button kick starting the brick into life.

I expected the pack of hankies to be sat on top of the many contents in her bag but amazingly enough they weren't and fishing around I heard the buzz again. I don't know who was more surprised when I returned to the table, Mum or the knob because in my hand was not the pack of hankies to stop Mum's nose running into her dinner but a phone with messages and pictures that I was not meant to see. I don't swear in front of my parents if I can help it but I'm sure both of them did not bat an eye lid to my language as the knob's antics had suddenly become public.

"Who the hell is sweet cheeks?" I shouted across the table to the sad pathetic sod who dared not even look at me never mind answer my question. I remember him just looking down into his food as his fork controlled by his right hand moved a solitary sprout for one side to another. Mum and Dad didn't say anything and were torn between watching him and watching me. If they would have had prior warning they could have made a pact for one to watch one of us whilst the other watched the other and then they could have compared notes later like the pundits analysing the teams on Match of the Day. Not that I watch Match of the Day but I have done if the knob watched it and being the dutiful wife trying to take an interest may have thrown the odd comment in, not that my efforts were ever appreciated. 'The reds are the better team 'cos the goalie is cute,' is maybe not the effort he wanted but I tried nonetheless. The off side rule was explained to me years ago and my pretence of understanding was short-lived as I pointed out it couldn't be offside as there was still one player between the attacker and the goal. I thought it slightly unkind that he called me thick as I hadn't realised that he was the goalie and was quite legally stood there. From that day I remembered the one in the different coloured top was the goalie, annoyingly to him I didn't realise that the man in the middle was the referee and not an extra goalkeeper. All very technical this football game. Rugby is much easier and I have to say although the players weren't as good-looking due to the fact that they run into men built like brick walls for a living, their legs are much nicer and I have to say their shorts are slightly tighter too giving all round satisfaction to a young girl like me stood watching Bradford Northern from the terraces with Uncle Barry. I didn't go to Rugby that much but I did quite enjoy the atmosphere. Stood side by side with men and Uncle Barry watching the cauliflower ears explode as the huge man machines collided was great fun. Uncle Barry had a voice like a fog horn and when he shouted you knew about it. He stopped going after a time and I always thought that the team had told him to stop going as they couldn't hear each other talk about their game plan. I'm sure that was not the case really and probably more down to the fact that he got gangrene in his leg which had to be amputated quickly followed by his other leg, and then he died. The team had a minute's silence for him which was nice so I'm sure they appreciated his support more than I gave them credit for. It turned out that he had played for them when he was younger, a fact which had escaped me and one which I could have bragged about at school had I known about it, not that it would have got me any sort of preferential treatment in a school where everyone supported Leeds United or Leeds

Rugby League club but I would have used it had I have had it to use.

Anyway I digress again. In answer to the sweet cheeks question I received no reply. I asked who the hell Lou-Lou was. This time a muttered answer of just one of the models came across the table to greet me almost turning the food rotten as it did. Dad put down his knife and fork just at the same time Mum had said that they should go and leave us to talk. I couldn't talk and if I had been able to I would have told them not to go. I did not want to be alone and being with him at that point made me feel more alone than I had ever done so in my whole life.

Chapter Ten

Mum and Dad waved as they disappeared from view half way down the street as the road bends round heading out towards the main road. I watched from the window just wishing they would come back and that it was him that I was watching heading out of sight. I knew I had to hear his poor pathetic excuse and I suppose I couldn't blame him after being surrounded by half naked women most days. Surely at some point he was bound to start touching them. The thought made me feel sick. The thought that the same hands that he touched me with, albeit occasionally, were the same ones that were all over some other woman's body. The fact that he was old enough to be her dad didn't even make it worse as it couldn't have been any worse. All I could think of was the sight of him rubbing his naked body against another woman. I would say that I felt sick but I didn't even get any warning before the vomit erupted from my mouth covering all before me. Luckily it landed on the windowsill and not the Sofia three seater settee as it would not have come out. You can still see the stain from the glass of red wine that was spilt there last year after the knob decided the week after we bought that and a matching two seater settee that it should be christened. As he lifted my leg and tried to take my knickers off I knocked the glass of wine out of his hand which went down the side of the settee. It washed out of the cushion quite nicely but pouring white wine over the red wine to get it out before it stained only worked to a point because the stain can still be seen if you look for it, not that anyone would know about it because it's not the topic of conversation that we address with guests. He blamed me for quite some time after that although I'm not sure if he was more annoyed with the stain on the settee or the fact that he never got sex. He quite clearly didn't need me for that though, did he? I've actually thought over the last couple of months that he'd stopped pestering me for sex. He used to sulk like a child if I said no.

"Do you fancy a bit of play time tonight?"

"Not really, no," I'd say. Well I didn't really but I wanted to. Instead I was more diplomatic.

"Not really, I don't feel that well."

"Again?" he'd say, "I've never known anyone to be poorly all the time like you." How could I say I don't want you to do it. I'm bored by the whole sex thing, it's the same all the time. He puts his hand down my pants and then the next thing he's laid on top pumping away whilst I'm wondering about the next day or the job that I'm working on or what shall I do for tea tomorrow, anything but 'Oh that's good'. It simply isn't that good, he simply isn't that good. The usual course of action was that he would be nice to me. He would make me a cup of tea or a sandwich for lunch, although never tea 'cos he couldn't cook anything any more adventurous than beans on toast. Even at beans on toast he would burn the beans to the pan which would go black on the bottom and smell like a bonfire for weeks. I once bought a pan and threw it away within a few weeks because he was once off work due to a fire in his studio. The weather wasn't good enough for outside shoots and he was waiting for the insurance company to fund the repairs so he was at home for a while. He had beans for his lunch a few days due to his lack of cooking skills and my pan was destroyed. I don't know why he couldn't buy a microwave meal or just make a sandwich but that's what he's like. Apparently one of the girls left her hair straighteners plugged in overnight causing the fire which also damaged the changing rooms. I very much doubted at the time that the changing rooms were ever used anyway 'cos he was always commenting on the way that models undressed and how good they looked no matter what they wore which he didn't need to point out because I already knew they'd look better than I ever would. People say life begins at forty. Well if that's the case, I've had nine years to practice and I'm still rubbish at it.

I do ponder what life has in store for me sometimes. When you are younger it just seems so simple. You date a few, you find one you like, you get married, have kids and then work until retirement either gives you time to do things together or you look after each other 'cos you're knackered and can't do anything. Nobody tells you about the plan B if things don't go that way. There's no manual that you can flick through the troubleshooting guide and repair it if it is broken or a call centre to ring for 24-hour emergency advice. Mind you all the call centres that I've used lately I couldn't understand a bloody word and you end up trying to sort it yourself anyway. Just like my life now. I have to try and find the way myself. The only people I would ever ask for any sort of help are my dad who's not here and the bastard who has just destroyed me. Anyway I digress, he would go on about us having sex until I gave in and let him.

The 'Nag for a shag' became his trademark tactic. The few days before, no, who am I kidding, the several days before he would act like a child, huffing and puffing, banging around, sighing before going on the charm offensive.

"You look nice."

"I like that top." This would then turn into more direct things.

"I love that top, really shows your fabulous figure."

"That skirt shows off what a great body you've got." This would then be stepped up to level three and now going for the kill.

"You have great boobs."

"I can see down your top when you bend down."

"You have a better body than any of my models."

"You look really sexy." As if that's going to do anything for me. What about taking me out and buying me a meal and then complimenting how I look instead of talking rubbish. How is that meant to turn me on. I want to feel like a woman not a tart. He really has no understanding of how a woman feels. Maybe his models like it when he says things like that but they're only a step away from being a prostitute anyway. He pays them to take pictures, he might as well sleep with them too.

So there I am with vomit dripping down my chin onto my blouse, some splattered on the windowsill and some on the windows and he's stood behind me saying it meant nothing. It meant nothing! That's the worst thing that anyone in that situation could say.

"You mean you threw away everything that we have for something that meant nothing?"

"No I didn't mean it like that," he said. "You're

overreacting as usual."

"I'm overreacting." I was now at the red rag to a bull stage and quoted the gay uncle Derek in the Catherine Tate show.

"How very dare you?" In fact I added a few extra words of my own. He had no comment. His eyes looked into mine. I could see tears, more so in my eyes than his although I saw tears in his eyes after I slapped the dirty sod right across his face. I have never felt so good as I did then, so I hit him again. I caught him with my ring just above his eye which ripped open the skin quite easily. I felt no sympathy for him as the blood started with a trickle, turning into a heavy bleed within seconds. He held his hand there to try and stop the flow but not once did I hear the word sorry come from his lips. I am not sure that sorry would have cut anywhere near the most basic of scratches into the damage that he had done. My heart hurt so much I knew it had been broken. So many years I had given my all to our marriage and for me to find out like that was the most humiliating execution of my feelings he could have done. To see texts with words like sexy, gorgeous and can't wait to see you on his phone, the same phone that he texts me on to say he will be late home was beyond cruel. To see pictures of Lucy Lovejoy sat in all sorts of naked poses was dirty, disgusting, degrading and disrespectful to me. He offered nothing in return, just a sad pathetic look on his face knowing that he'd been caught. How long it had been going on for was anybody's guess, he wouldn't tell me. I just cannot see what was in it for her. He gets a beautiful, if not a little bit false, twenty-five-year-old to show off and who looks fab. I say false not because I believe she has had a boob job which according to the pictures I don't think she has but because her makeup is a little bit on the trowelled on level. I'm actually surprised that I noticed her makeup after seeing the pictures of her very neatly attended-to lady garden. That's another thing that escapes me, I know we like to trim the hedges in the garden outside but I don't get the taking the lady-garden bush down to minimal or even zero. I just think that it is wrong and can't understand any man who would want to visit a bare playground.

I packed his bag for him, just the basics, T-shirts, jeans, undies, socks and toothbrush and after throwing the bag down the stairs at him and screaming for him to go. I watched as he walked down the drive, avoiding the tirade of verbal abuse that I threw at him from the bedroom window, launch his hurriedly packed bag in the car and drive away. Part of me wanted him to turn around and come back and at least try to talk me round. I was not for the turning but he didn't really try. That hurt too. I wanted him to be on his knees begging me to let him stay but he didn't and there was only two places that I could think of where he would go, to his brother, who was on holiday, and hers. I didn't even think about her living situation. She maybe still lives at home with her parents who were probably around the same age as her new boyfriend. I couldn't imagine it being a happy family environment; in fact I couldn't imagine anything other than my husband sleeping in another woman's bed that night.

My dad came back after he'd gone and I could see the pain in his eyes at seeing me upset. My dad and I always had a bond broken by no-one. He had destroyed my world but had destroyed a part of my dad's too. I knew one day I would recover from the pain he had caused me but hurting my dad was one thing I could never forgive. My dad was there for me on many occasions throughout this ordeal. Whenever I was upset, whenever I cried and whenever I was at my parents' and we talked about it, he would drive me home and stay with me. I still need him now but feel his presence and feel his strong arms around me. I love my dad more than I have ever or will ever love any man. He never let me down.

Chapter Eleven

So I am still left with a dilemma. Do I go to meet him or do I not? My gut instinct is telling me to stay well away but as I have already said I am curious to know what he wants. I have now texted him back and said I would meet him just to buy me some more time and then at least I can change my mind if I decide not to. If I say no now it's harder to change my mind without messing him about. Funny how I think that I don't want to mess him about, I think he messed me about slightly more than I would changing my mind about Costa. I do love a good coffee and meeting him probably won't be as traumatic as meeting Sally for one. She had a Costa Ice once and caused a right fuss because she didn't like it – having decided she preferred her coffee hot.

"Well I didn't realise it was going to be cold," she said.
"What did you think the Ice part meant?" I asked.
"Have you ever had an iced tea?"
"Of course I have," she said looking at me indignantly.
"I'm not thick."
"I never said you were thick, but it's obvious to me that if an iced tea is like cold tea then an iced coffee would be like a cold coffee." She then spent the next ten minutes winding the replacement soya milked hot chocolate in a large cup around the long teaspoon without a word. Yet again I was the one who had to make amends and apologise although quite what I had to be sorry about was way beyond me but the grudges that Sally holds tight in her hands are like babies that she doesn't want to lose, they will at some point make an

appearance which are not always in the same day or even the same week, but suffice to say they are well and truly stored for another occasion. I find a piece of Tiffin makes a great half way stop to an apology and by the time the last bit went in she had forgotten all about it. Thick is not a word amongst the many words that I would use to describe Sally. Selfish, self-centred, controlling, materialistic, grumpy and grudge-bearing amongst them, but not thick.

I've been glad of the time off work, I needed it to recharge. I hate feeling that I don't particularly give a damn anymore. Sometimes though I really don't give a damn and the idiots that I deal with have two effects on me. Number one, they make me feel better about myself as the situations and circumstances of their private lives are difficult and I think that maybe my life isn't so bad after all and number two, I realise that some people are so petty about things that shouldn't even be an issue. Why we have to bother with people who complain 'cos their neighbour has erected a fence which they think is six centimetres onto their land is beyond me. I wouldn't even notice if my neighbour's fence was twelve centimetres onto my land never mind six, mind you twelve centimetres does seem quite a lot after being married to the knob.

"Hi, Mum," I said as I picked up the phone and swiped it to answer. It always amazes me when you pick up your mobile phone to ring or text someone and at the same time you receive a text or phone call. I wonder if there is some sort of sixth sense in us all 'cos it's happened to me a few times. I wish the same sixth sense would become active when I pick my lottery numbers but alas, I haven't won a sausage for some time. I always do the Wednesday and Saturday lotteries which I now have to do online as I either forget to put the tickets on or forget to check them, and the only time I remember to check the numbers is the times when I forgot to put the tickets on in the first place. The beauty of online playing is that they check the numbers for me. I only do the euro when it's an amount that's worth winning, actually I would be quite happy to win anything over £25.

"Hello, Mum," I probed again. I could hear a scrambling sound and it was ages before I heard her voice.

"What happened there?" I asked.

"You sounded like you were miles away," she said. At this point I couldn't work out why she hadn't heard me, my signal was fine. I assumed that as with many previous occasions she had put the phone to her ear upside down. I had seen her do it so many times when I was in the house, and even Dad had sometimes got up and turned it around for her. The handset had a little notch near to the ear part of the phone for some reason and Mum always thought that it was the bottom of the phone, this confused her to the point that when she picked it up it felt natural for her to put it at the bottom. I'd like to point out at this part that my mum is by no means suffering dementia but it's just sometimes she gets a bit confused. Confused is a good word to describe anyone from thick to daft and covers my mother on so many levels.

"Can you hear me now?" I asked reassuringly.

"Yes, I'm not deaf, dear." My mum is not an old eighty and doesn't suit the old lady label that much, but on occasions she does excel.

"Do you need me?" I asked.

"No why?" she replied.

"You rang me."

"Did I?" This wasn't going well. "Oh, maybe I did then."

"Well what did you want?"

"Err," she paused, obviously frantically trying to search the farthest reaches of her brain for her final thoughts before ringing me. "What are you doing today?" I don't know if that was the real thought or if it was just a poor substitute one.

"The knob invited me to Costa to talk. I did tell you 'cos you said I should meet him."

"Oh, is that today? Yes, dear, I think you should and I do wish you wouldn't call him that word. He does have a name." Reaffirming her position made me doubt it more and I started an unwanted and quite unnecessary debate in my head of why she would want me to go and meet with him. I think she always liked him and I think she still does. If she doesn't like me calling him knob, I'm damn sure she wouldn't like my other names for him.

"Anyway, Mum, what did you want 'cos I need to decide if I'm going or not."

"It doesn't matter," she said. If it didn't matter why did she ring me in the first place I just didn't know. "I like going to Costa."

"I know, Mum, I'll take you next week."

"I like those Al Pacinos that I had last time."

"Cappuccino." I corrected her for the umpteenth time. Most people have a memory of a time when they have been embarrassed to have been with their parents at some point in their life. Most people would mention a disco where Dad took to the floor and did the dancing that every dad is born with the capability of doing, but my tales are all about my mother. How she mixes words up and confuses things with other things is legendary. Sometimes I laugh about it but always after the event and never at the time. The poor man in the phone department of Tesco must have thought there was a hidden camera when I took my mother to get a mobile phone for the first time. I asked for a bog standard basic one that even my mother would be able to use. The man kindly and helpfully passed me the most basic of mobile phones that had ever been built. It was perfect and fitted in her hand as though they had designed it around her arthritic thumbs. Then the best line ever that had the man frantically looking for Jeremy Beadle.

"Where do I put my money in?" I have never wanted the floor to swallow me up as much as that day. I'm not entirely sure if the question was as bad as the fact that she stood waiting for an answer to what she obviously thought was a perfectly normal question. How he kept a straight face when he explained the pay as you go top up system, as I rolled up into a ball and died, is beyond me. Suffice to say, I have never taken her to Tesco again. In the days following this incident the pay as you go system in my mum's head became the passing go system. Now when we are out together, avoiding Tesco at all costs, I keep thinking she needs a wee when she says she needs to pass go.

The streets are busy this morning which is maybe something to do with the weather being okay for a change and this being my last day of not working I have to decide whether I will ruin it by going to see him or if he will have something for me which will make my day. I can't imagine it would be the latter as he cannot possibly do anything which will make my life better other than divorce me. Then a thought comes over me, a cold hard thought that digs deep into my mind planting a seed that with a bit of watering will grow into something horrible. What if he brings her? What if that is exactly the reason why he wants to see me, he is the one who wants the divorce to marry her. That morning if I'd woken up and someone had told me that he wanted a divorce I would have been happy beyond happiness, but now in the face of something which may be a possibility I don't like the thought at all.

What will I do if she is there? How should I conduct myself? Should I pretend that I'm not bothered, have a boyfriend even – that might work. Thoughts race through my head so quickly that I find comfort on the bench outside the post office my head spinning with thoughts of looking at her over my Al Pacino, err cappuccino, Oh god, my bloody mother has a lot to answer for.

The Costa is in sight and as sleek as a Royal Marine Commando I walk slow and tight into the building, guarding myself from enemy sight. I will get as close as possible without being seen and conduct a recce to check on enemy numbers. If there is one I am going in, if there are two and if he's brought that tart with him I'm pulling out.

The problem with my plan is firstly I am no Royal Marine Commando and I stick out like a sore thumb, especially as I have decided to wear my Diesel animal print cardigan which, unless you are expecting to see a Leopard walking down the high street, makes me more noticeable than if I was naked, and secondly, and again I am no Royal Marine Commando, my small confident killer instinct steps towards my intended target before being blown apart by a tap on my shoulder. This causes me to scream and the knob to put his dirty filthy arms around me to either comfort me or to stop people thinking that I'm being attacked. I'm not sure which one and I'm not really bothered but I pull away as soon as I regain control of myself.

"Good to see you, Em." I do not like being called Emmy as this is what Sally calls me but I have never minded Em. However, hearing him say it sends a sick feeling to my stomach.

"My name is Emily," I correct him and he repeats his greeting using my Sunday name.

"Would you like a coffee?" He points to the familiar red sign a few shops down.

"What do you want to see me for?" I am not sure I want to sit opposite him in there, I'm not sure I'm ready for this.

"Can we go and sit and talk?" He asks me like we are going on a date. I wonder if this is where he takes her before deciding that he has probably never been to a Costa shop before. He has no class, no culture and no inkling to go to places like that, unless she has injected some into him. I don't want to think about what he has injected into her, and throw the thought out of my head and banish it into the wilderness. I feel sick, flustered and hot, panicking beyond all reasonability but yet strangely safe that someone is with me. I feel faint and in need of fresh air and as the pavement comes towards me the fact that I am already outside makes no difference to my need for it. I feel myself hit the floor and then I feel calm and nothing else.

Chapter Twelve

The air blows gently on my face as I open my eyes and see the knob looking at me. I try quickly to get to my feet without his help but as I wobble he steadies me so I unwillingly accept his offer of assistance. I feel a bit shaky but everything comes back to me as to why I am there. I did mention that I am not a Royal Marine Commando and I stand by this as I get myself together and walk slowly towards Costa Coffee. I feel his arm around my shoulder, the very same arm that has molested Lucy Legs-wide-open on what will by now be many occasions. I nod at his suggestion of a regular hot chocolate and sit looking around the shop gathering myself together, my thoughts and feelings at conflict with one another. I feel cold and can feel intermittent shivers travel the whole length of my spine. I check my phone hidden away in the very depths of my Gemma bag hoping that someone will have texted me with words of advice, but nothing. No words of wisdom from Sally and no dippy attempt of advice from Dawn, I am doing this alone it seems. A couple in the corner act as though they have been together way too long and they sit playing on their phones as though the other person isn't there, and in the few minutes that I have observed them, not one word has passed between them. I wonder if me and the knob ever looked like that, we had been together twenty years and had quite clearly completely run out of things to say. Maybe if I had shared his interests more we would have survived the quite obvious rocky patch that we'd had although I'm not entirely sure I would have offered much in my liking for young attractive naked female models. This was one interest he most definitely did keep from me for obvious reasons. I never liked photography or the technology that become associated with it and he often said that he would take pictures of me. When I said I looked awful in pictures as I wasn't as slim as I had been, I waited for the 'you're perfect to me' answer which would have made me feel at least a little bit attractive but the reply that I got was 'don't worry about that. I can airbrush it out.' I never did do the pictures. We once did some pictures when we first met and I found out that he was a professional photographer. At first they were normal photos on days out and at parties but then they started getting a little bit more risqué. My dad would have killed me if he had ever found out. At the time I was mortified with myself for doing topless pictures and I was convinced that he would show them to people so I kept them in my knicker drawer. I only got rid of them when he left me as I clearly wasn't that nice anymore. I did wish I still had that body in the photographs and had a good last look at them before I tore them up and set fire to them in the garden. Shame old Patrick didn't get his hands on them before they went; the pictures not my boobs.

On the far side of the shop I can see Owen, one of the twins from No.43, with a man. Are my instincts about him being gay right, I wonder? They look cosy and unlike the other couple they are deep in conversation and very attentive of each other. Oh, I'm sure I just saw the other man touch Owen's hand, maybe accidental, maybe not. I do love people watching.

My fun is spoilt by the knob putting a tray on the

table in front of me. He moves one of the chocolates and places it in front of me and the other in front of himself.

"Bought you a present," he says pushing a giant chocolate marshmallow towards me.

"Thank you," I say politely.

"My pleasure," he says. Well this is all very polite and nice. He looks at me and I look away. I don't want eye contact if I can help it. I still have no idea what he wants and as long as I don't make eye contact or ask questions I will not find out. I start to have butterflies in my tummy and I'm not sure why. This is the first time I have seen him properly since he left and I don't know how to behave. Are we supposed to act like friends or do we shake hands at the end of this 'meeting' as I'm not sure what I would do if he hugged me. Would I push him away or pull him closer? I just don't know.

"You look nice." I try not to believe him but I do look nice, I spent extra time this morning straightening my hair with the present that I bought to console myself after he left. I love my purple GHD hair straighteners, they have now become my favourite present that I have ever received, even if I did buy them myself. They cheered me up at the time until I realised that I had the most perfect hair straighteners in the world but nowhere to go after I'd used them. Luckily Dawn and Sally stepped in and included me in their social lives, not that I wanted to tag along but I knew I had to get out of the house instead of spending all my time crying. Everything reminded me of him in that house and even though I bought a new bed and new bedding I still thought of him in everything I did for weeks.

"Thank you," I replied. I wasn't going to say that he

looked nice too because although he did actually look a lot smarter than he used to I knew it was for her benefit and not mine.

"How've you been, Em?" I didn't want to get on a rant about how my world had fallen apart and that my heart had been ripped in two and stamped on and that I have cried buckets of tears since he went and that I felt my life would never be the same ever again!

"Fine thank you. You?" This is easier than I thought. He looks stressed. Maybe I'm not making this easy for him and I'm glad. I don't want to make his divorce request easy at all. In fact I want him to squirm and sweat before he gets it granted. I decided in the few minutes watching Owen and his boyfriend and the couple not talking that if that is what he wants then I should not stand in his way. Everyone deserves a wedding and although he'll be greedy for having two, that little tart Lucy deserves one at least, even if it is with my husband.

"Yeh not too bad." Do I detect a hint of unhappiness in his voice or is it more wishful thinking on my part. I need to probe further.

"How's Lucy?" I didn't mean to mention her at all. I wanted him to bring her up as I knew he would at some point. You can't ask for a divorce without mentioning how happy she makes him and how he wants to give her that ring that she craves for. He puffs air through his top lip.

"She's fine." Damn, I didn't expect that. 'She's fine,' I mimic his voice in my head but change it to make it sound like a teenage girl. I wanted him to say that she had run off with a man her own age but my disappointment hopefully didn't show on my face.

"That's good, I'm glad," I lied. "How's your mum?" The fact that I asked about his mum must have given away the fact that I had nothing constructive to say, but I didn't want to sit and talk about Lucy and him nor did I really care how she was. I hated his mum and he laughed as the question left my lips.

"Why are you asking about my mum?"

"Just wondered how she was?"

"Em, you've not seen or spoken to the old witch for over ten years." I laugh and he laughs again. It was the ice breaker needed and the tension left my body in orgasmic proportions. We talked about nothing in particular until the hot chocolate had vacated our tall glasses, the holidays we had, his witch of a mother, he asked how Jasper was which I'm glad of because I know she still misses him and we laughed about things in the past. The time we went swimming and he wanted to save his chewing gum for later and for some God forsaken reason he stuck it down his trunks and went swimming. On his return to the changing rooms he went to take out the chewing gum to put it back in his mouth and found it had attached itself to his pubic hair. He said nothing until I walked in the bedroom and he's there with my lady-shaver shaving his bits, he didn't even use his own shaver. At the time I went mental but sitting in Costa Coffee about eighteen years later I laughed until my bladder nearly spilt its contents.

"Would you like another drink?" I didn't really want one but I'm actually having a slightly better time than I expected to do so I offer to get them I like to keep topping up my Costa card with points. I'm in the queue waiting to order when I feel someone standing close behind me, almost brushing against me and I don't like it, I feel that my personal space is being invaded and I try to move which doesn't help as the person seems to move with me. I turn to say something and the person is looking the other way, but from the side of his face I can tell it is the Italian stallion from Frankie & Benny's.

'Oh no, what shall I do? What if he sees me with the knob? He might think I'm married. Well technically I am but not in that way. I'm single and ready and available, Oh, take me now.'

"Sorry." Oh, he spoke to me. I am gushing with all the feelings that I haven't had for so many years. He actually spoke directly to me. He said sorry. I look at him and he smiles at me and turns away. He doesn't recognise me, does he? I am filled with the gutted feeling of rejection without even offering myself to him on the proverbial plate. I wanted so much for him to take me in his arms and do with me whatever he wanted. I would not have objected to any of it. Why didn't he notice me? He is gorgeous. And in that one small sentence of three words I have answered my own question. He is gorgeous. I am not. I feel silly, small and shattered for even putting myself and him in the same thought and as I carry the tray of two hot chocolates back to the table I just feel that I want to go home and curl up into a ball and disappear. He has shattered me with just one word: sorry. I will never eat at Frankie & Benny's again. As if I could not feel any worse, I watch the knob as he clocks someone walking through the door and I can tell by his eyebrows rising that he likes what he sees and as low as I feel I cannot cope because I know this is the point where Lucy Love-of-his-life comes in and joins us. I now see the plan. He butters me up with memories of yesteryear and then BAM! the divorce request is granted 'cos I'm in a good mood. Well he can get lost if he thinks I'm falling for it now. However, as I watch his eyes there is no smile to accompany the sight as he would have inadvertently given had it been Lucy. I turn to follow his gaze to see the most amazingly beautiful woman I have ever seen with long, and I mean long, jet black hair with an unfastened long black coat flowing behind her like the trail of a wedding dress, tight blue jeans with long black knee length boots and a black silk top showing the heavenly cleavage of perfectly shaped boobs that any man would die to have a private viewing of. I cannot fault the knob for watching this vision who would knock spots off Lucy Love-myself as well he knows and I can tell this is what he is thinking as he drools causing a bit of saliva to drip into his hot chocolate. I watch as the remaining bit of my world is destroyed before me as she sits down with the Italian stallion and kisses him over the table. I now know beyond all reasonable doubt why he would never give me a second look. He has an angel for a girlfriend. What am I thinking? I now have nothing to lose and go for the kill.

"What did you want to see me about?"

"I just wanted to see you. I've missed you."

"Missed me? Pull the other one it's got bells on it." I've not used that expression for ages and feel a sense of pride that at a time when my life is in tatters I can pull it out of my 'expressions to use in certain occasions' box.

"Emily, it's true, I've missed you since day one." He

only calls me Emily when we argue or he wants to stress his point, and I guess he is now trying to stress his point. I cannot help but watch over the knob's shoulder at the stallion laughing and smiling and touching her hand, he seems happy but is he in love and does it really matter, he clearly wouldn't notice me anyway.

"Whatever," I throw in casually.

"Em, I have made the stupidest mistake of all time and seeing you today makes me realise. Will you take me back?" Well, I really didn't expect that. If I had made a list of all the things that I thought he was going to say to me, that wouldn't have been anywhere near the top fifty. I thank him for the chocolate and make my excuses. I'm not feeling very strong at the moment and a bit of nostalgia can do silly things. I don't want to do silly things so distance is the best form of defence. I practically run to my car ignoring his attempts to ring me. I see a text from Dawn and reading it makes me smile.

'Don't go x.' As always Dawn is late with her advice but at least she texted me back. Sally will be getting either wined and dined or rogered senseless by Marcus. Note to self – Find new personal advisors.

Chapter Thirteen

It is what I would class as mid-afternoon and I'm not sure if I feel sick from my hot chocolate, seeing the knob again or seeing the Italian with his girlfriend. It may not be the real sickness but more an apprehensive feeling about my future. I had thoughts of single being the new married and fifty being the new forty but as I face this part of life alone I'm not sure either is true. Here I am a rapidly approaching my half century and spending my days with my mother. My friends seem too busy for me, my husband is seeing a girl practically our daughter's age and now he claims it's all a mistake and the man I dream of taking me to bed and sending me to the moon and back has a girlfriend. I have several missed calls from the knob and I will let them remain that way, I will not answer them. Jeremy Kyle always has a way of helping me feel better and as I put on the TV and kick start the kettle to make myself a redbush, I hear a banging on the door. Without thinking to check who it is I open it to an out of breath knob stood on my door step.

"Oh Shaun, just go away." That is the first time I have used his real name for nearly two years.

"Em, I need to speak to you. Hear me out and I will go. I promise." Oh what harm can it do? As the second cup hits the worktop and is filled with his favourite coffee, heaven only knows why I still buy it when he doesn't live here and I don't drink it. Note to self – Make the house more mine.

I keep Jeremy Kyle on as it may give me something to talk about to avoid his conversation if it gets too uncomfortable. He sits next to me on the sofa but that is too close for me so I move and I can tell by the look on his face that it hurt him. Good!

"I'm really sorry for what happened. I was weak and it just happened." I hate it when people say it just happened as though one minute he was sat talking to Lucy Little-miss-innocent and then the next a part of his body is stuck inside her, it just doesn't happen that way. No matter how intense the passion is you can always say no. This sounds good in my head so I decide to use it.

"No matter how intense the passion was you could have always said no." I like it, and it worked.

"I know. You're right. You didn't want to sleep with me and she showed an interest, I'm so sorry. I just wish I could undo it all. I want you back so much it hurts."

"So it was my fault? Thank you very much. Well if I was so bad you'll be glad to be away from me then?"

"I didn't mean it like that." He's squirming now.

"We were married for twenty years," I remind him just in case he's forgotten, "and couples who have been together that long don't have sex all the time."

"It wasn't just about the sex; I couldn't even come near you without you moving away, not even for a cuddle."

"The only cuddle that you ever wanted was a naked one." I have to point that out because it is true that a man only ever wants a cuddle when his penis is sticking out and will be the first point of contact. I notice he is quiet and can't or won't answer it. I decide to step it up a bit now.

"Anyway, does Lucy know where you are?" Brilliant. What a shot. Top corner that one.

"We don't need to talk about her, do we?"

"She doesn't know you're here, does she? You naughty boy. You will never change, will you? Only this time it's her that's being lied to not me."

"Emily, I came here to try and talk to you, to ask you to forgive me and take me back."

"You are wasting your time, Shaun, I would rather be alone for the rest of my life. And probably will because I will never trust another man after what you've done to me." I pick his cup up and take it with mine into the kitchen. When I come back through to the room he's standing up to leave, he looks hurt and rejected which makes me happy. I feel powerful. I think again about him sneaking behind her back and that only adds to my happiness. I am in charge in this house and what I decide will happen, happens. Without thinking any further I pull him to me and kiss him. I smell the same aftershave that he always wore and I like it. He is stunned but I press my tongue into his mouth and kiss him like I haven't kissed him for a long time. I pull his shirt so that the buttons pop off and throw it to the floor. I grab his hand and put it on my boobs and feel him groping them. I undo his trousers and can tell instantly that he is excited and totally aroused. I step back for the tease as my top comes off over my head and my bra gets unclasped. I know my boobs are nice and I know he wants to touch them but he will have to wait until I take the rest of my clothes off. Within seconds we are naked on my living room floor. He is enjoying it, I can tell by the noises that he is making. I am not. This is my game, me exercising my power and putting myself back on top. I have made him cheat on a beautiful twenty-five-year-old model who has a body to die for. As soon as it's over, my game is won. This is the ultimate payback and something that I will hold over him for the rest of his life with Lucy the marriage wrecker.

Not for the first time I watch him walk down the drive and away from the house. This time he has a smile of accomplishment and waves as he goes holding his shirt together with his hand replacing the buttons torn off in my leadership, I on the other hand have a smile of power and determination and the tears of upset and hurt have been replaced by a deep sense of one-upmanship that I have never experienced before. He walks away thinking that he has made progress in his quest to get me back, whilst I stand firm knowing that I am at last the king or queen of my castle. To sum up; I am firmly in charge in my house.

After enjoying my own self indulgence for a little bit longer I start to come back down to earth with a bit of a bumpy ride with feelings twisting in my head as to what just happened and why I let it happen. I knew I had a point to prove to myself that I could regain control and a point to prove to the knob that I am a woman with feelings, someone who was not there to be used as a doormat and I know that he had just had sex because I decided it would happen, not him. In the shower I wash every trace of him from my body which psychologically I need to do and by the time I get out of the shower and look at myself in the mirror that same feeling of the new confidence that I had experienced last week came back. I am a woman in charge of my own destiny.

Note to self – Be a bit more believable when trying to convince myself.

On the way to my mum's for tea I think about going

back to work tomorrow, not something that I'm particularly looking forward to doing but it will be nice to get some sort of routine back into my life.

Jasper cried 'cos I said she couldn't come as we were going out for a tea, a slight lie, but is it wrong to lie to a dog? She had been cheated out of a proper walk but the promise of one later didn't seem to register with her and the look of 'yeh you've said that before' washed across her face. I find it a shame that sometimes my only companion is a dog and when even the dog seems to be pissed off with me I think what chance have I got of making a man happy. Two things then come to mind, when they said a dog is a man's best friend does this exclude women? And it doesn't really matter that I have got no chance of making a man happy as I have no man to make happy. I know though deep down that I have a lot to offer a man, I have said before that I'm not ugly, not that all good-looking men go for looks which is a good job but immediately my thoughts turn to the Italian stallion and his girlfriend almost disproving the point I have just made to myself. I don't have a bad body, again my thoughts refer to the Italian stallion's girlfriend and even Lucy loose-pants come to think of it, again disproving my point as next to those two my body is hideous and almost immediately I can see in my mind the flabby tummy that I hide behind my clothes. I am good company and good for a laugh although now my thoughts refer to me having a huffy dog and my eighty-year-old mother as the only people I spend time with. The dog doesn't particularly have a choice and my mother only wants to spend time with me 'cos I'm her taxi driver not because I am good company. My note to self has been reinforced, I do need to be more convincing to myself. I am a nice person and nobody can take that away from me.

"How did your meeting go with Shaun?" There was no hello, how are you? Just straight onto him. Nice to know whose side she's on, that's all I can say.

"It was okay, we just chatted."

"What did he want to see you for?"

"Nothing really," I lied. I didn't want her to know that he wanted me back 'cos she would badger me on his behalf.

"You should take him back, you could do a lot worse."

"Thanks, Mum," I'm getting annoyed now so I breathe deeply. "I can also do a lot better than being married to a lying cheating dirty scumbag."

"There's no need for language like that," she says. Good job I held back. I have words for him that would knock her glasses off. I never used the 'C' word until that day when I found out about his affair and shouted it at him from the bedroom window. Mrs Cartwright opposite was amazed that such a word came from my mouth, but it did along with other words too. I wonder if she mentioned it at the parish council meeting. Good job I didn't go to church. I bet the Archbishop of Canterbury would have driven to my house in person to have excommunicated me. Mind you, the big fella would have got here sooner so he would have probably just come himself.

My cheese and pickle sandwich made by mum for tea was eaten in relative silence and made only a slight more exclusive by adding a few sour cream Pringles to the side of the plate as I continued to dodge the occasional comment from her about the knob. I cheated myself out of quiche for tea that I had in my fridge to spend time with my mum only for her to inform me that it was WI night and that she needed a lift to the church hall where they would be jam making and finger knitting. I know that it wasn't the same lot as the stitching and bitching crew but some members are the same and after the tales of colostomy bags I decided there and then that I would not be eating any jam. Finger knitting did make me wonder cruelly maybe, but how women with twisted and bent fingers can finger knit without it looking like a pattern out of zig-zag magazine.

Yet again I find myself driving Emily's taxi for my mother and the new found problem of whether to go home or sit and wait.

"Just come in and wait."

"No, it's okay, Mum, I'll go home."

"Come in and do something useful and make some jam." As I study my list of things that I would class as important I fail to see jam making, in fact, it doesn't even make it onto my list at the bottom in the section marked 'after thoughts'. As I drive away I wonder what ingredients are put in the jam but before I make it too gross, I change my thinking to Dawn. I am about to drive past her house so pull up outside. I don't like people who make unannounced visits but I am about to embark on one myself.

Chapter Fourteen

Walking up the drive I squeeze past Dawn's car. I like her car as I have always liked Astras and in particular black ones. She complains that it shows the dirt but I like it and think the style is much better than my own Corsa. I think Jasper would prefer the Astra too but I have learnt to live to my means and selling my Audi A2 was not an easy choice but a necessary one all the same. My Corsa is economical and cheap to run so said the man in the garage and I had no reason to doubt him. It's only £20 a year for the road tax too which is a bonus. He was nice and friendly and I'm sure I detected a prolonged handshake at the signing of the deal. Whether he fancied me or not I don't know, I'm sure it was more my promise to return one day and buy another car from him and give him a good review on the online customer satisfaction survey that all customers are asked to fill out. I was true to my word and described him as friendly and helpful and Yes I would buy from again. I did go maybe a bit too far with the *'I think Gerry is an asset to your business with a smart appearance and outgoing personality which gives the customer a good first impression of your company. I was unsure what I was going to buy,'* which was a lie as I knew I had to buy something cheap and economical*, 'but Gerry gave me great advice taking the time to help me with my choice.'* In reality he asked me what I wanted, I said something cheap and economical and he said 'here we have a Corsa which is economical, cheap to run and in the £20 tax section,' I said 'I'll have it,' he said 'Brill,' and that was that.

"Hi, Emily."

"Hi, Dawn." Fairly routine so far I thought.

"I wasn't expecting you."

"No I'm passing. I've just dropped my mum off at the church hall for her jam making session with the WI."

"Oh," she said, clearly impressed.

"If it's awkward I can come back another time. I just didn't want to go all the way home and then have to come back so I thought I'd call here."

"Err," she paused. I was now beginning to feel the tension in the air, quite obviously from her not me.

"It's fine, Dawn. I'll see you another time."

"I've just got visitors, that's all. If I'd have known." Before she could finish her fobbing off sentence I was half way down the drive knocking her wing mirror as I went. I wasn't bothered as I distinctively got the impression that she didn't want to see me. As my car started and as if on purpose my radio was playing a song by someone I recognised as Michael Jackson, I didn't at first realise which song it was until the 'Leave me alone' lyrics started. I had certainly got that message from Dawn and would remember it. One thing I can't stand is the creeping around behind people's backs. I much prefer the upfront approach. Wondering if Sally would be any more welcoming I stopped outside her house. Seeing her car in the drive I thought that maybe she was in alone as I assumed Marcus would be driving a top of the range car and no such top of the range car was parked outside. I knocked on the door which was opened by Nancy, Sally's daughter.

"Hi, Auntie Emmy." The nerve still twinges over that

name.

"Hi, Nancy, is your mother in?"

"No she's at Dawn's." My words of 'Oh is she' must have sparked off some thoughts in poor little sweet Nancy's head as she started back-tracking. "Err well I thought that's what she said, maybe I misheard."

"No, love, I'm sure you didn't. Tell her I called, I won't interrupt their evening." I was mad with rage. If one of them stood in front of me now I would take off their head with one chop. Betrayal isn't a nice trait, even less when it is a friend who executes it. I now realise who the visitor was that Dawn was so tongue-tied in defending. Sally and Dawn my two closest friends had betrayed me. More so Dawn as my tolerance of Sally is not too good at the best of times, and slightly less now, but at this moment when my friends list is extremely low in terms of figures, I thought I could rely on those two. Returning to the church hall I decided that at this moment in time in my sad little life I would rather be in the company of finger knitting jam making grannies than two Judas style best friends although sticking by my instincts, I would not be eating any jam. That night as I dropped Mum off at her house I asked her one question with a request that she give me a truthful answer. My mother is someone who even when you request a lie to spare your feelings will hit you with the truth as hard as she can possibly hit it and give it one final tap for good measure.

"Do I go on a bit too much about things?"

"A bit too much?" she says. "I'd say you go on about things way too much. People have things in their own lives, dear, and have their own troubles, they don't want to listen to you going on about the doom and gloom in your life. Barbara was only saying tonight that her granddaughter has got to go and have some more chemo for her cancer so you just think yourself lucky." As I said, my mother hits things home as hard and as truthfully as she possibly can and this was no exception. I now knew that the reason Dawn and Sally had left me out was that I go on too much about my own doom and gloom and don't give any thought to theirs. I complain about their friendship being crap when in actual fact it was mine. Note to self – Stop being a selfish cow.

When Sally split with Jonathan was I there for her? No I was not. I was far too busy taking the mickey that she was being too dramatic whilst I was still married and being part of what I thought was a couple. Dawn is no better and the fact that she would sit with me talking about how Sally was all 'woe is me' and how Jonathan is better off without her now makes me realise that I am now the topic of conversation and that they will be feeling sorry for Shaun. I'm not quite sure what I have done wrong to warrant that sort of talk as I am the victim in all this. One thing I have to make known about Sally is that she thrives on gossip. She not only thrives on gossip but is good at character assassination. Sally is the manager of the Human Resources department at the council where I work. I do not see a great deal of her at work but our paths do occasionally cross. Once I attended a management multi-departmental meeting about the future structure of the council and how budget cuts would affect the way we had to work. As we sat around the table I noticed something that made me laugh out loud. Embarrassingly I was the only person who spotted it therefore all eyes were on me. Sally stood and did her spiel as did other heads of departments and at the end of the session I had deep bite marks on every finger. Did it work? It helped me to stop laughing out loud but could not stop the sniggers. My object of amusement? The name plates. We all had our names on plates in front of us. Mine smartly displayed E.MATHESON ASB; which is me in the Anti-social behaviour team. All other name plates were as smart as mine except Sally's which read S.LANDERS HR. This made me laugh. Sally as previously stated is a gossip and great at character assassination and her name read as one word confirmed this. I didn't tell her or anyone else what I had seen as I like to keep myself to myself. However, it amused me for days.

Dawn is – somewhat in her own opinion – an inadequate police officer. She claims to know very little about the law, knows nothing about which act or piece of legislation she is using at that particular time but does what she thinks is right. She is funny, witty, ditzy, gorgeous and dim. My first memory of her was on a job that I was dealing with. Most of my jobs are neighbour disputes. I mentioned earlier that people are so petty about neighbour's fences being six centimetres into their garden and I jest not. It is fact that people really are that petty. I had been called to deal with a neighbour dispute as the anti-social behaviour officer for the council and requested Police attendance as apparently threats had been made and I was fearful that it may kick off when I was there. This lady police officer pulled up in a police van and I laughed as she could hardly see over the steering wheel. It wasn't that she was small, just the fact that when she sat down her head disappeared down into her stab vest making her look like a tortoise with the top of her head popping out. As she exited the van her radio fell from her stab vest and when she bent down to pick it up her pen fell out of her pocket. And when she bent down a second time to pick that up her hat fell off. That was my first introduction to Dawn Winchester, our community bobby. That job, as with many others that I have since attended with Dawn, turned out to be a big pile of pathetic pettiness.

"Hello, Mrs Graves," said Dawn professionally, hat placed back on her head and pens put back in her pocket.

"What seems to be the problem?"

"Well," says Mrs Graves, "she has chopped my bush." We obviously snigger at her choice of words. The lady points to a large bush in the garden.

"Where?" asks Dawn

"That one?" she says pointing at the bush.

"How can she have chopped it down when I can see it?" Dawn said with a puzzled look on her face.

"I'll show you," says the lady. All three of us go into the garden and look at the bush standing a healthy five feet tall with leaves and flowers to suit. The lady points out five places where it has been cut neatly. I am no gardener but I know a neat cut when I see one and communicate this to the lady.

"It looks to me like it has been pruned."

"Well she must have done it."

"Who?" I ask.

"Her." She points next door.

"Why would she do that?"

"Because she's jealous."

"Of what?" Dawn says.

"My garden." Now again I say that I am in no way an expert on gardening but I know a tip of a garden when I see one.

"Why should she be jealous of your garden?" I am now intrigued to find out why she would be jealous of a garden that in my humble opinion is nothing more than an untidy piece of land. It has flowers I will grant you that but are they the most beautiful flowers I have seen? No they are not. It reminds me and I can tell by the look on Dawn's face that she is thinking along the same lines that she has stolen some wild flowers from a cemetery and planted them in her garden not because they are beautiful but because they are colourful and free.

"Well, have you seen hers? There's no colour in it and that's why she's chopped my bush down. She's jealous" I was about to give this lady some home truths when Dawn stepped in.

"I am a police officer here to investigate criminal damage to a bush. There is no damage for me to investigate."

"Well, she has cut it here and here and here." All the neatly cut twigs were pointed out as though a check list of shopping was being ticked off.

"She obviously thinks that the bush is so nice she wanted a cutting." Dawn said. The next five seconds were the most amazing I have ever experienced. The lady said.

"Well if she had come to me and asked nicely I would have given her a cutting because I am chopping it down next year." Those words signalled our intention to leave until her husband came out. He resembled something out of a 60s pop group with a flower-power shirt on but he himself looked like a corpse who had borrowed it.

"You'll have to excuse my husband, he's blind." I had no idea why we would have to excuse this gentleman for being blind but I had to stand and be party to their conversation of how next door were criminals as he had seen her walk past the house every day for five days with plants and plant pots which could only have been stolen from around the town.

I have never before in my life been in a police car until this point when I could not hold my laugh any longer. I would not have made it to my car which was another ten steps away from Dawn's patrol car therefore, as I scrambled into the front seat and filled the car with laughter, I will not lie; I literally wet myself. The scars of childbirth for me come in the form of a week bladder which let me down this time. The criminal damage to a bush which wasn't damaged paled into insignificance behind a blind husband who had seen the elderly neighbour carrying stolen plants. After calling off at home for clean clothes I wrote the job off as complete with no further action from me. I never did tell Dawn about sitting in her car and weeing myself despite the numerous times we have relived that incident since. That day started a friendship that through my own selfishness has been damaged. I now appear friendless, but on a positive note, it's OAP line dancing tonight!

Chapter Fifteen

For the first time I start to think that my life isn't that bad really and things could be a lot worse. This thought came to me whilst watching the line dancing session tonight. There was one old bloke who, Mum said, was a Major in the Army. I watched as he manoeuvred his Zimmer frame to copy the moves of the instructor who herself was in her eighties and struggling to complete the steps. I have a lovely daughter who had texted earlier to say that she was coming home as she had a week off so would be staying with me for a few days before heading to London to see some friends. I didn't even know she had friends in London. My mum is still grieving for Dad, as I am, and I know I have to keep up the support for her. I know how bad I felt after the knob left me but my parents were together sixty years. She got chance to say goodbye, which was a slight consolation. It's nice that she's getting out but I worry that she is beginning to forget him. She doesn't cry like she used to and when I go round now the TV or radio is on, there is no more sitting in silence. I don't want her to forget him I want her to be sad and upset 'cos that's how I feel. I feel guilty as soon as those thoughts come into my head and I astound myself by my own harshness that I almost resent her for going out and trying in some small way to take her mind off things. What is happening to me?

Harsh realities hit home like fireworks exploding in my head, I think I'm turning into a right selfish unsympathetic cow. My imagination places me into a fictional conversation between Sally and Dawn and I do not like what I hear. I cannot blame them for not wanting to spend time with me.

'Fancy tea out one night next week? My treat.' I send the text to multiple recipients, well two but it is better than one and I take comfort from that. I keep my phone on silent not to disturb the line dancing and watch the Major who struggles at the best of times to move let alone keep up. I still cannot stop myself from being amused by a group of elderly infirm people line dancing. They seem to enjoy it and do it in their own way but not one of them is in time with either the music or each other. One chap at the far end of the room has clearly had enough and is fast asleep on the chairs put out for the blood donating session in the morning. My thoughts disappear into the past thinking of Dad when I was young and how he would do everything with us, and going to the park on a Sunday morning became a weekly routine. Even from that young age I remember Mr Baldwin from next door asking Dad if he wanted a round a golf one Sunday morning. My dad refused his invitation stating that he wanted to spend time with the kids. This was my dad's idea of a perfect weekend, just chilling out and spending time with the kids. It was me mainly 'cos Charlotte would do her own thing. I would hang around him like a fly around shit; I adored him. We would always do something on a weekend. Sunday mornings we would go on the park for a bit then walk back past the shop where he would buy Charlotte and me some sweets and a newspaper for himself. We would then go home, sit with him and eat our goodies. He'd read the newspaper whilst we played.

"What the hell!" Someone screaming brought me back

to earth quicker than a space rocket on speed.

"Emily, get an ambulance." I realise that the music has stopped and my mum is shouting at me. She says it again.

"Emily, get an ambulance." I jump up and rush the length of the hall whilst some others seem to carry on dancing not noticing that the music has stopped and a medical emergency is unravelling before their eyes.

"He's dead." My mother is not known for making things into a drama so the sense of desperation in her voice makes me realise that something is wrong, that and the words that she chooses of course. Dead is always a strong word, I find. I try and remember the basics of the first aid course that I attended through work and as the nominated person to do the first aid on my department I should know what to do. I rack my brains sorting through the useless information stored there whilst picturing myself doing the mouth to mouth on the horrible smelly rubber bodiless dummy with the moving head and detachable mouth and try to think if we covered potential dead bodies. I am not very good on training courses and find myself drifting away to more interesting subjects of food and wine leaving the important life saving skills for others to listen to. I agreed to go on the course never imaging that I would one day be called on to do first aid. I have to confess although secretly to myself, that my thoughts were: if my mum says he's dead there's not much point in me doing anything. My mum shouting in my ear to do something made me realise that I had indeed got to do something and I checked for signs of breathing. There was no movement on his chest, no noise coming from his mouth and nor could I feel breath on my cheek pressed against his mouth. My body started to move itself into survival mode for dealing with its first casualty, namely a dead body when he coughed into my ear causing me to scream and run away letting his head drop down and his glasses smashing on the floor. I ran around frantically in a circle in and out of the few remaining dancers still unaware of anything happening around them ending up back near to the former dead body and another body laid out on the floor.

"Mum." I shouted loud, still with a hint of a scream, but there was no answer.

"Mum." Louder and louder I went until I saw a black screen in front of me. Looking up I saw something from my youth. I saw the green goddess. I did not want to partake in any exercise session – I was quite happy lying here.

"Hello. Can you hear me. My name is Mandy and I'm a paramedic."

"Oh no, Mum!" I wanted my mum.

"Oh, is this your mum." The green goddess was speaking to me. I stayed lying down waiting for the news that Mum had also died. I held my breath as I thought I might accept it easier if I didn't breathe. It was all that stupid old man's fault I thought and decided that I will never forgive him for killing my mother.

"Mum." I thought if I shouted loud enough she would come back to life.

"Shut up, you stupid mare."

"Mum, you're alive."

"Course I'm alive." I was so pleased. I didn't want to lose her. I wasn't ready to be an orphan just yet. I wanted to hug her but Mandy the paramedic told me to stay lying down until she had checked me over. Her hands were soothing as she checked all and down my body even though she wore blue latex gloves. I remembered this bit from the first aid training about checking for broken bones and wished I had paid more attention. Finally I was allowed to sit up and helped by Mandy I looked at my mum. I could not stop the tears that accompanied my happiness that my lovely mother was still alive. I wished my dad was here; I just needed one of his hugs right now. Mind you, if he was alive we wouldn't be wasting our time line dancing with coffin dodgers.

I thanked Mandy, she was nice and Mum said Mick, who helped her, was lovely too even taking time to mention how good looking she thought he was. For my mother who had just suffered a shock to take time to notice how good looking the paramedic was surprised me, she had clearly moved on from her twenty-year-old love affair with Joe Longthorne. I remember telling her that Joe Longthorne was gay. She thought I was being nasty due to the unpleasant thoughts of her having a crush on someone. I'm not even sure if she believes me now or not despite seeing him in the newspapers with his partner. I actually thought that Mandy the lady paramedic was very attractive but I didn't think to broadcast it to the world, although I did wonder what my hair would look like in her style. She had it tied up at the back in a pony tail but looped back through and the front coming down either side of her face. What a time to steal hair tips from someone! I quite liked her shiny lip-gloss too.

Note to self – Make more of an effort to look nice. (If Mandy can do it for work I'm damn sure that I can do it for a night out).

Outside there were two ambulances, one of which must have been Mandy's and Mick and I commented to Mum that they must have thought she was a goner for them to send two.

"No dear, the other one came for the Major. Line dancing was one battle too many for him. He croaked." I felt sick, faint and short of breath as I got into the car. That huge breath that scared me half to death causing me to run around like a idiot and my mum faint causing me to faint had been the poor old bugger's death breath. Oh my god I feel sick. Note to self – I must listen more on first aid training courses.

Back at Mum's I washed my face over and over again. I felt the Major's death breath would stay with me forever. My life was rubbish enough at the minute without catching the dreaded black death from someone. I looked at myself in the mirror seeing if any part of my face had changed into an old man with a handlebar moustache and started thinking about how he had fought the enemy for several years of his military life only to die in front of a group of line-dancing codgers. It just didn't seem fair to me.

Mum sat in silence when I went downstairs. I liked having a shower at my old home as there was much more space with her walk-in shower. I say walk-in shower, it was more of a sit-down shower with an adjustable seat, but on the few occasions that I had sat down on it and turned the shower on I felt as though I would die from water filled lungs. At least when you stand up you can move out of the direct line of fire from the hose.

"What's up, Mum?" I asked but she remained silent. As I walked further into the room I could see the light sparkling in her eyes. When I got close it was the tears in her eyes that made it noticeable rather than a normal sparkle. I asked the same question but her bottom lip quivering seemed to stop the answer from coming out. I had never shown a great deal of physical affection towards Mum since my adult years as most of it had been directed at Dad and despite the clubs and groups and sessions she now attended, here before me was a lonely old lady.

"I'm just being silly," she said in between wails. I had no idea at this point what was wrong with her but seeing her like this made the tears start to fall from my eyes.

"It's just so sad." I had to agree it was sad to see the Major die like that.

"I know but he had a good life and had a career doing what he loved to do. I'm sure his family are very proud, I mean it's not everyone gets to the rank of Major and goes to all the places that he's been to."

My mum's crying had become almost hysterical. I could only hold her and let her cries and tears find their way into the curve of my neck. I wasn't aware that my mother knew the Major that well other than to say hello to him at the geriatric line dancing group although I can imagine most of the old ladies would be upset at his passing as it looked to me sometimes like he was holding court with a bevy of ladies by his side hanging on his every word listening to his tales of heroic adventure. In reality there is a shortage of elderly gentlemen so the good old Major had his pick of the bunch.

"I miss him so much." I'm getting worried now. As I've just said I didn't know she knew him that well but to be so upset at his death is beginning to make me worry. Have I missed something, has my eighty-year-old mother been having some sort of, I hope non-sexual, relationship with the Major? I can cope with her having companionship but anything else is too much and the thoughts of it must end there in my head before I start having nightmares.

"Who?" The look that she gives me reminds me of being a naughty child all over again. The wait 'til your father gets home look, the sit on the naughty step and don't dare move look, the look that says you have become the child of the devil for not picking your toys up, the look that says I have just missed something so damn obvious look. She is of course talking about my dad.

"I still wait for him to come home every night. I leave the toilet light on so that he can go to in the night without disturbing me because he always used to wake me up putting the light on. I still say goodnight to him before I go to sleep." I know how she feels, I still miss my dad terribly, I cannot find the words to describe him, there are no words worthy enough.

I sit with Mum talking about their life together and I feel close to him. I sit in his chair rubbing my fingers on the arm rest that once bore his elbows as he read the paper and supported him as he climbed out of the chair to stand to cuddle his favourite daughter every time I visited. He would frequently tell me that and I often wondered if he ever told Charlotte the same thing when she visited. I didn't care if he did; I know he meant it when he said it to me. The fact that I visited more than her means that he told me more often, which is important to me now. At the end of the night I didn't want to go home, my dad was with us in the room that night listening to the stories and enjoying the trips down memory lane. I just know he was.

"He was a good man your dad and he idolised you."

"I know, and I did him."

"He was such a proud dad always taking you out for walks to the park."

"I remember my little bike and going to the park with him and Charlotte whilst you made dinner. I remember washing the car with him, I would spend ages washing the wheels 'cos it was the only bit I could reach." My childhood was so happy I could not think of any negative parts. I am lucky, I know I am, for the childhood that I had and the loving parents that I had. Many of my friends and colleagues had crap childhoods. Note to self – Be more thankful.

Chapter Sixteen

The clock is fast approaching midnight as I decide that it's time to make the move home. I lied to Jasper about going out for tea and she will now be going mad. I hope she hasn't howled like she does sometimes to annoy me, well not directly annoy me as I'm not there, but she must know that when the neighbours start coming up to me complaining I get a bit embarrassed by it all. The other week Mrs Cartwright stopped me in the park. She had her granddaughter with her and I think she maybe used her as a human shield knowing I would be on my best behaviour and not use words that she doesn't like.

"Coo-ee." I hate it when people shout that. I have a name and she bloody well knows it.

"Oh, Mrs Cartwright," I said trying my hardest to sound friendly. "How lovely to see you." I have to explain that as a bit of a personal joke due to the fact that I have no-one to share jokes with anymore, I mimic Hyacinth Bucket as I think Mrs Cartwright sounds like her.

"Can I just point out that dog of yours was howling all day yesterday."

"Well I don't know what's up with her, I do apologise. I think she may be on the menopause." Mrs Cartwright's face was a picture as she grabbed her granddaughter's hand and hurried off. The little girl who is about three years old looked back and I waved, making her wave back at me. I heard Mrs Cartwright telling her off for waving at strangers. Well if I am a stranger, Mrs Cartwright shouldn't be speaking to me, should she? What a bad example she sets.

All the way home I am thinking about Dad and the Major and how his family are feeling now, if indeed he has any family, and then I start thinking how sad it must be to get old and have no family to visit, mind you if some of the old buggers that I meet through my work were my family, I don't think I'd go visit them either. People are strange these days, and Facebook has a lot to answer for. I go on Facebook and do the whole pictures and status updates with sad faces 'cos I'm going back to work, which reminds me, I need to do that when I get home before bed, but I wouldn't dream of having public profile arguments with people.

"Oh she called me a slag." You either are a slag or you block her on Facebook and delete the post from your timeline. I have to be honest though, I am quite happy to read the public arguments.

'get lost u biatch.'

'you carnt sey dat.'

'hoo sez?'

'me sez.'

'wot u guna du bout it?' It's hardly surprising that kids can't spell. Rightly or wrongly, Sally occasionally likes to show an example of the future generation's grammar around the office when they apply for jobs, and I have to say we can see the funny side.

Give an example of a time when you have had to use your knowledge, skills and experience to make a bad situation better?

I woz wunce working for a shop and dis man cum in and asked for a hot roast beef sarnie. I told him dat we dint have any beef and told him we ad chiken. He had a roast chiken sarnie instead. He woz well happy and smiled as he left.

The mind boggles. I remember once when I went to a parents' evening at Beth's school and during discussions with the teacher I pointed out that I was concerned about her spelling. He didn't seem concerned at all saying that she was average. I told him that I had to correct her spelling every time I checked her homework. He told me that they didn't correct spelling anymore in case the children felt like a failure. I nearly gave him a word or two to correct. Biggest load of rubbish I've ever heard. I'm glad I corrected her 'cos I'd be ashamed of her filling in application forms like they do these days. I know working as an air hostess has its critics, but she has a great job which she loves and she gets to fly all over the world.

"I bet there's some real nice pilots love?" I said to her not long after she had passed her training.

"Not really, they're real old," she said. I have been on flights many times I thought, considering her comments. "Most of them are about your age." There it was – the killer blow. I still have those words in my head as my fiftieth shouts its imminent arrival and I'm sure in ten years time those words will be deafening as my sixtieth approaches. I can't say I am overly impressed with being forty-nine and alone knowing that I won't even get a birthday present marked '*with love*' or a birthday meal where I can gaze into his eyes over the table knowing that when I get him home I will devour his body, which is not something that I would have thought had the knob still been here on my birthday. I would have probably wished he'd go out so I can watch telly in peace. Although if he was here and he went out on my birthday,

I know who would be getting the *'with love'* gesture and it wouldn't be me. I wonder if I will get a card from him this year what with it being a biggie and with him wanting me back. I try and think what he thought of our little, and to be honest, fairly quick family reunion for two on my living room floor. I have mixed emotions about it. I am proud that I know his weakness and after all these years I still have the power to control what was once my man. I know how to get him to do what I want and I know I am strong enough to turn this to my advantage. I don't want him back but the thought of her having him doesn't particularly fill me with joy. I don't think I have any bad feelings towards her and would be civil if I saw her in the street with him but I think the knowledge that he slept with me behind her back is a much too powerful piece of information to just let it go. I will keep it tucked away for the day that I need it. I cannot imagine why I would need it as he says he wants me back but you never know if one day she says the wrong thing to me, BAM, she'll get it both barrels. I have heard people who have been the other person try and justify their affair and how things just happened and that it wasn't planned but if he or she cheated on their partner with you, how can you be sure they won't then cheat on you. A cheater is a cheater right? So how do I stand? I am the cheated on and now the one who is the other person. I think I prefer being the other person if I'm honest because things are on my terms. I think I could call him tomorrow and get him to come around. Is that bad of me? I don't know or care. What I know deep down is if I admit my true feelings, I am hurting and I want someone else to hurt too, I want her to know how I felt and that's why I need that piece of information..

Jasper is not happy and this is maybe the reason why she has left a wee at the back door. I probably wouldn't have noticed but it looks like she must have just done it as it still looks wet. She probably waited until she heard my car pull up, the little tinker. Despite my attempts to smooth over our dog / owner relationship she runs past me and into the garden and disappears into the dark. My garden certainly isn't the biggest but I have no light at the back so without walking round the garden I just have to be patient. I don't like letting her out to do her business in the garden as the grass is only just about looking better from last year when her nitrogen fuelled piss destroyed it leaving it patchy in places, but the joys of having her far outweigh the negatives.

My head seems full of all sorts of stuff making it near on impossible to nod off. Usually I put my head in the middle of the pillows in the nook and I'm out like a light. Tonight it seems that the on/off switch is broken in the on position and thoughts race around my head like Lewis Hamilton and his friends are playing out. For some reason the knob is in my thoughts which brings a smile to my frustrated early hours in the morning face that's staring up to the ceiling in some forlorn hope of finding the trigger that will make me sleep. There is no such trigger and I'm beginning to think that beyond my sinister motives behind the game I played with him, I actually quite enjoyed it. It was good to feel like a woman again and I think the need for sleep has been replaced by the need to feel wanted and devoured.

Note to self –

I think my note to self this time must be: do not do

notes to self in bed as you are likely to fall asleep before you can do it properly. I need a man that's for sure, well, I will rephrase it, I want a man, I most certainly do not need one, not unless there is a shelf to put up or something. Shelves are something that, as a married woman, I have never needed to do and when I have watched the knob do it he makes it seem like a rather long drawn out process as he measures from the ceiling to check it's at the right level and that is in addition to using a spirit level and shouting me to stand back and check with my eyes. I think women definitely have a better eye for things like that; it's just inbuilt more so than in a man. Men are singular beings and can only see what they are doing at that time and not the bigger picture. When he was getting his end away with her he didn't see what he would lose, only what he would gain, but a fit twenty-five year old girlfriend is no match for a wife of long standing who has been with him through thick and thin and seen him at his worst. I am simply more accepting of him than she will ever be and the minute he pisses her off with his blokey attitude she'll be off like a shot. I have nothing against marriage break-ups as long as they are someone else's, and I have nothing against twenty-five year old girls being with men older than their dads as long as the man is not mine, but will she stand in the kitchen on a Sunday morning cooking lunch whilst he goes to play golf. I do not think she will.

My getting up process this morning is taking me forever, perhaps it's the excitement of going back to work, not! But receiving a text from Beth wasn't what I expected. It is always lovely to hear from her but shortly after my alarm went off with the flashing LEDs from my phone lighting up my bedroom like a Christmas tree I felt a thud inside my body. It felt as though someone had just hit me with the biggest piece of reality check ever.

Hi Mum hope ur well. Tell Dad not to take his tart to the golf club. Tara said it made her sick watching him slobber all over her.

I didn't read any more of the text because my eyes kept going over the same bit. He took her to the golf club? He never took me to the golf club in all the time we were married because he said it was his thing, something to do independent of me. It became routine that he would get up early on a Sunday and go and play golf whilst I did the cleaning and cooked dinner and in just over eighteen months he is at the golf club with her. I sit on the bed with my phone in hand as the second alarm sounds. Staring into the flashing lights I feel betrayed all over again. He made out to me that it had been a mistake and that he wanted me back; I am now beginning to wonder which one of us is playing the game. I refuse to be hurt again.

"You'll never guess what the bastard has done now," was not the sort of greeting Sally was expecting after my two weeks off as she filled her lungs with enough nicotine to get her to the 10:00 morning break. I haven't known anyone before who is so fit and healthy and eats all the right things, goes running, even doing half marathons for charity and yet who smokes like a chimney. Funnily enough, whilst I'm quoting idioms, she also swears like a trooper. Sadly I don't get a chance to rant about him as Sally informs me that her and Moneybags Marcus the great have split up so I now have to be a friend to a person I currently have a low tolerance

level for. She has recently reciprocated my low level of tolerance as she dumped me to go off with Dawn. I now feel cheated as I only wanted to rant about the knob!
Note to self – save the rant for tomorrow.

Chapter Seventeen

A hundred and eight emails I have come into today. I've only been off work for two weeks; mind you it seemed a lot longer to be honest but am I glad to be back – not one bit. Nothing has changed. Kippers is still sat opposite me. She is called Marion but we call her kippers for obvious reasons, not to her face but certainly behind her back. I think God forgot to upload the instruction manual for washing your own fiddle when he made her. Luckily she sits far enough away for me to dilute the smell with the plug in air freshener that sits in the plug socket in winter to be replaced by the fan in summer. As I have been away from my desk for two weeks her smell seems to have got into the fabric of the building and this is my challenge of the morning to rid the place of it. So the fan is unplugged and the smelly thing is plugged in. She also has another little quirk that I will never grow to love; chronic fatigue syndrome. I mean why do we employ someone to sleep at work, how do we benefit as an organisation from that? She can't go upstairs because she gets tired and can't work a full day, but she wouldn't work a full day anyway even if she came in 9-5 'cos she sleeps for most of it. She doesn't even work in Anti-Social behaviour so why they put her in my office I have no idea other than Sally said she has to be on the ground floor. She didn't put her in the HR office though, did she? See what sort of friend she is? The majority of the hundred and eight emails can be discarded but having learnt a lesson a few years ago about deleting emails without reading them I open each and every one before deciding to delete or keep. It is a story that I must tell to explain my positioning in this subject. I once got an email from Ray Crabbs who was head of legal services at that time and as I had been off I deleted it without reading thinking that my out of office message was enough. It did state in case of emergency contact Audrey on … and then her extension number. Audrey, who is my colleague, handles things for me when I am off as I do for her. Anyway Crabbs or Apples as some call him or STD as others call him had emailed me about a serious case that we had going on at the time telling me that I had to deal ASAP (stressed in RED CAPITALS). I deleted the email and it kicked off: the person had a breakdown and overdosed. Error and lesson learnt after having my arse kicked rather severely. So now my first day back is spent reading the first couple of lines of every email to see if it is to be kept or not. I still think he should have sent it to Audrey to deal with but in this culture of it's not my fault it's his / hers / theirs etc and the fact that he was head of legal services, I lost and admitted fault on all accounts.

By morning break I had just about caught up on my emails and made a list of what I should do for the remaining hour and half before lunch. Sally texted me asking if I fancied a walk into town for lunch at Spoons. I like lunching at Spoons but sometimes, depending on how busy it is, it's difficult getting back to work on time. The last time we attempted lunch was about Easter and I organised a fake site visit with Dawn who just happened to be off-duty that day although this was not broadcast around my office and Sally booked herself out for a meeting; we stayed in Spoons beyond the one hour lunch break. It was nice to relax and have a laugh until Creepy Colin just happened to walk past the window and saw us. He took our wave in reply to his wave as an invitation to join us. Sitting himself down at our table for three, he made himself at home by borrowing a chair from the table next to us and slotted himself down in between Dawn and me. Dawn, who was wearing a tight jeans and boots, must have looked a lovely sight for male eyes as Colin could not take his eyes off her. She is a good looking woman with a fine figure who uses her long blonde hair to her advantage swishing it across the air making most men take note of her presence and Colin certainly noticed. If he had dribbled any more into his drink it would have flowed over the top of the glass and flooded the pub. His eyes watched her every step of the way as she left the table to go to the toilet and shortly after he also got up and said he needed to visit the little boys' room. This caused Sally and me much amusement for two reasons; firstly the thought of the little boys' room seemed so appropriate for Colin and secondly Sally's whisper that he was going for a wank creased me and made everyone else in the pub look over. I just could not stop laughing and as the tears streamed down my face making me look like the chief mourner at a funeral, except for the laughing, Dawn returned to the table closely followed by Colin who went straight out of the door.

"He just asked me out," Dawn said, making Sally and me laugh even more. She couldn't understand what we were laughing at but joined in providing beyond doubt that laughing is infectious.

"What did he say?" Sally asked once composure

returned somewhat to the room and all the other customers had got over their annoyance of us.

"Cheeky sod said that he felt we had a connection and would like to take me to the library next Tuesday for the literary society's reading of The Importance of Being Ernest." The laugh started again, louder and more exuberantly. I could see people slamming down their knives and forks in protest, unmet by the attention of the staff and unheard due to our laughing. My sides began to hurt so much I had to get up holding my arm across it for support. My legs felt as though they were supporting too much weight and my head pounded. Sally's laugh turned into the roaring laughter matched only by Brian Blessed, and Dawn's laugh made her sound like a pig on its way to slaughter. All in all, what must have been a most horrendous noise continued for some time until a lady with a look suited to Headmistress status stood before us.

"Can you please keep the noise down?" We stopped and as the pub enjoyed the few seconds of silence before the breath held so tightly by Dawn exploded down her nose bringing with it the sort of stuff that you don't want to see laid out before you on a table.

"I really must ask you to leave if this behaviour continues." These words were like a trigger in the most unfortunate way causing us to bellow out the laughter again. Whilst in the process of laughing and clutching bellies for support we made our way out into the street where the laughter continued even beyond the point of Sally going over on her ankle causing her to fall into the road perfectly landing on the zebra crossing. Cars, buses, and pedestrian footpaths were full of people witnessing what looked like three drunken woman displaying anti-social behaviour. By the time we had fully recovered, two and a half hours had passed and Sally returned to work from her meeting and likewise I returned from my site visit with the neighbourhood police officer. Creepy Colin who works as a cleaner in the building avoided me for some time after that, changing his hours to start earlier so that my floor was finished and he was upstairs by the time I started work. He must have blamed me for the whole incident as he remained on speaking terms with Sally and if he was ever walking towards me and I saw him he would double back or change direction. Very strange man and probably in truth quite well suited to Dawn.

As we left work for lunch I reminded Sally of this incident which started the laughing again. Quite simply it is one of those moments where you had to be there to appreciate it and one which was as funny after the hundredth time of laughing at it, as it was being there at the original incident. This time we lunched in relative peace compared to that but Sally was not happy and it showed as her usual order of Tennessee Burger had been sidelined and replacing it from the back of the closet was a Skinny Chicken Burger with side salad. It has always made me wonder how Dawn, as a trained police officer and therefore not without a bit of knowledge, could actually believe that skinny chicken burgers were made out of the thinnest chickens in the brood. This became known as a Dawnism. The definition of a Dawnism? *A word, sentence or phrase created and understood only by Dawn where everything she says makes complete sense in her own mind but not to others.*

I didn't know whether she wanted to talk about it or not and with the knowledge that she had complained about me when I went through my split that I had talked only of this – and more in-depth than anyone had clearly wanted me to without having the bottle to tell me – I kept a safe distance from the subject waiting for her to bring it up. I wasn't waiting long.

"He's left me, Emmy." The first four words out of her mouth left me without having a reply ready. The only thing I could think of saying was Oh and it didn't seem to fit. I waited. Then the tears started. I got out of my seat and walked around the back of her and putting my arms under hers I gave her a cuddle of support. I remained silent whilst my brain clocked up a few air miles by flicking through the sympathy phrase book that was used so often on me until they got bored of reading it.

"I know you understand. They're just bastards, the lot of them." Whilst I am sure that sentence is true in some respect I am equally sure that some men are quite nice. I refer to my dad who was the best and nicest, loveliest man who ever walked the earth. I'm sure that the Christian Church would question that but it is not only my opinion but also the truth. Sitting down I made myself comfortable for the story. My cheese and ham panini looked much more appealing than the impending tale of woe but I had a duty to do and do it I will.

"I thought things were going good and we were getting on really well."

"So what happened?"

"Last week he asked me for the credit card back."

"Oh, things must be bad." The tongue in my cheek

during the comment stayed there as I went through the process of showing my concerned face. In reality the reason why Moneybags Marcus had dumped her now struck me. She is a gold digger and always has been. I went through the list in my head of ex-boyfriends. Bank Rolling Bobby, Loaded Laurence, Rich Richard and now Moneybags Marcus all of who got fed up with her spending their money. The £10,000 spent on decorating her house was one of many warning shots that Marcus should have taken note of. He didn't but had finally learnt, it seemed. There were a couple of exes that I couldn't think of nicknames for but who'd still got fed up with her trying to live like a millionaire. The nicest man that Sally had ever been with was Adam who worked in a factory and had nothing, but he adored her. Being adored is clearly not what she wants.

"He was so horrible to me." The tears started again, not that they actually really stopped.

"Well it obviously wasn't right, huni." I was impressed with that comment 'cos it sounded sincere. I learnt a lesson about myself as she was whining the story through a stretch-out mouth adding to the whine sound. I learnt that I have no sympathy for this lady in front of me at all.

"I know you understand and that's why I can talk to you." She had said it again that I understood. I'm not entirely sure what I should understand, the fact that my husband left me for a younger model is in no way a comparison with that of losing access to a credit card and copious amounts of twenty pound notes. I never even saw the knob's credit card never mind spend anything on it and I am a hundred percent sure that she misses that much more than the man himself. Then it came.

"But I loved him." What a load of tosh. She loved his money.

"He was so nice to me." When he was spending thousands on her, yes!

"I miss him so much." Again the money.

"We were supposed to be going away together." Again the money.

"What am I going to do?" Bank roll your own life like everyone else does. I can feel myself biting my lip. I have to stop myself saying things but usually with me, out of every five thoughts, at least one will break through the defences of my mouth and make its way into the world of verbal noise.

How she managed to eat and whine and cry her tale of woe is beyond me but I would have given a straight ten for effort. I nibbled on my panini thinking if I took my time eating it I would always have food in my mouth and because my mum always told me not to eat with food in my mouth the thoughts would not come out and would stay safely in my head thereby confirming my place in Sally's mind as a loyal friend and sympathetic listener who can be called on in her hour of need. I have to say it's slightly like an arse covering exercise but one which only I know about.

My phone, although turned on silent, vibrates like an over excited washing machine and not wanting to feel rude and answer it I try and ignore it but it just keeps going. I start to panic thinking Mum has fallen again so make my apologies and get it out of my bag. Without looking at who it is due to my panicking I go through the automatic motions of answering it.

"Hello?" It's always made me laugh how you can make one word a question by lifting the tone at the end.

"Emily, I've just spent two hours on the phone with Sally getting the tale of her and Marcus, if you see her stay out of the way 'cos you'll get it too. Does she not realise that no-one cares? I'm surprised he put up with her that long." The problem with mobile phones is that private conversations are a thing of the past as the look on Sally's face confirms she just heard every word.

Chapter Eighteen

I so wanted to tell Dawn that I had inadvertently dropped her in it. Obviously I hadn't intended to but the afternoon meeting dragged on far too long and I thought Sally would have got to her first. She hadn't and as I told Dawn the story of what had happened with me answering the phone her reply was typical Dawn.

"Oh well, it's nothing I wouldn't say to her face." Conversation over as far as Dawn was concerned. I always wanted to tell her about the knob taking little miss Lucy to the golf club, somewhere I was never taken, but somehow it didn't seem that important anymore. I had a rather strained awkward friendship if that's what you could call it to repair and I knew I had to start soon.

"Shall we have a girlie night out and just forget about today?" Sally was quite reticent and I felt that soon I would get blood from the proverbial stone.

"I'm a bit busy," said Sally. Three words sprang to mind. Taken the huff. I suppose she felt a bit like me when I found out that Sally and Dawn had been going out behind my back to avoid my ramblings about Shaun and Lucy. I noticed that my recovery had started as I had just used their real names in my thoughts instead of knob and slag. Progress!

"Aww, come on, Sally, we didn't mean anything by it." I threw myself into the equation to try and soften the bad feelings, if any, towards Dawn. I am learning how to be a good friend again.

"How about we go into town on Friday and just have a

laugh? It'll be fun and just what we need." She ummed and ahhed which I took as her softening her stance so I left her to think about it and then texted Dawn and told her we were going into town on Friday. Her reply came back almost before I'd sent the text accepting the invite and saying she needed a good night out.

It was walking Jasper that evening that made me take stock of my life. Nearly fifty, I can't escape from it, it's coming faster than the Flying Scotsman and what do I have to show for it? I have my house but no-one to share it with, I have my independence and no-one to share it with, I have a little bit of money and no-one to spend it on and I have nice boobs and no-one to show them to. I have mentioned my boobs before but I think at the age I am and still having nice boobs is an achievement. On the odd times I have seen topless models, I have thought mine are just as good as the twenty-year-old on the page and I have seen pictures of her on the knob's phone, I noticed I have not mentioned their names this time, is that a backward step? But mine are just as good and more so, he knows it too. When we had sex in the living room, an incident I try not to remember that often although I have to admit I enjoy the thoughts, he couldn't stop touching them. He remembered how nice they were. They're quite sensitive too and he used to make a circle with his finger or tongue around my nipples that drove me wild. I noticed he didn't do that last time so she obviously doesn't like it and he'd forgotten that I did. He did have a few new techniques though, which I liked and quite obviously things that she must have taught him.

I have to say that in the cold light of day or evening

as it is at the moment I am quite fortunate. I have my health and so many people my age have all sorts going on in their lives. Kippers must have health problems as not only does she stink like raw kippers and fall asleep for most of her shift, she has psoriasis and her elbows looks disgusting as skin flakes off onto her desk which is opposite mine. She also has real bad dandruff to the point that she could sell it for snow for the model villages playing out winter scenes with snow five feet deep. She could probably supply countless model villages just with one brush of her hair. The very thought of it makes me retch. I dread to think of all her other ailments, but one thing that she has over me, she has a man who adores her. Heaven knows how!!

I listen to my voicemail. It's an elderly woman in panic mode and I return the call.

"What is it?"

"Why don't you take your phone out with you?" See I am never going to be too old for a telling off from my mum so maybe I should see that as a positive.

"Why, what's happened?" She is clearly upset by something.

"Are you coming over tonight?"

"I wasn't going to, why?"

"I need to talk to you. Something real bad has happened."

"What? What's happened?"

"I'll tell you when you're here." The phone was put down answering the question that she posed in the first place. Of course I'm going to go over now, this better be important. She sounded upset though. Guilt started to ride across my mood, my mum rang needing me and I am being cynical of her intentions.

Jasper was pretty much thrown into the house and the door closed behind her, and within minutes I am exceeding the speed limit by far more than I should be to my mother's house. Abandoning the car in Mum's drive in a more diagonal than straight piece of parking I open to the door to the smell of baking.

"Cup of tea, dear?"

"Mum what's wrong?"

"Nothing, dear, why?"

"Nothing?" The baking does smell nice but now isn't the time to appreciate it. "I have just driven at a hundred miles an hour to get here 'cos you sounded upset. So what's wrong?"

"I'll make us a drink and then we can talk. You need to calm down, Emily, you'll give yourself a heart attack." I'll bloody give her something was my thought, which I kept to myself as I waited impatiently for the kettle to boil. My cup of tea was placed on a coaster on the table in front of me. It was my dad's favourite coaster and reminded me so much of him. A picture of a man sat in a chair with slippers on drinking a cup of tea with the words 'World's best Dad'. He really was and although Mum had put it in the cupboard as it reminded her of him, she got it out every time I came. It seemed to be coming out quite a lot lately as my life seemed to have started to be centred on her.

"What's so urgent, Mum?" I asked wanting to find out what she had summoned me for.

"It's Mike, dear, from the blind club."

"What blind club and what Mike?" I had never heard her mention either to me so both came with an equal amount of surprise.

"I sometimes help out at the blind club – going on trips with them."

"When?" This was news to me.

"I went to Blackpool last year to see the illuminations."

"You went to see the illuminations last year?"

"Yes."

"With the blind club?"

"Yes, me and Joyce helped out with escorting."

"Why would a blind club go see the illuminations?" This was a perfectly normal question to me but she looked at me like I was being unkind.

"It's a nice ride out and we met with the Blackpool blind club for chit and chatter." Chit and chatter, knit and natter, stitch and bitch and moan and groan, god the activities of reaching a certain age are endless, no wonder old people piss themselves, they can't contain their excitement.

"Well that makes more sense than going to see the illuminations."

"We go to the garden centre on a Tuesday morning for coffee and cake."

"Oh good lord, take me now. Mother will you get to the point of why I am here."

"I thought you'd come for a cup of tea, dear, you're always coming here, I think it's about time you got yourself a man."

"Mum, I wasn't going to come tonight but you asked me to come because of something bad happening."

"Well don't force yourself to come if you don't want to." I'm getting annoyed with this poor sweet little helpless defenceless old lady sat before me.

"Mum, you rang me asking me to come because you wanted to talk to me about something bad happening and now you're telling me about a trip to Blackpool and the garden centre. I'm sure you didn't ask me to come to discuss your outings."

"There's no need to be hostile, dear."

"I'm not bloody hostile, I just came here 'cos you said something bad had happened, that's all."

"There's no need to swear either, I'm your mother. You're not too old for a smack you know." I really can't believe where this conversation is going and the way I'm feeling at this particular moment, I'd love to see her try.

"Mum, please, I'm tired, I've just gone back to work and had a really bad day, and I just wanted to go home, have a bath and a glass of wine."

"Well don't let me keep you if you've got things to do." I decide to leave it there and finish my tea and if she hasn't said anything then it can't be that important. One thing about my mother is she likes to run the show. She likes to be the one holding court, being the important one in the room, whereas I am like my dad, we just sit at the back and bother no-one. Charlotte is just like Mum. If they walk in a room full of people they want to be noticed, not necessarily be the centre of attention but like people to know that they are there. I think there is a difference also in wanting people to know you are there and people just knowing you are there. Bethany could walk in a room and the room would light up. People would notice her even though she wouldn't make an entrance or announce her arrival or anything like that, but she is stunningly good looking and stylish in her dress sense which she obviously inherited from moi, but people would notice her. She has a presence. Mum and Charlotte would make some drama to make people know they are there. Dad and I would just sneak in at the back and not move, maybe only speaking to a few people in our immediate area. My dad as I have told you was very popular with the ladies at the WI and all of the ladies would wish their husbands were like him but I think that was more because he was just a lovely man and would do anything for anyone especially my mum who he adored.

"Right, Mum I have to go, thanks for the cuppa." I put my cup in the sink and put Dad's coaster back in the top cupboard at the side of the cornflakes. My mum doesn't eat cornflakes but she still buys them just so it feels like he's still there I think. As I walk back through the room to get my bag, I notice Mum's eyes glistening in the light.

"What is it, Mum?"

"I'm just being silly, dear, ignore me."

"Tell me what has happened."

"I feel like a silly old fool sometimes."

"Why?"

"I couldn't remember why I had asked you to come round."

"Have you remembered now?"

"Yes, it's Mike from the blind club."

"What about him?"

"He's been sacked."

"What for?" I feel like I am going to be privy to some groundbreaking news story before the BBC has got hold of it.

"Eileen the secretary told Bernard who runs it that

Mike swore at one of the members and he wouldn't do that. He's a nice man and without him we can't go on our trips. He wouldn't swear at anyone, he's so helpful and thoughtful and he always helps us off the bus and buys us flowers on our birthdays." I watch as she gets more and more upset at the thought of Mike losing his job.

"Does Mike get paid to be your driver; surely he will be in a union or something." My thought process is corporate and thinking along the lines of employment law and representation.

"He's a few years younger than me and is our community volunteer."

"Oh I see, scrap my idea then."

"It's a travesty," she says through tears and cries. "I'll tell you what it is," she says.

"What?" I ask.

"It's a bloody misjustice of carriage, that's what it is!" Even in the darkest times a few mixed up words of my mother's or a little Dawnism from PC Winchester and my day just doesn't seem as bad.

Chapter Nineteen

Fresh from the news of the misjustice of carriage I find it hard to sleep and lie tossing and turning my way through the night. I battle with thoughts which are attempting to penetrate my brain and take up my thinking time. I don't really want to think as I'd rather sleep but sadly I am not in control of that part of my brain. For some reason I think of Shaun lying there next to his perfect princess and I think that I do not need him, he is the habit that I am finding hard to kick, the finger nail that I always bite and make sore, he is the itch that just won't go away but is hard to locate to scratch. If he was lying next to me right now I would be lying awake thinking I hate the way he snores or how he farts in the night so loudly it wakes me up and yet he sleeps so soundly. I soon come to realise that it is just the whole thought of him lying next to her that irritates me in some way. I know that I can cope on my own, I get by, and even to a point I feel content but I don't know if it is her age that irritates me as it reminds me that I was young and beautiful once. Sometimes I could just do with a cuddle and one of those needing a cuddle moments is right now. Then it hits me like a bolt from the blue, I am jealous. Not jealous in the way that I want him, she is very much welcome to him, I am jealous of her age and beauty, I have lost mine to a point and I will never get it back. I have given him the best years of my life and I find it hard to think of what I have to offer any man now. I have realised that at my age I will probably never fall in love again not like I did back then, I will not ache to see someone and pine for them when they are not here, yet if I can find someone who I feel comfortable with and like to spend my time with I will bite the good Lord's hand off for it.

The clock hits six forty-five and explodes into a fanfare far too loud for my sensitive ears first thing in a morning. Lying there I wonder just how much sleep has passed me by and if I go back a few hours how much harder I would try to get some sleep. I have only been back at work for one day and my head is full of jobs that need to be done and things that I need to sort out. People's pettiness hasn't changed whilst I've been off, no-one has waved a magic wand and made all neighbours live in harmony together. At least I have a job. It's count blessings time again. I have my job, my house, my dog, my mum, my friends and an ISA stashed away for a rainy day. The saying about saving it for a rainy day was certainly not invented in England because if we stashed things away for a rainy day they wouldn't be stashed away for long.

Capital Radio certainly isn't the same without Hirsty in the morning and although it's still entertaining it seems to me that something is missing. Hirsty! My daily routine of getting showered, dried and dressed is missing the main ingredient, a good old fashioned dose of Hirsty wit. Jasper has to make do with a quick walk this morning as I am running late as always and yet again as every morning I am full of good intent and will give her a much longer walk tomorrow. This is a promise repeated every day, and I am grateful that she doesn't understand the concept of empty and broken promises. She watches me leave in my car from her perch on the top of the sofa and my feelings of guilt are slightly lifted when I drive past Frankie & Benny's and think of the Italian stallion. I wonder how he is getting on with his amazingly gorgeous girlfriend. My guilt over the dog changes into jealousy, real jealousy this time as I would love to be the woman he takes upstairs and makes love to. I can feel a rush of excitement, a tingling in my body, deep down into its fabric, a tingling in a place that hasn't tingled for some time when I think about someone touching me. Today I do something unthinkable yet exciting. I stop my car and text Sally telling her that I will be late as Mum is not well so I'm going over before work. I then turn my car around, go home and I masturbate. The thoughts of him taking me by the hand into my bedroom, his bedroom or to be honest any room, make me want to be loved in a sexual meaning more than I can ever remember before. I go in the house ignoring the welcoming yet slightly confused dog, run upstairs, get undressed and lie on my bed in my underwear and gently start to run my fingers up my legs stopping short of the place where I want him to be. I almost tease myself in a way that if he was doing it would start to drive me wild. Teasing myself is not part of the plan, I would much rather he did it but I'm sure the sight of me lying naked on my bed would not be enough to prise him away from his girlfriend. Would I sleep with him knowing he had a girlfriend? Too right I would. I have been the damaged person being lied to and cheated on, and hurt beyond the measures of pain but the fact of the matter is that I want him so much that I would be prepared to put a woman in my situation. Am I ashamed of myself for thinking it? I am now, I wasn't before.

I had forgotten about the knob taking her to the golf club until I was met by Sally in the kitchen at work. I didn't want to ask how she was in case I got the full chapter and verse again and tried hard to think of how to ask without asking so I apologised about being late and assured her mum was okay now. It felt naughty to lie knowing why I had been late in the first place but she brushed away my lateness.

"You okay?" I asked. Please don't give me the whole story.

"Fine. You?"

"Yeh," I said.

"What were you going to tell me the other day," she asked.

"Oh I can't remember now," I lied. Quite honestly I really couldn't be bothered discussing it again.

"You heard from Shaun?"

"No, he took her to the golf club though. He never took me." And out it came. Why do I do that? I fully intend to keep things to myself but out they come. It's like a compulsion to tell someone something. I have to try and be more sensitive at a time when Sally is feeling pretty low, but I don't want her to forget that I don't feel too great myself. I know it's been a while since he walked out on me to rub my nose in the fact that I am no longer young but neither is he, neither is Sally and yet I don't feel a great deal of sympathy coming my way.

"What, she plays golf?"

"I assume so, one of Beth's friends works at the golf club and texted her to say she had seen her dad with his tart. Well she said girlfriend, I say tart."

"Oh, Emmy," she said stroking my head as though she had called round for a cuppa and was petting Jasper. "That night out you mentioned is upon us." With that she walked out of the kitchen, arms waving around in a divaesque fashion singing the words 'I've got the moves like Jagger.' Sally certainly does have the moves like Jagger and on the many times she has demonstrated her moves like Jagger, the dance floor clears as people are astounded at her moves. Not in a nice way though which is where the interpretation problem comes in. She thinks people stop to admire when in reality they stop to ridicule, me included. However, Sally is one of those people who, when having a good time, finds common sense goes out of the window and the outside world is blocked out.

"Oh, Emmy, I forgot to tell you, I've got you a date," she said swinging her head back around the door.

"What?"

"I've got you a date."

"I don't want a date."

"Every single girl wants a date." I wasn't lying, I really didn't want one, especially one that is set up by someone else.

"Who with?" I ask because I obviously need to know as it may change my mind as to whether I need one or not. I'm wondering if by some twist of fate she has met the Italian stallion and invited him on a date with me and he, remembering me from our brief but memorable moments of passing each other by, could not refuse.

"Tony."

"Tony who?" He could be called Tony, many Italian Americans on TV are called Tony, not that I believe he is American any more than I am and my one visit to New York certainly doesn't qualify me for an American passport.

"The guy from Highways."

"Tony from Highways, are you kidding?"

"He's nice."

"Well if he's so nice, Sally, you go out with him."

Tony is the guy who runs the Highways department. It is hardly surprising that he is single. His belly hangs so far below his waistline his belt must be swamped into his flab and I'm sure Lord Lucan was high-flying around town the last time he saw his feet never mind anything else.

"Just go out with him, it might be fun."

As though perfectly rehearsed, a large round man with round specs and a large round plastic see through sandwich tin walked into the kitchen.

"Hello, ladies," he says with theatrical presence. "Em-il-ee, how are you, my darling?" I could not think of any words to answer without using the F word followed by the 'off' word so remained silent. His blue shirt, red tie and black trousers causing the starkest contrast ever as though a child had picked his clothes.

"Morning, Tony." Sally just had to encourage him to speak. I will remember this moment the next time she looks for sympathy as she will get none.

"Emily, I have booked a table at Castano's for seven, I hope that is okay. I will pick you up at six- thirty." Once again I could not think of the words and found my head nodding all on its own. This is turning into a nightmare. Sally smiled as he put his rather large sandwich box with enough sandwiches to feed the whole highways department into the fridge. I watched him walk out of the room his trousers falling three inches short of his shoes and at about five feet nine inches with a crown of grey hair which circled his head pushing his bald patch above it, I couldn't help but notice how ridiculous he looked. If someone would have put Danny DeVito and him together you would think three words. Separated At Birth. I cannot believe that I have managed with Sally's help to get myself in this situation.

"Aww it'll be fun." Sadly I did not share Sally's views but then a thought came to me that appeared to show a slight hope for my escape from this predicament.

"He doesn't know where I live."

"Oh, didn't I mention, I've given him your address. Six thirty, don't forget."

"I hate you." I really do at this point, I could kill her. I wouldn't dream of doing this to anyone so what gives her the right to do it to me. I have never hurt anyone, I have lived a good honest life, I have respected my parents, well, Dad more than Mum and I have never stolen anything, and I am nice to people. Why am I being punished. I have just spent two minutes in the company of a man who I can honestly say after that two minutes that I don't like, I have never spoken to him nor would I look at him twice no matter how desperate I was. Why couldn't I just say no? Why am I too soft? I hate Sally.

Note to self – Stop being soft and speak my mind.

Chapter Twenty

I watch as the clock in the kitchen points to twelve and six respectively as I wipe Jasper's feet after yet another short walk. I cannot believe that I have agreed to let some bloke who I wouldn't look at twice take me out. I just don't know what is happening to me at the moment. There'll be no casual sex in the living room like there was with Shaun although it poses the question, is it classed as casual sex when you sleep with someone you've been married to for such a long time? It may be questionable whether it would be classed as casual sex for him as he has a new partner but for me it was sex with my husband although estranged, and boy is he strange. I notice the clock counting down the 29 minutes until he comes so I decide I must make some effort even if only small as it is not his fault that my so called friend is a bitch. Not only has she set me up, she has also set him up as he thinks he's in with a chance, so I will tell him from the start. As I ascend the stairs I inadvertently find myself practising the line out loud.

"Tony, I've had a lovely night; thank you so much but I don't think we should do it again." Too hard.

"Tony, I'm sorry if you've got the wrong idea but you don't want to be with me; I'm an emotional retard." True but not right.

"I need to tell you from the start, Tony, I'm not really interested in any sort of relationship, I'm sorry if I've led you on." That's a bit better. Blame myself and then he'll be sympathetic, making it easier for me.

"Tony, I'm really sorry, I have just been through a real

bad split so I'm not looking for anything just now." That sounds the best one so that's the one I'll use, but the conversation continues as I hear his reply in my head.

"No it's been lovely, I've had a lovely night. Thank you."

"Yes of course I like you, Tony, I think you're very sweet."

"No you can't come in for coffee, I need to be up early."

"Well it's my mum; she's staying with me 'cos she's not well."

"She's got a really contagious disease. Doctor said she has to stay away from people."

"No you can't kiss me on the doorstep."

"You just can't, that's why."

"Cos I don't fancy you. Is that clear enough for you?" Oh god I hope I don't have to be so harsh. By the time I get ready, nothing too flash, just a dress that I have had for years albeit a nice one from Next, I see a car outside with its lights on. It's a nice car; rather large and would look nice on anyone's driveway just not mine. Luckily it's on the road and not in my drive 'cos I know that Mrs Cartwright will be watching. If he was a half decent looking bloke, and for a laugh, I'd pull him out of his car and snog his face off just to give her something to look at, but that is not going to happen.

I keep him waiting the customary five minutes not through playing hard to get or anything but the sheer fact that I am never ready on time. I faff about, I have been told many times by many people that I faff about. I am just about ready to go out of the door and I decide to check once more in the mirror that I look okay, not sure why, but a girl likes to look nice even if for her own benefit not his, but then I have to check Jasper's water bowl. She looks at me as though she is getting sick to death of me going out. I can't even pretend I'm not going out. I know she's a dog but she's not thick.

"Mummy's going to work. I won't be long."

"Lying sod," she says. Well, her eyes tell me that's what she says. The door clicks as the lock does its job and I walk down the drive. I am beginning to feel nervous and I cannot imagine why I am doing this.

"Emily darling you look delightful." My words, he sounds like he's going to eat me. That's the sort of thing I would say about a cake in the baker's window.

"Thank you," I say trying not to sound like a woman getting into a car with Hannibal Lector.

"Castano's is a favourite place of mine; have you ever been there?" He has clearly got the wrong impression of me if he thinks I can afford to eat there. I'm more a KFC type of girl. I am more than happy to eat at Castano's, I'm not so common I don't know how to behave in these places or anything like that; I'm just more comfortable with a boneless banquet and coleslaw as a side order.

"No I haven't, I'm looking forward to it." I lie of course and consider at what point I should use my well rehearsed line about not wanting a relationship. It certainly is a nice car with plenty of room and as I look around at the dashboard lit up like an aeroplane cockpit, I can't help but notice that Tony's belly is wedged neatly in between him and the steering wheel. It is not an attractive look and I hope beyond hope that no-one sees me and thinks he's my boyfriend. Oh gosh, can you imagine what that would do for my reputation. Not sure what reputation I speak of as I'm not sure I have one but I don't want the first thing of my reputation being that I date men like Tony. Am I being shallow? I probably am but a girl needs to have some sort of standards. Shame Lucy didn't have standards before jumping into bed with my husband but we can't judge everyone else by our own standards can we. Am I being hypocritical because I slept with her boyfriend? Nah, he's still my husband. Something else which needs sorting out, I still want a divorce. I hate the word boyfriend being used on someone of his age. He's already made that jump into his fifties and I would not class him as a boyfriend. Partner maybe, other half yes, but I can't see how boyfriend can be used for someone who is fifty. On the other hand I'm not sure I would like to be referred to as someone's partner as it makes me sound like a lesbian and lady friend makes me sound like a hooker. I almost certainly would not like to be the other half so whilst I am trying to find another word I'll have to stick to being a girlfriend when I find myself a boyfriend.

Conversation is flowing, well at least from his side it is, but I am far too busy thinking of what I should be called when I get myself into a relationship to pay much attention. I have noticed a few gaps in his talking where I have politely inserted a 'yes' and a 'mmm' but I honestly have no idea if I have signed up to anything as I really wasn't listening. I sit with my hands clasped tightly over the top of my handbag and watch the shops pass by.

"So that's pretty much my story really. How about you?" Oh god I knew this would happen.

Note to self – Pay more attention.

"What do you want to know?" This is a good way of getting him to re-ask the question without me sounding too ignorant but I don't want to sign up to any full-on conversations as I really don't fancy him.

"Your story. Your background. Your situation." My perfect time to get the line in.

"Well, I went through a tough time in my recent split from my husband which I don't really want to talk about as it's still quite raw." There, it's out there now. Just a few tweaks and the message will have got through.

"That's why I'm not looking for anything. I really couldn't contemplate another relationship."

"I understand." Brilliant he understands. Pressure off.

"Allow me," he said as he forced his belly out of the car and hurried to my door to open it for me.

"Thank you." His manners are certainly old fashioned and I like it. He even holds the door open for me too, what a gent. We walk inside to be greeted not only by the warm air and soothing classical music playing in the background but a tall slim lady with a white shirt and black skirt and hair tied up with a pen stuck through it.

"Good evening Mr Jewell, Madam," she said nodding at first him and then me."

"Good evening," we said in unison as though well rehearsed. I could feel Tony's arm on my back gently guiding me to the table which I didn't need as I was following the hostess closely but it felt somehow reassuring. He pulled out my chair and gestured for me to sit down before helping me push my chair in.

"You must come here a lot if they know your name."

"Not really that much. It's just that sort of place, they take time to get to know their customers." It was a nice touch I thought and very welcoming. I had started seeing past Tony's rather large belly and grey hair and instead started to focus on the man within. I hadn't known him that long at all but I felt safe and relaxed and well, I felt like a lady. I followed Tony's direction when ordering my food as I felt slightly out of my depth with the choice but he clearly knew about food and that's not just referring to his belly, but the conversations that he had with the hostess were way beyond my level of culinary knowledge. I opted for the Mushroom and Tarragon Soup and Buffalo Ricotta and Spinach Ravioli.

"Tell me, Emily. Why did you agree to come out with me tonight?" Damn, I didn't want to get into this sort on conversation. I nervously played with the strap on my Cotrell shoes. Something else which fell into my hands on a regular shopping trip displaying the sale sign and yet another bargain at £60.

"To tell you the truth, Tony, Sally kind of set me up." I didn't want to sound like I didn't want to be there but didn't see any point in lying about it.

"Yes she seemed very keen to get us together, didn't she?"

"What exactly did she say about me?" I have to know.

"She said you were lonely after your spilt and needed something to take your mind off things."

"I'm not a charity case." I can feel myself getting a bit annoyed. If it didn't feel like a set-up before, it sure does now.

"Look, Emily, I'll be honest with you. You are a very beautiful lady and you look fantastic tonight." I am speechless. In the space of half an hour he has said two things to me that Shaun didn't say in years. I am beginning to warm to him. He is a true gentleman; there are not many left in this world in my educated opinion. It's a shame he couldn't have taught Shaun how to behave but I hope for sure I meet a man like him. The hostess brought our starters which seemed to kill the flow of conversation coming from Tony and I had expected more compliments after the last one. It was as though he had lined himself up to deliver more but then stopped himself. I'm a patient soul, I can wait. It seems to me that Tony's compliments are meant entirely and will therefore be worth waiting for.

We spent the rest of the mealtime talking about work. I had obviously seen him around but not really spoke to him. We talked about Sally and he laughed at her name as he too had noticed the S.Landers in a meeting.

"I think for the amount of time she slags people off it is the most appropriate name for her," he laughs. He is funny, witty and charming. I laugh at his jokes not because I feel I have to, like I did with Shaun, but because they're funny. When the desserts come to the table I feel fat. I have shovelled away everything that was on my plate and not surprisingly Tony did as well.

"Have you noticed that the waitress takes my plate away real quick. I think she's scared I'm going to eat that too." He pats his bulging tummy as he says it and I laugh. I cannot help it. Laughing at himself because of his size may well be a defence mechanism but I like him. I feel bad for being so wrong and judging him by his appearance. He dresses smart it's just that he'd need to buy two identical shirts to stitch them together.

I look into my Apple and Poppy Seed Strudel with Vanilla Ice Cream and think about the saying judging a book by its cover. Tony is the nicest man I have ever met in every sense of the word. I know I have been in a relationship for a long time but even men I have come across in any aspect of my life do not match the charming man I have before me. His arm comes across the table attached to a long dessert spoon. I taste his Vanilla Crème Brulee from his spoon – something I have never done before, and I can feel myself blush. As we talk for the rest of the evening over coffee and a mint chocolate, I know that if anyone looked at us together I would be proud for him to be called my boyfriend.

The tone of the night is interrupted by my phone calling out for my attention.

"Sorry, can I just answer this?"

"Of course you must," he replies.

"Hi, Mum." I pause whilst she requests what is more and more becoming my daily visit.

"No, I'm out with my friend Tony." That word alone surprised me as it exited my mouth as I hadn't thought of him as that.

"A friend from work." I'm hoping that he cannot hear what she's saying.

"Yes, Mum, he's lovely." I blush again.

"Yes I'll see you tomorrow."

I sit back into my chair and roll my eyes. I then look at Tony opposite me who is smiling sweetly back at me. They certainly broke the mould after making him.

Chapter Twenty-One

"I have had a lovely night, Tony, thank you so much." I felt guilty that he hadn't let me pay half of the bill; in fact he didn't even let me see how much it was. He gave me his liquor chocolate that was brought to the table with a complimentary Brandy which he also gave to me when the hostess brought the card machine for him to pay.

"I'm glad you've enjoyed it."

"Would you like a coffee?" In a million years I would not have thought I would say that but it was in some way a contribution to my half of the bill. I have learnt a lesson tonight not only to look at the book cover but open the book and look inside and get a feel for the contents. Read it in context and not just take a glimpse of the snapshot given to you by the author.

"Thank you, I would love a quick coffee, then I must go." I wonder if Mrs Cartwright is looking and I can quite honestly say that I hope she is. Jasper makes a fuss of Tony confirming the fact that we don't get many visitors and whilst they play I make coffee and think about the lovely night and lovely company. Tony is not normally what I would go for but if he was I would have hit jackpot with him for sure despite his size. I sip my coffee watching Jasper play with her new friend. It is the first time for a while that my house feels alive.

"Emily, I thank you for a most pleasant night but I really must go now. I will either see you at work or maybe we can talk on the phone at some point." He certainly didn't seem to be pushing things and it all seemed very formal still.

"Thank you, Tony. It was a wonderful night, honestly." He stretches out his hand to shake but I plant a kiss on both of his cheeks in true European style and stand in the drive until he goes out of sight. Jasper heads into the garden indicating that in her opinion it's bed time. I can't say that I'm tired but as it's work in the morning I know she's right. In the time it takes me to get undressed and showered and get into bed wearing my nightie as my pyjamas irritate my legs for some reason, I realise that I have been thinking of Tony the whole time. As the quilt pushes out the air and lands gently on my legs after a quick fluff up, I cannot believe that I actually feel turned on. There is no way that I fancy Tony but I think I fancy the gentleman within.

"How did it go?" I am greeted with fishing questions the second I get in to work. Gossip is all Sally is after. I will be truthful.

"It was lovely, he's real nice." The shock on her face tells me that her attempts at a wind-up have backfired somewhat.

"Really? You seeing him again?"

"I hope so. It was good. Castano's is lovely; have you ever been there?"

"No, Marcus always said he'd take me but he never did." There is a tear appearing in the corner of her eye and I make my retreat before it turns into a full blown cry.

"I'll see you later; I've got some work to do." I don't know if I am more happy with the fact that I really did enjoy the night or the fact that it backfired on Sally. I try and get all my papers in order and sort out my appointments on the computer. I have a few jobs that I need to speak to Dawn about which I earmark for later. By the time it comes to the ten o'clock morning coffee time, I have checked my phone so many times to see it there is a text. There isn't and I find myself slightly disappointed.

The canteen is full of talk and as the food smells drift across the room to the door as I walk in I feel as though the talk stops for my entrance and I feel slightly paranoid that they are talking about me. I have nothing to be ashamed or embarrassed about so I walk in and choose a cheese and pickle sandwich. I sit with Theresa and Chris who I have barely spoken to before only because I find them boring and after giving a nod I open my sandwich and start to eat. Chris and Theresa do not mutter a single word, giving rise to my paranoia. Chris and Theresa have been married for a few years, he is a computer nerd and she is an accountant suggesting that the conversation in their house isn't all that interesting. On a weekend they go orienteering which doesn't do much to change my opinion of them. He was once offered a promotion package but because it meant being on call he turned it down as it would interfere with his weekends. I know work isn't everything but I like to think that I work hard to afford the nice things in life. Although the nice things I have at the moment amount to bags, dresses and shoes only. One day I know that I will have a nice man to share my life with and a nice man springs to mind again as I check my phone. Again no text from Tony. I am beginning to think that he doesn't want to see me again but just wish he'd have told me last night rather than wait for me to get the message through his silence. I could always find an excuse to visit his office I suppose, but does that smack of desperation? I think it does. However, I have a parking dispute which I need to run by the highways department, it may be the excuse that I'm looking for.

Knocking on the door I can feel myself turning red, even more so because Creepy Colin smiles as he walks past in a 'I know what you're doing' kind of way. I am not doing anything but feel as though I am as I look guilty, I can feel it. Even if I was guilty of something I am single and can do what I want. However, I do kind of feel naughty.

"Come in." I do as I am told and enter the highways office. The first thing I notice is a huge map on the wall with blue dots, red dots and yellow lines. It looks very official and stylish.

"Emily, can I help?"

"Yeh sorry. Is Tony in today?" Phil is Tony's assistant. He takes off his glasses which are perched on the end of his nose, points to Tony's desk and answers.

"He's out and about until this afternoon, can I help?"

"No it's not important, I'll catch him later." He nods and puts his glasses back in place and returns to his work. I leave the office but not before smiling to myself about the banana and apple on Tony's desk. I am so hopeful of another date that by the time I return to my own department I have booked myself in for another appointment with Kirtsy for my hair colouring. I think I want to go slightly lighter than what I am and this time I omit the three weeks of debating about it and will just do it. If I don't like it I will just go darker again. This is time for taking control of my life even if it is only a hair appointment.

The thing that I like about the canteen at work is that there is a lot of choice and usually a lot of healthy options. I like salad and sometimes just to be naughty I have a few chips on the side. Some people – and I would expect Tony to be no different – will fill their plates and get their subsidised monies' worth. I sit in the corner on my own hoping for a quiet lunch break. Kippers is asleep in the other corner. I'm glad as I would not be able to eat my lunch if she was sat next to me unless I was eating tuna to mask the smell of her. She does tend to be always sitting on her own unless Creepy Colin is in and he will sit with her, usually because no bugger will talk to him either. How amusing that he asked Dawn out, she really does attract them. You can guarantee if you walk through a shopping centre with her anyone with any sort of learning disability or mental health issue will home in on her. I always thought it was the uniform that attracted them until we went shopping in the centre of Leeds and it still happened. One guy who looked like Friar Tuck with his bald head growing out of the top of his hair latched onto her and asked her back to his room. She asked where he lived and he said that he lived in a shared house. Dawn thought it was a room in a house with supported living but I thought it was more likely a hostel for psychos and nutters and she would never have been seen again. She thought he was sweet but sweet in my book does not constitute making the slavering sound that Hannibal Lector makes. He'd have slit her throat and drank her blood, no mistake. You'd have thought with her being the police officer she would be more sceptical than me of people like him but she seems to give everyone the benefit of the doubt as though she doesn't really get the fact that there's a lot of weirdos out there. Like I say, she would not be the one you picked out in a crowd as a police officer. He followed us around for most of the afternoon and when we went in a shop he waited outside. Even when we went into Costa for a drink he waited outside, occasionally looking through the window. I honestly never saw him smile but his eyes looked right through you when you looked at him.

"Aww, bless him, he's just lonely."

"Lonely? Yeh 'cos he's probably murdered and eaten his friends."

"Don't be cruel." She just couldn't see it. We finished our drinks and continued with the stalker back towards the car.

"Can I carry your bags, lady?"

"No it's fine thank you," I answered for her. He followed about two paces behind us. I went to pay for the parking and when I come back he was on the floor with his arm twisted up his back and held by Dawn who was knelt with her knee digging into his shoulder.

"Anything you do say may be given in evidence. Do you understand?"

"Dawn, what's happened?"

"Dirty bastard tried it on with me. Get my phone out of my bag and ring Jon." I did as I was asked and scrolled down her contacts to find the only Jon in her list and before long Jon, a dashingly handsome sergeant, arrived to take him away.

"Is he single?"

"I don't tend to ask as it's not part of the caution," she said.

"I meant your sergeant."

"Oh, no."

"Shame."

Luckily our shopping had finished as Dawn had to drop me off at home and go to the station to do her statement. For someone who is usually a bit dippy, she was on the ball that day and that scroat will think twice next time he decides he wants to grab some woman's tit. I still laugh when I think of him on the floor with Dawn on top of him and not in a way that he would have chosen with his arm twisted into next week. I really can't take her anywhere.

I returned home with pictures in my head of the handsome sergeant in uniform with his handcuffs. At least I know I still have urges.

The afternoon came and I met with Dawn to discuss a job where the neighbours had been arguing over whose bin went where. Yet another neighbour dispute over a most pathetic issue. A semi-detached house where both parties had a garden path down the side of their house which then ran round the back ending in a small fence between the two gardens where both bins were stored. There was no issue with this but the dispute started on bin collection day. Three weeks ago Mrs Ryman went to put her bin out at the front to find that Mrs Hobbs had already put hers out in the place where Mrs Ryman liked to put hers. Mrs Ryman claimed that Mrs Hobbs had put it on her side and Mrs Hobbs claimed she did not. Both ladies, if I can call them that, are in their late sixties and started shouting and swearing at each other in the street, which is on a main road, and at school time. Dawn was called out and as she got there saw Mrs Ryman tip Mrs

Hobbs' bin over and start throwing rubbish all over the street. The final straw was seeing Mrs Ryman hit Mrs Hobbs with a cornflake box resulting in Mrs Hobbs falling over. This incident was witnessed by several five-year-olds coming home from school with their parents. Dawn took the decision to arrest Mrs Ryman for a public order offence and assault and the children cheered as she was put in the police car and taken away.

"Has there bin any further issues?"

"No," I said trying to work out why Dawn was in fits of hysterics.

"Has there bin, get it." She has clearly tickled herself and I do see the funny side now she's explained it although is it funny when a joke has to be explained?

"Oh, Em, I made a right fool of myself yesterday at the pubwatch meeting." Dawn is responsible for the pubwatch in the town which bans people acting in an anti-social way within the pubs. If you get banned from one you are banned from all of the pubs on the scheme. I have to know this. I like stories of Dawn making a fool of herself and something which seems to come natural to her.

"We were discussing the issues in the pub beer gardens and one of the councillors said that he wanted to ban people going in the beer gardens with glasses after nine o'clock. I took issue with this and said, 'You can't ban people from going in a beer garden just because they wear glasses'."

"You are joking; you didn't say that did you?" She nods.

"I wasn't listening." I join her in the fits of hysterics. How does she do it? I love her to bits but I wonder sometimes how on earth she gets through life.

Chapter Twenty-Two

Arriving home I realise that I forgot to go back to Tony's office. There is still no text from him and I decide that he doesn't want to see me again. I feel a bit offended if I'm being honest. Never in a million years would I ever date a man like Tony and I very much surprised myself in liking him, but how dare he, an overweight balding bespectacled man, dump me. He hasn't told me but in effect he hasn't phoned, texted or spoken to me since, which in my eyes constitutes a dumping. I found his personality more attractive than his features and think had I seen him in a pub I would not have given him a second glance except to do a double take at his belly. As much as I try to be disgusted by his size, I'm not. I don't like overweight men at all but there was something about him that made me feel safe. I didn't feel that he would jump on me, which is good as he would have squashed me, but most men would just turn on the charm to get you into bed and he didn't. I didn't exactly go to any great lengths to wear my best knickers just in case as I knew there would be none of that but I can guarantee if I went out with the Italian stallion I would wear my best matching set of underwear. Red is more tempting for a man I think and if he got a flash of them he would want me more than wearing virginal white. I haven't thought of the Italian for a few days but it's time I did. He made me feel like an electric current was being passed over my body. I'm going to go to Frankie & Benny's again, sod his girlfriend, I want to flirt. No-one cared about my husband having a wife when he was offered it on a plate; it's all fair in love and war.

I hold my phone all night whilst I watch TV, waiting for texts. I really have no strength to do much and can't even be bothered talking to Mum. It will do her good to entertain herself for a change. Who thinks about me when I'm running around after everyone else? No-one, that's who. I nearly jump out of my skin when my phone buzzes and vibrates in my hand even though I was wishing it to.

'Been thinking about you. Can I come and see you? xx'

Why would Shaun want to come and see me when he has a perfectly young vibrant girlfriend.

'What about?'

'Just want to see you.'

'What about?'

'I've missed you.'

'Yeh, shuttlecocks you have.'

'Been thinking about when we slept together. xx'

'Oh so you think you can come round here and sleep with me whenever she doesn't want to?'

'It's not like that at all, Em. It was good though eh? xx'

'I've had better.'

'What do you mean? xx' I knew that would do it. He doesn't want to think of me sleeping with other men yet it's okay for him sleep with her. That makes it 1-0 to me, I think.

'Just what I said.' I smile to myself as I text my reply and the texts go quiet. He didn't like that. It was good but I'm not telling him that. It was good because he knows what to do to me and how to get me going. That comes with being together a long time. I bet he doesn't enjoy sex with her like he does with me. I will put money on it. It's not that we do anything weird although she probably does all sorts of weird stuff, but it's because we just work. Maybe the excitement wasn't there like it was when she made her interest known but it was good, comfortable and it fit and that in my opinion is good sex.

My phone stays silent now so I have no idea if he will turn up or not. I don't really want to encourage him but I kind of like the idea. Part of me wants to change and dress a bit provocatively but then the sensible side wants to tell him to sod off.

My question is answered by a knock at the door. I can see a car parked on the road outside and it is not a car that I recognise but I assume due to the texts that it is Shaun. As I open the door Shaun is leant against the door frame with a bunch of flowers. Not my favourite ones but I wouldn't expect him to remember I love orchids but these are actually quite nice and slightly better than the garage flowers that I have had in previous years.

"I'm sure something was happening today." I remember him saying that a few years ago. I knew what was happening but left him to pretend that he didn't know it was my birthday. He had done similar things in the past and then at the last minute he would spring a surprise after pretending all day, rather badly, that he had forgotten. Only that time he had forgotten.

"Well I can't remember," he said, "maybe I arranged to meet the lads down the pub."

"Maybe," I said pretending to be taken in by his 'bad

memory'.

"Right well, I can't remember so I'll pop out for a few jars." I watched him walk out of the drive and down the street. I was so convinced that he would come back I took Jasper for a walk and staying in the bushes as cover followed him so that when he turned around I could jump out on him and scare him. He walked all the way down the street and turned right. He really was going to the pub! I followed him to the pub and watched him go inside. Jasper seemed to know where she was going too which made me think if I go out I know where he takes her for a walk. I went back home and watched TV in a bit of a mood. A couple of hours later he returned half cut stinking of beer with a crappy bunch of dead flowers that he either got from the garage round the corner or nicked off some poor bugger's grave at the cemetery. He tried so hard to make it up to me in the days after but failed. I enjoyed the attention actually but it's something he didn't learn. Give a girl a bit of attention and everything else will be fine. I'm not even bothered at getting presents, a card and a 'happy birthday, love' would do for me but preferably on the morning of my birthday and not on the border of someone else's.

"What do you want?"

"I told you I wanted to see you."

"Whose car are you in? I've not seen that one before."

"Laura's," he says sheepishly.

"So you text me wanting to see me and then turn up in your girlfriend's car. That's class, Shaun, even by your standards."

"Can I come in then or what?" I stand aside and let him in. I'm not one to conduct my business on the door step.

I stand with my back to the door and watch him as he lives in new depths, lower than even having sex with me went. He takes off his jacket and hangs it over the white glossed square piece at the bottom of the steps. I don't like things being put there and he knows it but I stay quiet trying to show him that even the small things don't bother me anymore if he indeed remembers that it did in the first place.

"Can I have a cuppa?" His familiarity seems out of place as he acts like we are long lost friends. He maybe forgets sometimes that he ripped out my heart and chopped it into small pieces but I realise that I don't seem as bothered by it as I was. This must be what people call the healing process.

It all seems very polite sitting in the living room drinking tea together. I have gone off the idea of anything happening with him as seeing her car outside my house has annoyed me no end, but I have to accept that he is with her now. I'm not even sure what he wants to talk about as we cover various topics from my mum to Beth, who hasn't texted him for a few weeks now, but I have to say it all seems normal. I'm happy that Beth hasn't been in touch with him as I don't want them to be friends, I want him to know exactly which side she is on if indeed there is to be sides. I am dealing with my pain and am almost getting on with my life now. Tony has helped me see that men do and will find me attractive and that is a nice feeling. I did think that approaching fifty which I haven't mentioned for a while was too old to be attractive to a man and I have horrible images in my head of wrinkly sex but I don't class myself as a wrinkly yet. I would have been disgusted by the thought of a fifty year old woman having or even wanting sex when I was younger but now I am that fifty-year-old woman, well nearly, and the thought excites me.

"How's your mum?" He has never bothered asking how she is before so my suspicion increases like some game where you have to score people's answers to find the guilty party.

"She's fine thank you." Apart from being a bit mad that is but he doesn't want to hear about that. I long to ask him about taking her to the golf club but bite my tongue. I resist. Although not for long.

"I hear you're taking Lucy to the golf club?" His face flushes a rather embarrassed red to the point that I feel like I am having a conversation with a tomato.

"Err, she wanted to learn to play golf."

"So did I."

"She insisted."

"So did I." A dark red tomato now sits in front of me squirming with the loss of words.

"I didn't come here to talk about Lucy."

"Well what did you come here for then? And why don't you want to talk about your young gorgeous girlfriend with the very pert breasts?" Where did that come from? I didn't intend any of that.

"I just wanted to see if you were okay."

"I know why you are here, Shaun, and it isn't happening." His muttering took the form of a man in desperate need of a hole to swallow him up. The hole did not appear in my house and he remained there as large as life. The only thing that broke the sound of his gums flapping was a knock at the door.

"Tony!" Of all the times for him to turn up he has to

pick the time when Shaun is here. Awkward!

"Hello, Emily dear, sorry to just turn up like this, I hope it's not inconvenient." What an understatement but I try hard to hide my shock at seeing him.

"No it's fine, Tony, I have a visitor that's all, I wasn't expecting you otherwise I'd have baked a cake or something." Oh how corny did that sound. I turn into a bumbling idiot right in front of him made only worse by Shaun appearing behind me.

"Oh!" Tony said.

"Err." I said.

"I'm her husband." Shaun said. I'm not sure this could get any worse.

"Oh my, I had no idea you are married, Emily."

"I'm not," I said.

"She is," Shaun said. I pull Tony to me and kiss him. He nearly suffocated due to not having any warning to breathe first.

"Emily, you are unbelievable."

"Tony, this is Shaun my soon to be ex-husband." Shaun didn't seem to like that comment and as his cup banged down on the work top he pushed past Tony and walked off down the drive. I was just about to try and explain to Tony when Shaun returned.

"I suggest you go on top, Em, he'll crush you." In those few minutes I had gone through all sorts of emotions from embarrassment to awkwardness yet I'm still standing. What a life!

"I'm so sorry to turn up like that," he said trying to make normal the situation.

"Tony, it's fine honestly, he comes round now and again for a cuppa, we still talk; we have a daughter together, but I'm sorry that I embarrassed you."

"Not a bit of it," he says brushing away his obvious embarrassment. "There's so many things that I don't know, well that we don't know about each other." He still seems to be a bit knocked back, almost standoffish now. Even after we sit and chat over a cup of tea he seems distant.

"I'm sorry that I didn't call you, my mum hasn't been well and I lost your number." I tried not to sound too bothered, I mean he's not exactly my usual target audience when I look for boyfriend material, not that I have looked for some time but I instantly liked the Italian hunk the minute I saw him, but with Tony it was more his personality that I liked. I wanted to say that he could have sought me out at work but decided to leave it.

"It's fine, Tony, honest. I know all about caring for a mother." We talked for another twenty minutes or so about our mums but then it felt to me like he was making excuses to leave. He did take my number with him but said because of his mum not being very well he couldn't commit to another date at this stage. Once he'd gone I felt a bit deflated if I'm to be honest. Maybe I have an opinion of myself way above my station but I would have thought that Tony wouldn't get much attention from women and not to blow my own trumpet, would be grateful for a date with a woman like me. I don't have to list my good points again as I have done it before but I'm not that bad for a woman of forty-nine with a half decent body, nice boobs, my own hair and teeth and independency. I am clearly not good enough for him which makes me wonder what men see when they look at me. Note to self – Take a reality check, girl!!!

Chapter Twenty-Three

"I thought you'd forgotten you had a mother."

"Of course not, Mother." Tony thinks his mum is a burden, I bet she isn't as bad as this one. I'd swap him for a day and see; I'd probably end up being much better off.

"I remember when you used to come and see me."

"I've been busy, Mother."

"Yes I know, seeing your friends, no time for me. I don't even get a phone call now." The guilt trip is not going to work, I will not give her the satisfaction of making me feel shit. My life doesn't evolve around her despite what she thinks. Before I can stop myself the words have come out of my mouth and my car keys are in my hand as I head out of the door to see my mum. My only bargaining tool was that Jasper is coming with me. At least I will have one friendly face to look at if my mother starts to pick on me. Oh I wish my dad was alive, he would tell her – he used to do that.

"Leave the girl alone, Peggy," he'd say. Peggy was a nickname that she had been assigned when she had a broken leg and was in pot hobbling around. It had taken some time to heal due to the severity of the break so she had limped for quite a while. Peg-leg had been shortened to Peggy and that name stuck.

You'd think my mother is completely dependent on everyone the way she carries on sometimes but she is more independent than most people are her age. Despite having large lapses in common sense she's quite switched on. Thinking about it I wonder if Dawn and I got swapped at birth; something which I would seriously consider if Dawn wasn't quite a bit younger than me. My mum says silly things as does Dawn and both are quite embarrassing to be around at times.

"I'm here," I call out as I walk in the door. Jasper knowing that she isn't allowed at Mum's stays hesitantly at the door.

"Mum," I call again. Silence fills the house. There is a light on but no TV and no sound of my mum answering my call.

"Mum!" My call is getting louder but still no answer.

"Where the hell is she?" I say looking to Jasper who is still standing by the door, for inspiration. If her tail was any longer I'm sure by now it would have been between her legs. She is waiting for the bollocking that clearly isn't coming as my mother has disappeared. I now start to panic as her door was unlocked. It usually is when she knows I'm coming but if she knows I'm coming why isn't she here. In my head something is drastically wrong and I begin to get scared. If someone is still in the house after murdering my mother I should not be in there and although there are no signs of blood, guts or even a body I make a tactical retreat and try and get my phone out of my pocket. It's hard when your hands shake at a million miles an hour. I have tried to ring the police before and it seems to take forever to get through to the 101 number so I use a direct line.

"Hi, Em, I was just talking about you. I'm in Tasties getting a kebab and Ahmed is asking about you. The cute older one so I assume it's you."

"Dawn please tell me you are working." She laughs obviously not realising my emergency.

"Well I'm at work but as I'm in Tasties waiting for a kebab I wouldn't exactly say that I'm working."

"Dawn, do you have to talk so much all the time!" Damn, did I just really say that? That was meant to be a thought.

We have had some laughs in Tasties after a night out. One of the lads in there who is about Beth's age started chatting me up one night. I got a free kebab with his phone number written on the box. I thought it was the number of the item on the menu and remember thinking that you go in the Chinese and ask for No.109 with chips, if you want Beef in Green Pepper in OK sauce obviously, but this item number was a long line of digits. Call it the drink or call me thick but when Dawn, who is known for her dippiness, points things like this out to me it makes me feel a bit of an airhead. I never texted him but every time I go in he writes messages and his phone number on the box. Dawn thinks I should just do it but three things are stopping me.

1) He is the same age or roughly the same age as my daughter.

2) He probably does it to loads of girls and I'm not into becoming a slab of kebab meat for his entertainment.

3) I just don't fancy him and that's probably the clincher.

"Right, Em, what's the problem?" At least she's still interested after insulting her, what a good friend.

"Dawn, I'm scared. I think someone has broken into my mum's house and might still be there. I was meant to be going round and when I got there she's not in. I daren't go and check the house as I think someone might be there." The phone went dead. I can't believe in my hour of need she puts the phone down on me. I take back what I said. I stand deciding what to do when a screech of tyres shits me up big time. A police car with lights flashing stops about two centimetres away from me. Dawn gets out ready to spring into action. She looks so professional that I am gobsmacked. The Dawn that I know would have run over my foot forgetting to stop. There are definitely two sides to this woman. Before I have had the chance to retell the story, Dawn and her colleague – who just happens to be the gorgeous sergeant – had rushed into my mum's house with tasers drawn. I stand for what seems like an eternity listening for any shouts of 'get your hands up' or 'drop the weapon' but there is nothing but silence. I say silence, that is apart from the small audience now watching in this small quiet cul-de-sac where nothing ever happens. Well tonight they're getting a treat.

"Emily." Dawn is shouting from the door beckoning me over.

"Is she dead?" I can hear the gasps of breath from the crowd waiting patiently for some gossip for the Monday club or is it the Tuesday club that survives more on gossip, either way they're getting a treat. Jasper stays loyally by my side as I walk back to the house. Either loyalty or the fact that she has got her lead on or she may have done a bunk. I wish I had done one. I am still heartbroken from losing my dad I can't lose my mum now. Entering the house there is a different feel to it. I can't describe it but it is different. I follow Dawn into the living room with my eyes almost closed as I don't want to see my mum's dead body. This is not something that I had planned to do this evening. In fact I just wanted a nice quiet night which thanks to Shaun, Tony, and now my dead mother I haven't had. Oh god I need a drink. I don't feel well.

All sorts of things are going through my head at this moment in time and I feel some sort of thud on the back of my head. I feel like I need to open my eyes but I can't, I feel dreamy, lightheaded, and a bit sick. Maybe I should have had some tea before I came out but I couldn't, my mum needed me. Oh my god I may have heard her final few moments before she was murdered. I don't want to go on TV to appeal for witnesses and information because it's always the people that appear on telly that are the ones who have done it. I know for a fact that I haven't murdered my mum but the great British public doesn't know that. They will think I killed her to get my hands on her money. I don't even know if she has got any money, I assume she has, my dad always talked about stashing away for a rainy day and he gave me a few handouts when Shaun left. Bless him I wouldn't have survived without him really. Always Daddy's little princess. So how could I have killed my mother. Oh god I'm beginning to talk like I did it. I didn't, I have an alibi, two alibis really, they will stick up for me, won't they? It would be a good way for them to get back at me though. Shaun was jealous when I kissed Tony in front of him, why did I do that? I was showing off and that few seconds of showing off with a fat man could have cost me my freedom. And Tony was clearly upset when he saw my ex-husband in my house. He must think I was sleeping with him, which I have done but not that day. The two of them could work together and stitch me up. Who would look after Jasper?

She will have to be put down. This is going from bad to worse. This is a living nightmare and it's me that's living it. All the people who know me will desert me and talk to the press and get their stories in the newspaper and get large five figure sums for doing it and dishing the dirt on me.

'I always knew there was something sinister about her. She had a dark side, you could see it in her eyes'. I can see the headlines now. Tony said I had lovely eyes and I wonder if he will tell that to the police now he's working with Shaun to get me banged up for life.

'FROM ASB TO HMP'. Front page of *The Sun* and all the other newspapers. It's got a nice ring to it and will be a headline winner above all the other newspapers.

"Oh, Mum, I'm so sorry, if I had been there for you, you would be alive now. I'm so selfish. All I wanted was a quiet night instead of coming to see you. What a terrible daughter I am. Mum if you can hear me I'm so sorry."

I think back to all those times when I didn't tidy my bedroom or I was cheeky, (I was only ever cheeky to Mum, never Dad. Ever!) Or when I was fighting with Charlotte and Mum didn't like it. She always sided with her anyway but being in the same room as my mother's murdered body is not the right time to discuss that now. I am sorry for all the times I feel I should be sorry for even the ones that I can't remember off the top of my head and there will be loads. Getting told off by Mum and sticking two fingers up at her behind her back, I'm sorry for that too. There was one time my dad saw me do that and I think that's the only time he ever told me off. After the telling off he smiled and said he understood why I did it and sometimes wished he had the courage to do it and only the fear of her turning around and seeing him stopped him doing it. I still feel lightheaded and dreamy but the need to pray is too strong to hold in. I did go to Sunday School when I was younger and if that influence has made me reach out to the good Lord when I need him the most, I just hope he hears me.

Chapter Twenty-Four

I feel a gentle slap on my cheek which seemed to get harder the more I become aware of it. It is accompanied by a screech.

"Emily."

"Dawn?" I think to myself.

"Emily!"

"Dawn?" I still think to myself.

"Emily!" I wonder how long this can go on without one of us losing interest. I open one eye and see a lady policeman standing over me.

"What are you doing?" Yet again another example of me saying instead of thinking but she scared me. Can you imagine going to sleep and opening one eye gently and seeing two big blue eyes peering back at you. It scared the shit out of me!

"Emily are you okay? You've fainted." I gathered something had happened as I don't normally sleep on the floor. It all comes back to me. Then the tears start.

"Mum, poor Mum, how did they do it?"

"Do what?" Dawn asks. Dawn is such a love trying to protect me from this horrible thing. I'm not even fifty and I'm an orphan.

"How did they kill my mum?" I just can't help becoming one of those over the top wailers at funerals. It is uncontrollable. It happens again. She actually slaps me!

"What the hell did you hit me for?"

"Listen to me." I try, and I have to say she has a voice of authority and the tears begin to slow and the wailing quietens down. She strokes my hair.

"Look." She points.

"Oh god it's a ghost." I feel the colour rush from my cheeks, I really can't take all this in. She gets murdered and when the police are here investigating her death she appears as a ghost. Bloody typical of my mother. She can't even die normally.

The next slap is hard enough to knock me into next week and I cry. Not because I'm upset, although when one of my best friends slaps me I naturally feel upset, but this cry is because it's so damn hard my head turns with the force.

"Shut up, you stupid cow, and listen!" Now I have worked with Dawn on jobs before but I have to say she has never called anyone a stupid cow, not to their face anyway, she has had many choice words for a few, not to mention the ones she came up with for the bin disputing neighbours.

"Your mum is here. Look." I can certainly see my mum, it looks like her but I don't understand what's going on. God I sound like Dawn, the dippy side of her anyway, when I think about the amount of times I've heard her say that with a confused or blank expression on her face.

"I don't understand," I say. I feel strong enough to sit up and push my body back to the door and rest against it. Dawn stands in front of me and I can see the gorgeous sergeant stood behind her. They'd make a nice couple I think to myself, he's maybe a bit young for me. They don't call me Shaun; going for the younger generation or two. Behind him almost hiding in the kitchen is my mother. My rapid blinking tells Dawn that I still don't understand so she steps in.

"Your mother is alive and well and was pretending to be dead to teach you a lesson," she takes a long pause before starting again.

"She's had a telling off and won't do it again." I catch the look that Dawn gives my mother and know that she will have had one hell of a bollocking. My mother looks sheepish and for some reason which is now very clear, she cannot look me properly in the eyes. As Dawn and the sergeant leave the house I wish I was going with them because right now I want to kill my mother myself, or at the very least rip her head off.

"You've got some explaining to do, Mother!" Her line of vision descends to the floor avoiding my gaze.

"Look at me when I'm talking to you." It seems there has been some role reversal her today as I am speaking as a parent and she is looking like a naughty little girl.

"I'm still your mother," she retaliates.

"Well damn well act like my mother then." In my forty-nine years I have never sworn at my mother directly. I did this time and I meant it.

"I'd like you to leave," she says.

"Don't worry, I'm going. I can't believe how pathetic you are sometimes, Mother." I go and don't look back because I know she will be watching me go. I think at this stage I am more angry than upset. The depths that some people go to will never fail to amaze me, usually it's the idiots that I come across at work not my own mother. Half way home I pull in to the side of the road and burst into tears. I cannot stop it, I cannot control it but the realisation hits home that sometimes my mother is very lonely but ultimately she is my mother. Waiting until my eyes are dry enough to drive my car I think back to the times from my childhood that seem like only yesterday. I can remember playing out in the garden with Charlotte and Mum and Dad would sit watching us. If we fell or hurt ourselves, Charlotte would always run to Mum and I would go to Dad. Dad's hugs made me feel better, safe and special. I can still feel them now and I still miss them now just as I have every day since he died. I now understand that because Charlotte is away and Dad has gone, we are as lonely as each other; both hearts breaking in the same way yet feeling so alone. My car seems to know what do and finishes the short journey back to my mum's house. Jasper excitedly jumps up from the passenger's seat thinking we are home only to realise we are back at my mother's. As I walk to my mum's front door I do not know what to expect. I have calmed down and am no longer angry with her and as she opens the now locked door we fall into each other's arms, hug and cry.

She tries to explain that she wanted me to realise that she needs me, as if I don't already know that. We laugh about the line dancing classes and the people who go there and before I know it I have agreed to take her tomorrow night. I'm not sure how, other than using the guilt trip, she gets me to do things like that but it's only an hour I suppose and I have to agree over the last few months I have been thoroughly entertained by them. By the time I get back in the car Jasper is crying. When will I get some time to myself, the last thing I want to do sometimes is walk her at night. I have a routine of getting home from work and walking Jasper then I can have my tea and chill. It's just a shame others haven't got used to my routine yet.

It's amazing what you see when people leave their curtains open when it's dark. I have to confess at being one of those nosey people that can't help looking in people's houses as I walk past. I hate it when people do it to me but I am guilty of that same offence. The majority of people sit watching TV with a laptop or iPad on their knee or sit happily texting away which reminds me I must text Dawn, but one guy who I walk past is sat watching TV with his hand down his pants. I can clearly see his hand moving. He is oblivious to me watching him and I dread to think what sort of film he is watching. Jasper must think I've gone on strike as I stand there for about two minutes watching him. I cannot believe that people would do this with the curtains open. I'm not a prude by any stretch but I'm both disgusted and enthralled by him. Then as I watch it comes to an abrupt end and I don't know if he has seen me watching or the job in hand, so to speak, has been finished naturally or not but his hand comes out of his pants and is rubbed on his leg. My enthralled part has now disappeared and left me with only the disgust. I would hate to do his washing. Jasper pulls as if to tell me I have seen enough which I can't really argue with. The thoughts of that dirty man stay with me for some time and seem to creep back into my thoughts every time I forget. For some reason I have the compulsion to ring my mum and I'm sure it is more to remind her that I do think about her rather than check she's okay, she'll always be okay, she's a tough cookie really despite the vulnerable woman of earlier. I wonder how different things would have been if Mum had died in place of Dad. I know it's not a nice thing to think about but I quite often think of things like that. How different would my life be if I had married Rob instead of Shaun. Rob was someone I had a six month relationship with when I was seventeen. It was mad, it was passionate, it was exciting and my mother hated him. That was more the attraction for me. Dad was okay about it other than Rob had a reputation for sleeping around. He was my first sexual partner and despite the stories that I had heard about stars appearing in front of your eyes and head spinning with passion it wasn't that good. It bloody well hurt, I'll tell you that. I felt like I was being ripped open from the inside. I didn't start to enjoy it until the fifth month by which time he decided that I wasn't the one and was already thinking about how to end it. He got his friend to tell me that he was with someone else. Shame 'cos I actually quite liked him. I saw him a few years ago in town and we had a chat. He told me he was single, surprise surprise, and we went on our separate ways. Maybe if that was now I'd ask him out 'cos I've certainly got nothing to lose and the sex might even be better now too. He looked okay but I think he looked older than me which made me happy.

Jasper drinks half of her water when she gets back from the walk and that is something that she always seems to do. She also knows my routine 'cos she sits next to the fridge knowing that I will make a cup of tea and when I open the fridge I will more than likely throw her a piece of ham or cheese. With this done it's time to sit and relax until my mobile pings into action. It must be serious and I feel my hairs stand up on the back of my head. My mother never calls my mobile.

"Hi, Mum, what's wrong?"

"Just making sure you're still taking me to line dancing tomorrow."

"Mum, we only arranged it a bit ago."

"Yes, dear, but I know what you're like for double booking yourself."

I guess after our lesson in respecting each other's feelings today, it's now business as usual. The double booking incident that she so clearly remembers was over a year ago when I went out with Dawn and Sally after promising to take her to the theatre to see the local amateur dramatics society performance of Brighton Beach memoires. I don't think it was too bad a mistake on my part as the person who played the older brother in the play was a paramedic by day and because of some serious accident he didn't finish work therefore didn't turn up to perform in the play. The only understudy who also controlled the curtains was much younger than the main character so the older brother was really a younger man who had to read the lines from the script sheet. At the end of the first half the rest of the cast had to wait for him to finish his line and then run off stage to the wings to control the curtains so that they could have a proper theatre interval. My mother obviously forgot that bit as she vowed she would never go and see amateur dramatics ever again but is obviously quite happy to use it as a beating stick against me.

"You have my guarantee, Mother."

Chapter Twenty-Five

Phil tells me that Tony isn't at work today and I start to get the feeling of being taken for a fool again. I don't know what it is about him. He is by no stretch an attractive man, in fact quite the opposite, he hasn't got the physique that I would spend my day dreaming about nor the looks that would turn a head or two, but I am beginning to feel that I quite like him. Not in a lovey-dovey way and I certainly don't fancy him but his personality means that he is someone I would get on with and at my time in life I am not expecting love, stars or heart-skipping beats. I have to be realistic that at forty-nine and a bit extra I will never taste the love that I once did and never feel the passion that I have done before. Companionship is the answer to all my troubles. If I can be content and comfortable with my companionship I will be happy, right? Surely three Cs are better than just one L. Who needs love anyway?

"Don't broadcast it please, Emily, but his mother died last night." Phil delivers the news in such a matter of fact way that I wasn't expecting it.

"Oh, poor Tony." What else can I say? Surely he hasn't lost my number again but I suppose he has a lot on now with his mother dying. I wonder if she has really died or if she is just reminding him that she is still alive like my mother did. I still think it was a bit drastic for her to do it and wished that Dawn had given her a ticket for wasting police time. Maybe Tony will be at work this afternoon with his own tale of his over-demanding mother. I think I should maybe send him a quick text just to say how sorry I am, the last thing he will be thinking about is sending me a text.

During the community partnership meeting I try to sneak my phone out of my Fiorelli Bridget Tote Bag which has been relegated to my work bag after the sad death of my Nica bag, and although they look similar and are both tan colour, which is not my favourite colour, they're both big enough to get my files in. I look around the room to check no-one is watching me and slowly press the small keyboard to text him. A beep frightens the life out of me and I drop my phone on the floor making everyone look at me.

"I'm sorry," I claim trying to make it look an accident by dropping my lipstick too. Dawn laughs at me which makes it even more funny as she is usually the one dropping things. At least every time I have seen Dawn in her uniform something drops out of her pocket. Once she left the partnership meeting and went back out on patrol only to return an hour later as she had left her utility belt with her handcuffs and baton in the meeting room. She has left her hat many times and once even walked back to the station not realising that she had come in a police car which was still parked at the council offices. As she was going off duty her colleague asked her for the car key which she promptly gave him but he couldn't find the car in the station car park. It was a good job that Creepy Colin was cleaning late that day otherwise it would have been locked in 'cos he is too thick to notice a police car parked outside; mind you, in that case no more thick than Dawn as she'd walked past it too.

With the text sent I put Tony out of my head and concentrated on the meeting. I managed to put the vibrate facility on the phone in anticipation of Tony's reply. I had to check I was still living in the real world with the next conversation.

"We are having a lot of problems on the estate at the minute with gangs of kids running round causing anti-social behaviour outside the shops on Roebuck Street," said councillor Mack. He lives nearby and I suspect it is more his low tolerance than any complaints from residents as I have received no calls about it. He's a tall skinny untidy man with unbrushed hair and gaunt features. If I was a doctor I would be worried about his health. I could put him in touch with Tony and he could give him a few stone, which would help both of them.

"We should build a wall similar to Hadrian's Wall and put the shits on the inside," he continues. Very helpful and constructive comment from a local councillor I think as I write down a few comments about his complaint. But then a classic comment from Dawn.

"Who's Adrian and what's his wall like?" says Dawn. "I know someone called Adrian who's a builder, maybe he can help." The room erupts in laughter. Even me who tries to be more loyal to Dawn than professional cannot hold this one in. She has come out with some beauties before but this one tops them all. Dawn remains straight faced not knowing why we are laughing. I watch her face as the penny drops as though in a machine in the amusements; her cheeks go red followed by her forehead and the rest of her face. Councillor Mack looks ready to spontaneously combust as his glasses slide towards the end of his nose with the vibration of his laughter. It takes a while to quieten down and Dawn, still unsure of the hysterics that she created, launches into her speech of what the police will do and how. How anyone can now take her seriously is beyond me. After the meeting I speak to Dawn about her newest edition to the Dawnism list, she now finds it funny and starts laughing but she's on her own. The hilarity has worn off for us who have already had our thirty minutes of fun out of it and I leave her to it. I need to get back to my office and check my phone as I'm sure I felt a buzz. Before I get there I meet Sally in the corridor. I have to take time out from my mission to tell her the Hadrian's Wall story which she finds as amusing as I did at the time.

"Drinks tonight?"

"Err, I said I'd take my mum somewhere but maybe after I can."

"Right cool, I'll text Dawn," she says.

"You don't need to, she's still in the meeting room," I say. I leave Sally in search of the highly trained police officer who can't distinguish between common sense and sarcasm and head to my office where Marion aka Kippers is fast asleep as usual. At least it gives me the privacy I want, failing that it would have to be the toilets but they smell worse than she does at times, hardly surprising really with Creepy Colin down on the cleaning team! There is no message on my phone to say I have a text which disappoints me but I suppose I am not on his list of priorities at the moment, in fact I don't suppose I am on anyone's list of priorities.

"Silly cow," Sally appears at the door.

"What?"

"Dawn. She can be thick at times." I have seen the other side to Dawn when she came to my mother's house after she 'died'. She was efficient, organised and authoritative. I'm not sure that being like that would actually suit our Dawn, she was born to be dippy. I love her.

"I know, bless her." That's my contribution to the conversation.

"Eight this evening at Spoons." That was Sally's contribution. Short and sweet. Mum's line dancing session will be 7pm - 8pm and then I'll have to drop her off before I go to Spoons so it will be at least 8.30pm when I get there. I can't say that I'm that bothered about going really but I have to show willing after our recent fall out and I'm sure they can forgive me half an hour. I have ground to make up on the friends list so I will do it. I will tell my mother that I can't stay for the usual and customary cup of tea at her house after line dancing as I have work to do, after all a little white lie never killed anyone.

As usual I have to rush around like an idiot when I get home. I take Jasper out but this time I go the other way to remove the temptation of looking into the disgusting pervert's house. The walk is short and sweet but enough for Jasper to do what she needs to do and then it's back home to shower, change, have a quick bite to eat and go get Mum. Right in the middle of the organising, something else blows it apart. A text. From Tony!

'Can I see you tonight? Need to explain.'

This is all I need. I have just managed to juggle things in my head and sort them. What am I going to do now? Who do I let down? It can't be Mum otherwise she'll die again so it is between Tony and the girls. I decide that my loyalty should really be the girls so text

Tony saying that I have arranged to go out with Sally and Dawn and could we rearrange. His reply leaves me feeling even worse.

'Really need to talk.'

I text Sally saying that something has come up and I might not make it. Hopefully Dawn will tell Sally about my mother dying and that will cover me in the excuse. I cannot at this stage tell them that I'm dumping them for Tony.

'OK when and where?'

'How about Frankie & Benny's at 7?' Oh no! I can't go there, the stallion will be there. What can I say?

'Can *we go somewhere else I'm not struck on Frankie & Benny's or you could just come here for coffee.'* I lie but he can't look in my eyes when I text so I don't feel as bad lying. Lying is only wrong when people can see the truth in your eyes. That's a new saying and something I've just made up especially for this occasion. I quite honestly don't agree with it as lying is wrong full stop but there is no way on this earth that I am going to Frankie & Benny's with Tony when my dream man might be there. What if he notices me and takes an interest and then asks me out, what would I say, sorry I can't I'm with him. We agree on Barley's a nice little place where it is quiet and cosy as I'm not sure he likes the thought of being in my house with the jealous ex creeping around. I am intrigued as to what he wants to speak to me about but secretly hope that he will not declare undying love or anything that I am not ready for. I may have given some unintended signals when I kissed him in front of Shaun but I'm not ready for anything yet. I am quite happy with a few dinner dates for now. Now is the time for some serious juggling.

'Can we make it 7:10?' It's a bizarre time I know but it makes sense to me and thus my time schedule for the evening is in place.

6:50 - Pick Mum up and drop her off at the line dancing.

7:00 - Drive to Barley's to meet Tony at 7:10.

7:20 - Order a drink whilst I look at the menu (but decide really quick what I want to eat).

7:40 - Order the food that I had previously decided on.

7:55 - Leave the bar, drive to the line dancing class, pick Mum up, take her home and then back to the bar by 8:15 just in time for my food to be put on the table.

What could possibly go wrong?

Chapter Twenty-Six

The roads are clear with minimal traffic and the vision is good. Conditions are dry and things start well. Mum is ready too, thank God, which certainly means it's a good start.

"I won't stay tonight, I just have a few errands to do and am meeting some friends later so won't be able to stay for a cuppa afterwards." Terms and conditions boxed ticked. This is easy. She doesn't even argue which is the biggest surprise of all. As we pull up the usual coffin dodgers are gathering for their weekly line dancing work out. Mum is delivered to join the queue and looks quite sprightly next to some of them. I'll say one thing for my mother she may be 80 but she's still got her mobility and her faculties even if some are slightly damaged like the one where she remembers to be nice to her daughter. A quick check of the time tells me that I am on course to be at Barley's for 7:10, this is easy, my organisation skills have obviously improved. Shaun used to moan about my time keeping but funnily enough I am very rarely late for work. I have, in my time, been late for weddings, funerals, parties and even my mum and dad's anniversary celebration night but I believe it's a girl's prerogative to be late when you're trying to look nice. He used to always moan about my sense of direction as well. We once went to a football match and I got lost because I was annoyed at him for having a few pints at half time so I didn't listen to his directions. I ended up in Ripon when I should have gone home to Leeds. He didn't notice 'cos he was fast asleep. I told him that I'd called off for a coffee as I was tired so he never knew about that little diversion. I have to say that even I started to panic when I saw a sign for Darlington being 35 miles away, I may have a rubbish sense of direction but even I know that Darlington is the wrong way.

Time check – 7:07, perfect! Time to park and go inside. It's all working out perfectly. Maybe I am a bit cynical of life sometimes. Surely something will go right for me. It's 7:09 as I open the door and I can see Tony already sat down at the bottom. He looks at his watch and smiles.

"Emily darling, perfect timing."

"Yes I hope you're impressed. I'm not normally on time for anyone else." I say it in jest however there is truth in it as I have already explained.

"Perfect and you look stunning." He stands and outstretches his arms.

"Thank you," I say and welcome the embrace given to me.

"What would you like to drink?" he asks. I am now so obsessed by my list of strict times that I check my watch (7:15pm) before realising that I will have to miss a few sips to get me back on schedule as I didn't plan on ordering my drink until 7:20. I will have to hope that he takes his time getting served. He does and I feel relaxed as he sits down at the table at 7:20. I have already clocked the specials board at the back of the bar and have decided on smoked salmon with sliced new potatoes and baby sweetcorn on a bed of spinach for my choice of food so I am keeping to the schedule and it is all falling into place. My coke is full to the top as it lands on the table and a bit spills out as the giant ice cubes smash together as though waves crashing against the harbour wall. I mop it with a paper napkin as we make small talk whilst we sip our drinks, covering work, choices of food (I don't let on that I already know what I am having) and then I tell him that I am sorry about his mother's death and if there's anything I can do to help he must ask. He sits quiet. Stunned by my obvious forwardness. Surely he wouldn't expect me to sit and not say how sorry I am. It's strange how when someone has lost a person close to them, everyone says the same thing. 'I'm so sorry, if there's anything I can do just ask.' Firstly why do we say sorry? It's not our fault unless we were driving the car that ran them over or unless we pulled the trigger, and then to say if there's anything I can do. What on earth could we possibly do? We can't make things better, we can't bring them back, we cannot stop their suffering in any shape way or form. It is the British way to say something rather than just say nothing. Anyway I have conformed to the British etiquette and offered my services if there is anything I can do.

"I'm really sorry about this, Tony, but I will have to pop out shortly to pick my mother up, I will only be gone twenty minutes." I have slightly lied about the time as it will be more like thirty-five minutes but if I was honest he would probably just go home thinking I'm a cheeky cow.

"That's fine, Emily, there is something I need to discuss with you so you will come back won't you?"

"Ha! Yes of course I'll come back. She's not been well and I errr…" How insensitive am I? How can I tell him my mother has not been well when his has just died? I was going to tell him the story of my mother faking her own death but think it better to leave this one out of the conversation too. I'm not sure if I have anything else to talk about. Maybe it is best if I leave him to do the talking. Not sure how that will go down as he has hardly said a word. It's like he has got something on his mind. Oh god, Emily, how stupid are you? His bloody mother has died of course he has something on his mind. I think I am clearly spending too much time with Dawn.

The young lady comes round to take our order. It really is nice in here. I have driven past a few times but never been in. Its rather alluring green lighting doesn't quite make it to the street so unless you look in the window you wouldn't really get the proper effect. I order my food and Tony orders a rare steak. I laugh and privately embark on another memorable story of having a meal out with Dawn. Me, Sally and Dawn went out for a meal once and Sally went to the toilet after we had spent time discussing our choice of food from the menu. The waitress came to take our order. I ordered mine and Dawn ordered hers and then Dawn decided to order Sally's as she had told us what she wanted. Dawn promptly ordered a steak on Sally's behalf.

"And how would she like it?" the waitress asked.

"With chips," said Dawn.

"Okay, with chips," she writes that down. "How would she like her steak cooking?" The waitress quite rightly asked.

"You can fry it if that makes it easier," said Dawn.

"No, you misunderstand," said the waitress whose English was very good despite being from Lithuania or someplace like it. "Will she like it well-done or medium or rare?"

"Oh," said Dawn, "She doesn't like her food burnt so you best do it raw." I could not see for tears welling up in my eyes and the more I tried to hold in the laughter, the more tears came. You could see the waitress's brain ticking over wondering what the hell she had in front of her. If she had known Dawn was a police officer she would have probably given up on our country altogether. I corrected Dawn's raw to rare and the waitress went off to the kitchen wondering what had just happened.

"Haha, I thought she said raw," Dawn laughed, "It must have been her accent." I laughed along letting Dawn think it was the girl's accent rather than just another Dawnism but then she added to it with another classic.

"Is that why the steak is so expensive?"

"Why?" I asked.

"Because it is a rare one?" I love her so much, but more so because when Sally returned to the table she was still blaming the girl's accent for the confusion.

I decide not to tell Tony that story but I enjoy the memory. I check my watch and it is time to leave to go get Mum. I have a quick check of my mental list and the food is ordered and it is 7:54 so I am one minute ahead of schedule but a red light will see to that on the way there. I promise Tony I will return very soon and apologise again. He seems fine with it but I think he is quite happy to be in his own company tonight to think about his mum. I'm not sure why he asked me out because he doesn't really seem like he wants to be here. I'm still intrigued as to why he needs to speak to me and have thought of a few replies if he wants to get serious, as a way of cooling it down a bit. I like him and like his company and that is all I want right now. I think!

I arrive bang on time to pick Mum up and she is waiting outside as though I am late. I check my watch and it is 8:05 so I am not late.

"Oh it was warm in there tonight," she says. "We're organising a memorial line dance and party next month in memory of the Major." I remember the Major's passing that night, how could I ever forget. How would I ever forget? I seem to be surrounded by events and tragedies, dramas and dilemmas, accidents and incidents yet no-one to share them with except my mother. I think of Tony sat alone in Barley's waiting for me to return. I bet people who saw us together think I've walked out and left him. He might get the sympathy from the single women in there. I might go back and see him sat with a woman having a drink, talking and whispering into each other's ears. She might have her hand on his knee as she giggles childishly dropping her gaze down to the table with schoolgirl embarrassment making it perfect timing for him to lean across and plant a kiss on her cheek.

Why am I thinking this? Do I really care that much about him to be jealous of something that won't even be happening? Or will it? When I was with Shaun I was convinced for the last few years of our life together that if I had known another woman wanted him I would have gladly given him to her with the knowledge that she would have sent him straight back. Sat watching TV with him listening to him fart and watch him scratch his arse is enough for me to have thought nobody else would want him. I was confident of that. I was clearly also wrong. I wonder what I could have done to stop him straying. I knew he wanted sex and quite honestly I couldn't be bothered with it. The thing is, I actually enjoyed it once I got going, I just couldn't be bothered with the getting going bit. The thought of having sex did nothing for me even with the knowledge that I would enjoy it. Maybe it is the same as every other couple. The bloke wants it, the wife doesn't. He either plays with himself and puts up with it or he goes elsewhere. Shaun went elsewhere. Sometimes after working all day and coming home and cooking and cleaning the last thing on my mind was having sex. In hindsight, I should have made more of an effort because I am finding myself at forty-nine thinking about sex and I love it. I love feeling alive, I love the tingling and the thoughts of someone making love to me, I love the thought of someone seeing me naked and liking what they see and I like the thought that someone is turned on by their thoughts of me.

Note to self – Get a sex life!

Chapter Twenty-Seven

Mum is delivered safely to the end of her drive. She is nothing like Miss Marple but neither is she convinced that I am rushing to meet Dawn and Sally. She has asked more questions than I could imagine she would fit into the ten minute drive and I fend off as many as I can. Her parting shot tells me she believed not one single word.

"Don't forget to bring him to visit your mother." I say she doesn't believe a single word, she clearly believes the bit that I am meeting someone but doesn't accept my answer of who. Schedule is kept to and the minute the passenger door is closed I'm off for the drive back to Barley's. This has been the most amazing timekeeping schedule ever and I think it certainly entitles me to a job with the Royal Marine's battle time planning department. I just hope that Tony is still there otherwise I will look a bit of a lemon walking to a table now occupied by another couple. I park the car in the exact same spot as before and walk past Tony's car to the steps leading to the door. It's all gone perfectly well. His car is still there and the time is 8:14. I am amazed by my own organisation skills. Then something which I hadn't expected happens. I had meticulously planned this evening to the finest detail but could not have foreseen this thing happening in a million years. As I open the door I feel like I have been slammed in the face by a sledgehammer. I stand still and without even looking in the mirror I know the look on my face says it all. Of all the eating places in all the world he chooses to bring her to this one. How can he do this to me. I want to turn and run but my feet are stuck facing forwards. I know if I make any quick movements I will fall. Oh Lord, please spare me this. I just cannot face him. Oh no he can see me and is looking right at me. Right, act natural! A slow walk and avoid eye contact. Then it gets worse still, she is with him. The most gorgeous woman I've ever seen is with him. The Italian stallion is right in front of me, with her. I told Tony I didn't want to go to Frankie & Benny's because he would have been there and yet that's the one place I would have been safe because Mr Frankie & Benny is here. I can tell he's watching me, I feel his dark eyes burning a big love filled hole in my heart. It's like he's pulling me towards him and everything else around me fades into insignificance. I can feel myself getting closer to him and even without the eye contact which I am dying to give him, I know he is watching me.

"Hello." I hear the words but do not associate them with any face. I feel a bump and lose my balance. The next thing I know I am on the floor and he is looking down at me.

"Are you okay?" I cannot believe I am on the floor at his feet and he's asking me if I'm okay. I try out the answer in my head.

"Not really. I am completely smitten by you. I want you to pick me up and savage the very bones of my sexual being." I think this may be a bit strong so luckily I have enough wits about me to change it before I do my usual trick of speaking without thinking.

"Yes I'm fine, thank you. I must have tripped. I'm very sorry." That sounds much better although I'm sure a little bit of excitement just squeezed its way out of my body.

"Here, let me help you up." He puts his glass down on the table where the goddess is sitting watching me make a fool out of myself in front of her boyfriend.

"Thanks," I say, still avoiding eye contact. I don't need to see him. His face is imprinted on my brain.

"Are you sure you are okay. Can I get you a drink? A brandy perhaps."

"I'm fine, thank you. My friend is waiting." Shit why did I say that? He will assume my boyfriend. I should have said boss. Actually that sounds worse and makes me sound like someone who sleeps with the boss to benefit her career. I can't believe women do that. I wouldn't. Well if I worked at Frankie & Benny's and he was the manager I most definitely would. Anyway I don't know why I am so worried, his angel of a girlfriend is stunning. No, she's better than stunning and I reiterate the point of last time I saw them together, he would not look at me twice. In fact I'm not even sure he would look at me once when he has her to go home to, other than to look at me on the floor in front of him in my own pathetic mess kind of way. I can only imagine the sight of the two of them naked in sexual excitement, their bodies locked together in love, exchanging love, lust and passion all in one. I have never stepped into the world of lady-love but I would even go to bed and make love with her just purely and simply because she is the most beautiful woman alive on this planet. When I say I haven't ventured into the world of girl on girl, I did once sleep with my old friend Cat Pritchard on a weekend away. I was about seventeen and hadn't met Shaun then. We slept in the same bed and had a drunken kiss. We may have had a bit of a fumble too but it was only the once and we lost touch soon after that. I did hear that she had married a soldier and moved abroad. I wonder if she ever remembers that. Funny how things like that just come back to you years later.

My thoughts have digressed and I need to come back to earth. That man makes me feel alive and my whole body tingles. I did notice though that there was no Italian accent. As broad Yorkshire as me. Oh well, he certainly doesn't lose any points in my eyes. Anyway, back to reality and as I sit down at the table with Tony who is smiling after watching me fall over making myself look a bit of a tit, I take stock of things. It's a bit of an impromptu stock take but it makes me think that although I like Tony, feelings like that for other men (and woman in his girlfriend's case) shouldn't come into my head, because if I liked Tony enough nothing else would matter. It is time for me to have a search in my heart for the truth about being with Tony. Is it for companionship or is it to prove to myself and others that I can still be attractive to men? I am sure that I would never or could ever love Tony and for me it would be about having that companionship and I am sure that this is really not enough for me. I want to love and be loved. I want to feel the love and passion and excitement that I know I am capable of feeling and I would never get that with Tony. It's time to call it a day as sad as that sounds. On a positive note, the time is 8:20 and although I messed around being turned on by the stallion for five minutes the food has just arrived at the table. I can still claim it as perfect timing.

"I'm so sorry that I had to leave you, Tony, It was very

rude of me but my mother is very demanding sometimes."

"This is delicious," he says taking a bite from his steak, noticeably changing the subject. He went for the well done option not the rare or raw version which is clear from the dark brown burnt parts but if that is how he likes it they have done it to perfection. It looks nice and now I wish I had chosen steak. How strange that you always want what the other person has got. I'm sure I've said that before.

Note to self – let the other person order first and then choose the same.

We start eating our food and although five minutes behind my scheduled time it's hot and it's tasty. Tony isn't offering much in the way of conversation other than the odd 'Hmm' whilst eating. I try to think of something to start a conversation about but my mind drifts to my mum. A few months ago she was sad and still hurt from Dad's passing and the woman who often sat in the window watching him in the garden in her memories seems to have been replaced by a socialite. Last month she volunteered me to go with the stitching and bitching group to York shopping for the day and wasn't happy with my excuse of having to work on a weekend due to a large work load. She knows I made it up but I don't want to go. In fact, I'd rather chop my legs off with a credit card. I will end up following her and Muriel around whilst they talk about a nice frock that they've seen. Does anyone call dresses frocks these days, clearly they do, but hopefully it's a dying trait as it's an awful word.

"This salmon is lovely, would you like to try some?" He shakes his head. It's becoming a bit of an awkward silence now and one which I start not to enjoy. My phone beeps and I try very subtly to check it as I believe it is quite ignorant on a dinner date to check your phone but as it may potentially be important I check it and as well as the welcome distraction from the lack of conversation it unwittingly makes me smile. It's from Shaun. 'Thinking about Lakes 2011.' Probably the last time we did anything together was a long weekend in the Lake District where we hired a log cabin. We had a brilliant four days together just him and me. Beth was supposed to be coming too but she got a long haul flight to Australia so it was just the two of us. I was dreading it because the cracks had already started to appear in our marriage and in hindsight he would have already been seeing her; however we walked the hills in the day and talked and chilled out in the hot tub most nights. In his text I know he is referring to the last night where we had sex in the hot tub. It was amazing. We decided to go in the hot tub naked. It was a shared hot tub with the cabin next door but the couple staying there were from Liverpool, not that that matters, but her mum was rushed into hospital on their second day so they went back leaving the hot tub solely to us. Being in the hot tub naked was a massive turn on and we had a great night. The memories rush to the front of my head as I think about it. I reply very quickly and out of sight eating with my left hand whilst texting with my right. 'Yeh it was good.' I feel myself go red and I hope it doesn't show and strangely I feel a tad guilty texting one man whilst sitting with another. How strange the brain is, but at the end of the day Shaun is still my husband as he quite protectively pointed out to Tony. In between exchanging glances and smiles with Tony, and swapping flirty texts with Shaun, my eyes watch the not-so Italian stallion as he eats and chats to his girlfriend. Oh, he is so nice!

The silent meal was very nice and although I felt bad texting Shaun I don't feel any guilt for perving over the stallion. My fork slips off the plate and as I try and grab it I knock my glass over which doesn't smash but causes a ting sound audible for most of Barley's customers, most of whom turn around and stare at me. How dare I spoil the atmosphere with my clumsiness? I can only say it's a good job Dawn isn't here. Talking of Dawn, I wonder how her night is going with Sally. I kind of wish that I had gone out with them because Mum's death or not, Tony is pretty crap company tonight. I look for the toilets, I need a wee.

Chapter Twenty-Eight

The toilets are quite nice and probably one of the best I've been in for a while. Things like that, more than good customer service, make me return to places. I cannot stand dirty smelly toilets. In this one the basins are spotless and even the usual make up residue marks have been removed. There are no tampon wrappers on the floor from people who have missed the bin and couldn't be bothered to attempt a second time to hit the target. The mirror is without the smudging of poorly cleaned mirrors and the toilet roll is well stocked and of good quality. The floor is clean as there is nothing worse than going to some toilets and pulling up wet knickers from other people's piss on the floor as with some pub toilets. People say men's toilets are bad and on the odd occasion that I have been in men's toilets, more through desperation rather than loose moral behaviour, I have to agree they were pretty bad but some ladies toilets are disgusting. In fact you should be prosecuted under trading standards for false advertising for putting them alongside the word ladies. A final check in the mirror and I am ready to rejoin the rest of Barley's in the main part of the restaurant. I open the door and stop dead in my tracks. It's him. Stood right in front of me after coming out of the gents. I cannot tell you how glad I am that I checked myself before opening that door. Could you imagine if I had a bit of food in my teeth or a food stain down my top. I am confidently clear of both as they are the first things that I check.

"Hi," he says. Oh my words! I can feel my face going a

lovely plum red.

"Hi," I say, trying not to sound like I am talking down the telephone on a dirty sex chat line.

"Have you recovered from your trip?" I laugh and he smiles.

"Oh that, I'm a bit clumsy sometimes." He is gorgeous. His jet black hair is perfectly gelled into place in the shape of a quiff except for a curl coming down towards his right eye brow. He opens the outer door and beckons for me to go first. All I can think of as I walk in front of him is he checking out my bum? I certainly hope so I know it looks good in these tight black jeans and I think he will like looking at it, if indeed he is looking. Then reality smashes my dream out of my head. He is probably twenty-eight or something, why would he be looking at my arse when he's got his donna perfetta. I need to stop with the Italian references now as he's probably never even been there. I sit down to Tony's contorted face. Oh no don't be having a stroke on me, I'm rubbish at first aid. I am just about to jump up or scream, or make some other hysterical girl noise when he speaks.

"I'm really sorry, Emily. I must tell you something. I have to say it now otherwise the moment will have gone." I'm beginning to get worried now. I am waiting for the violins to start and for him to get down on one knee, I hope he doesn't, he'd never get back up, and I really don't want this to happen, not here anyway, well not anywhere really but especially not in front of the dreamboat.

"The thing is…" he pauses, "Errr…" he's sweating like mad. What on earth is he going to tell me. He looks nervous, petrified even, like a small child who knows he is in big trouble.

"Tony, what is it?" The stallion walks past again and oh god he just winked at me. He has seen me sat with Tony and winked at me. Is he just being friendly? My phone beeps again and as Tony takes a sip of his glass of water and pulls at his shirt collar I check it.

'Still thinking about you.' It beeps again just as the phone goes in my bag. 'Can I come round tonight?' I don't know what game Shaun is playing and I feel slightly confused. If he wants me then why did he leave in the first place? If Juicy Lucy is so lovely why does he want to come and see me. I am forty-nine years old and at this moment in time I have one gorgeous male winking at me when he is sat with the most amazingly beautiful woman, I have a man opposite me who is acting like he's trying to pluck up the courage to propose (I hope so much that he doesn't) and I have a soon to be ex-husband who wants to come round and see me. Is life winding me up or what? Am I on a secret camera show? It bloody feels like it. I decide to go with the flow and just see what happens except for marrying Tony, that's a definite NO! He has got a lot of money I'm sure of that as I have seen his house but money doesn't bother me. As long as I have enough for the important things in life, shoes, bags and hair and nail appointments I'm one happy girl.

"The thing is…" And Tony's back in the room. Will we get any further this time?

"After my mother's death I had to errm… take stock of my life." Oh no it's coming I can see it.

"I am fifty-two after all and have lived most of my

adult life except my university days looking after her."
Now it's time for him to do what he wants and he wants to marry me. I am poised ready with my very polite put down.

"There are certain things that I could not let my mother know for reasons beyond her understanding."

"Tony, what is it just tell me." This guy needs a bit of persuasion.

"The thing is, Emily," he fiddles with the paper napkin that he had placed so neatly on his lap which has now found its way onto the table and is being torn from one side leaving a small pile of fluffy paper next to his plate. The Italian walks past me again and drops a piece of paper from his pocket which lands just near my foot. I want to tell him that he's dropped something but I can't as I need to give Tony my full attention. It's a bit unfair to litter in the restaurant as the waitresses have enough to do but I'm sure he didn't do it on purpose, he doesn't look like a litterer.

"Would you like another drink?"

"No I'm fine thank you." He's stalling and it's beginning to annoy me now. Nothing can be that important that he can't speak.

"No, errmm, right." He takes another sip of his water which is still half full."When my mother died it gave me the opportunity to be myself." I watch as the waitress picks up the piece of paper. I feel so sorry for that girl she has worked so hard all night and on top of that he drops litter for her to pick up. Note to self – leave a good tip.

She walks fast between the chairs and tables and stops to talk to him. She's maybe a bit young for him but

211

she's pretty enough. His girlfriend isn't sat at the table with him. How typical that she has gone somewhere and he's now chatting up the waitress. It could have been me if Tony wasn't being such a stuttering fool. I haven't seen his girlfriend pass me to go to the toilets nor did I see her leave the restaurant. Mind you I have been trying to listen to Tony or I would have done if he had said something worth listening to. Last time he talked about cultural things like art and museums and the places that he had been to around the world, usually with his mother, but he's been all the same. He was interesting and full of excitement for the things that he had done and it made me want to visit them too. He said he would take me to Rome as I have never been and he told me of the Colosseum and the Trevi fountain and made it come alive to me through his thoughts, yet this time he has hardly said a word to me all night. The waitress comes back my way after speaking with him with a smile on her face. I bloody bet she's got a smile. He will have told her she's pretty and she will fancy him like mad because she's a young woman finding her feet in the world of female to male sexual connection.

"Excuse me, madam, I think this is yours. I found it on the floor by your feet and I believe it must have fallen out of your bag."

"Oh thank you. I'm ever so sorry." She goes and I think it must have been a receipt that was on the floor. Maybe he picked it up thinking it was interesting and when it was only a Morrison's receipt he threw it back on the floor. That, I think, is a bit cheeky looking at other people's things and just discarding them when they are of no interest. Cheeky sod. If it had been ten pounds

I bet he wouldn't have thrown that away. I play with the paper between my finger and thumb whilst I listen to my phone beeping away. I sneak a look. More texts from Shaun. I can only see the first few words on the display but they are all 'Can I, Will you, I want.' At this stage my nice reply to Tony's impending marriage proposal is losing its niceness. If he doesn't spit it out soon it will be more of a 'I'd rather slam my head under a piano lid' or 'I'd rather gouge my eyes out with a blunt spoon,' kind of answer. He is beginning to look like a pathetic man instead of the funny intelligent cultured man of last time. My phone is ringing now and I can only assume that Shaun is desperate for the answer to his questions. I just don't feel comfortable answering my phone just now. I sneak another look. This time it's Sally. Oh god what is going on tonight? Tony is still sweating and has now started using my napkin to wipe his head; he'll be pulling that one to bits soon. Our plates are cleared by the same waitress who picked up my receipt from the floor and she's smiling at me. She doesn't even look at Tony, her attention is all at me. I know I have had thoughts for the Italian's girlfriend but I am not interested in girls at all. She leaves our table and exchanges a few comments with stallion man on her way back to the kitchen. I am beginning to think even more now that there are hidden cameras everywhere. Maybe Sally was trying to warn me. I am going to answer my phone. It has stopped ringing by the time I pick it up and see four texts from Shaun and a missed call from Sally. I ring her back and all I can hear is laughing down the phone. I hang up. My brain is hurting with all the goings on and it is struggling to keep up and process the information.

"The thing is, Emily." Here we go again. I have heard him say 'the thing is' about four times and it led to nothing so I am not expecting any further words to come this time either.

"I shouldn't have led you on. I'm very sorry."

"What?" I am starting to look for the hidden cameras. I'll kill the sod that has set me up. Anytime now Jeremy Beadle's successor will come in dressed as a waiter or something.

"You are a lovely lady and need to find someone who can give you what you want." Lovely lady? What is he on about. That is the sort of thing you say if you are dumping someone.

"Tony, what are you on about?"

"I just think you are a lovely lady who deserves the best. In time you will meet someone."

Hang on, I've got the Italian giving me the eye and my soon to be ex-husband wanting to come round and have sex with me and you are saying I'm a lovely lady who will meet someone in time.

"What are you trying to say, Tony?"

"Errmm, I have to be honest with you, Emily."

"Well I wish you would 'cos I have no idea what you are on about."

"When my mother was alive there were certain criteria that I had to adhere to which, on her passing, I no longer have to."

"Right, and?" I prompt. The sweat intensifies and almost drips from his forehead. The Italian winks at me and smiles. I subtly smile back. Tony won't notice, he's lost in his sweaty thoughts.

"The fact is, Emily, I am gay." Well knock me down with a feather. I didn't see that one coming.
Note to self – Find a feather to be knocked down by.

Chapter Twenty-Nine

I am not sure if I am more shocked with his revelation or disappointed that he would prefer a man to me. I have had problems trying to picture Tony naked even more so now with the thought of him being with a man.

"Is this something you have known for a while?"

"Since I was about fifteen," he said.

"Hell of a burden to carry." He hummed in agreement. I'm surprised and shocked but also slightly offended that he would ask me out knowing that he didn't really fancy me, yet deeply touched that he chose to reveal himself to me.

"Emily, I am so sorry. I feel that I have led you on." I knew this wasn't going to go anywhere yet I suppose I find it easier being the victim here as it is awful having the end a relationship not that we have a relationship, well we certainly won't now. "I would ask one favour though please which I have no right to ask." His sweating has stopped and it must be enormous relief for him to finally get it off his chest.

"What?" I ask.

"Please keep this to yourself. I'm not ready to go public yet."

"Of course," I say reassuringly. I feel a deep connection with him probably for the first time. "Do you dress in women's clothes?" Again my thoughts come out without warning. I am curious though but I certainly couldn't imagine it.

"I'm not bloody Dr Frank-N-Furter, dear." I smile. His voice seems to have changed slightly to a more camp one and I wonder if he now feels more himself, not literally though as I'm not sure I'm ready for that thought yet.

"Did your mum not know?"

"No, she has always said how she couldn't wait for me to find a nice lady and settle down. I didn't mean to lead you on, Emily, I really do like you."

"It's fine, Tony, honestly, don't worry about it." My phone continues to beep away and Tony ignores my plea to pay half of the bill choosing instead to go to the till and settle up. The Italian winks again. I smile. My fingers are still rubbing the receipt given to me by the waitress and he points at it. I look around and he smiles. He mimics my finger movements. I open the piece of paper up and written on it is the name Kevin and a mobile number. He then points to himself. I decide to check it now and do something that I would never normally do. I get my phone out and after ignoring the texts from Shaun, I send a text to the number. 'Hi.' I keep it plain and simple and watch as he gets his phone out and replies instantly. 'You look good x.' I put my phone away as Tony returns and takes his coat from the back of his chair. My last date with Tony is over and there is a slight sadness as I do enjoy his company but that is pushed out of the way by my new excitement of having Kevin the non-Italian's number. I smile at the slight rhyme at his new name and accept the help from Tony, the perfect gentleman, as he lifts my coat over my shoulder. I blush like a schoolgirl as I walk past Kevin and blush even more when I walk past the waitress who bids us goodnight. She clearly knew what was on the piece of paper as she passed it to me.

"Once again, Emily dear, I have enjoyed your company and again I apologise for my misleading ways."

"Tony, it's fine, just be yourself and be happy."

"May I take you out again one night? I don't have many friends, Emily, my mother saw to that but I feel that I have met a true friend in you. I hope my actions haven't spoilt that." I like him, I can't help it.

"You have my number, Tony, text me anytime you need to talk." I plant a kiss on his cheek, bid him good night and walk to my car. Once there I check my phone properly. Shaun has texted seven times asking if he can come and see me and come and talk and Kevin has texted again too. It feels nice to be in demand. I know Kevin is just playing with me, there's a thought, and I know that Shaun is just texting because things aren't working out for him as he had planned. My drive home gives me chance to reflect on the evening. With the stress from my most meticulously planned schedule behind me and the desires of other men, I haven't had a bad night at all. I am now looking forward to getting home and putting my PJs on and chilling out before work tomorrow. As I pull into my drive I know it's not going to happen. Shaun is sat like a homeless person on my doorstep with his coat pulled around him, knees tucked under his chin. His face emerges from the tightly rolled hooded coat and he watches until my car comes to a stop and the lights turning off make his face disappear into the darkness.

"Where've you been, I've been texting you all night."

"Yes I know you have. I was out with someone which is why I started ignoring you." He stands up and looks at me. If I didn't know Shaun I would swear he'd been crying. However, I dismiss this as bad light and unlock the door. Jasper comes running to see me and jumps up knocking me into Shaun who puts his arms around me to steady me. I move away as soon as I recover my balance.

"I suppose you'd better come in then." I'm not sure if I want him in or not but I'm far too nice to leave him on the doorstep.

"What are you doing here?"

"I said I wanted to come round."

"Yes I know you did but I didn't say that you could." He follows me into the kitchen and flicks the switch on the kettle as though he read my mind. He takes off his coat so I know he's planning on stopping a bit. Just one cup of tea won't hurt then I'll kick him out. I am a strong woman now, I am in charge in this house! I am tired and all I want is a bath and bed.

For a little while it seems like old times, with him sat in his favourite chair, and me in the one under the window until my curiosity gets the better of me and I mention the L word.

"Where's Lucy tonight?" His face crumples into a wrinkled mess.

"Why do you always want to talk about her?" I laugh but prod further.

"You said she was the woman of your dreams. So why aren't you with her?"

"She's out with her mates, again." The word 'again' tells me that things are not good in the Shaun and Lucy love nest.

"Oh she's a bit of a party animal is she? Why don't you go out together?"

"I'm not that keen on her friends to tell you the truth."

"Why don't you take her to the golf club again, somewhere where you never took me." I want to bring loads of things up and score a few points but I really can't be bothered arguing. He looks quite pathetic sat there and I feel a tinge of sympathy for him. On the other hand I know it was his choice to leave and he's only here because things haven't worked out like he wanted them to. Yes, she may be more beautiful than me, yes, she may have a better body than me and yes, she may be great in bed and do wonders for his ego, but I am his wife and I am the one who knows him inside out and have taken the rough with the smooth. I am the one who fits him like a glove and I am the one who he knows he should belong with. But he chose to leave not me and he has to live with that. He lets the golf club comment pass over him without reaction just as my mobile beeps. I look and quite obviously without intention I smile as he comments about it being 'him'. I assume he means Tony, but he's wrong, it's Kevin. I don't reply as I'd prefer to be alone when I do.

Shaun makes conversation about the past and the good times that we had. I have to agree we have some good memories and only ones which we can share with each other. Had I been staying with Tony and with him being with Lucy, these are memories that will be lost in the vaults of time, locked away and never to be enjoyed again together over a glass of wine on important anniversaries. It's times like this when I think of the past that I miss Beth. She was a lovely little girl. I miss all the hours spent putting the tins back into the cupboard when she had pulled them out and putting the dirty washing back into the washing machine when she had thrown it all over the kitchen floor and I miss trying to get the pencil marks off the wallpaper when she had drawn on it but on top of that I miss my husband. I feel a warmth towards him as he sits there. I find it hard to dismiss the years that we spent together and that is something that he won't have with her for another eighteen years or so. My thoughts jump between memories of walking the canal with him and the dog, not Jasper we had a different one then called Benji a cross between a corgi and a whippet a great little dog but one whose memory has been faded by Jasper, and new thoughts of having a bath with a glass of Sauvignon Blanc with bubbles and texting Kevin. I still have doubts about why he would look at me but he's texting me so he must like me unless he's playing with me, a thought which doesn't put me off. I wonder what has happened to his girlfriend. I need to find out because I have been the cheated on I so do I really want to become the cheated with?

"I really need to go have a bath and then go to bed, Shaun. It's been a long day." He looks at me and then looks into his cup.

"Okay, I'll just finish my tea, thanks for the chat, you go up, I'll see myself out." He stands as I walk to the door and I give him a hug. "Take care," I whisper deep into his ear. I have no bad feelings for him and I suppose I want him to be happy. There is a small satisfaction that things aren't too good for him but I feel in the last few months I have come a long way on the recovery road that people speak of. At the time it seems it will never get better and you cannot get lower but someone once said to me that no matter how long it takes, they will always have a taste of how you feel now. It can take months or years but it will come. I now know this to be true because at the time I could not have felt any more hurt, upset, alone and depressed than what I did when he cheated on me and left. I now feel human and my self pride has returned, the texts from Kevin are helping, I am now a woman who is alive and vibrant and vivacious again. I say again although I am not sure I was in the first place but that's how I feel now. Nothing will hold me back!

The bathroom fills with steam as the water fills the bath to the safe point, a point that I have come to realise is the fill line for the bath so that the water doesn't spill over onto the floor once I get in. I like to have a full bath and have had desires on a new bath for some time as I love corner baths. The wine glass has steamed up too but the chilled wine enters and swishes around before settling down. My new Laura Ashley duck egg bath towel rests on top of the sink holding my mobile phone until I can get in the bath and reply to Kevin's texts. Shaun shouts bye and I hear the door close. I am now alone with my thoughts, wine and my mobile phone and I feel naughty. I slip in between the bubbles which separate to allow me to lie down. My hair is tied up and the glass of wine makes frequent visits to my lips. Let the fun begin.

Chapter Thirty

'You looked good tonight.' I smile; he thought I looked good, I didn't make that much of an effort to be truthful. If I had known he would be there and watching me I would have worn my black dress with the cut out back. It looks real nice if you have a good figure and although I lost a good few pounds with all the stress of the break up I'm sure it's all back on now. I'd certainly have worn it for him though had I known he'd check me out.

'So did you.' I reply 'cos he did, he always does. Every time I've seen him he has been wearing a white shirt with black jeans or trousers and a leather jacket. Not that he wears a leather jacket at work but he did when I saw him after work getting into his girlfriend's car. We exchange texts about the usual personal details as he didn't even know my name until he asked me in a text. He is called Kevin and he's thirty-one and lives about three miles away from me. In fact he lives just about opposite my work which is handy to know if we ever meet at lunchtime. I am surprised by my own presumption that we will meet as it is just a bit of flirty fun for us I'm sure. I cannot believe how good he's making me feel. He noticed my eyes are blue, which I suppose could have been a lucky guess, but if not, it proves he really has looked at me. I wonder if he has ever thrown his number at other girls and stop the thought there before it grows into a cancer of thoughts spreading like wildfire wiping out all the positive thoughts. At this stage I am not that bothered. I haven't properly flirted for a long time, not since dating Shaun and a couple of flirty texts with him since. I actually feel sorry for him but I am not thinking about Shaun at the moment as Kevin is all over my mind. I write out a text asking him to come over as I am lying in the bath and the door is unlocked. I wonder what sort of reaction I would get and almost dare myself to press send to see. I dare not send it really but I just want to see what it would look like written out on my phone. I am careful to delete it just in case my finger has an attack of a mischievous nature and sends it without my permission. I long to ask him about his girlfriend but decide not to, I am enjoying being naughty and if that means that he's texting me behind her back then so be it, it's only flirty texts, I don't intend to do anything about it. My second glass of wine goes down as good as my first and I'm beginning to feel tipsy, maybe because I am sitting in the heat of the bath drinking chilled wine at speed. Sometimes they just go down well.

Note to self – Take my time with the third glass and appreciate it more.

Further note to self – Take time to understand my note to selfs because the third glass goes the same way and just as quick after my initial intentions to drink it slowly disappeared after the first few sips. My thoughts stray back without me knowing to the ones where I text him to come to my house. Through the bubbles I look at my body and wonder what he would think if he was standing over me now. I push the water with my arm to create a wave to wash over my boobs removing the bubbles from them. I'm not sure if it is the hot water or my slightly clouded judgement through the many glasses of wine but they look nice. I have never been one to take pictures of parts of my body as some of the girls have done at work but the thought crosses my mind. Mel at work regularly takes pictures of her boobs and sends them to her husband when he's at work. She said one day she did it to keep his interest throughout the day so that he would be ready to have sex that night. That's all well and good but in my opinion a bloke is always ready for sex. The slightest little glimpse down my top and Shaun's little man stood to attention good and proper. It wasn't so bad when I was in the mood for it but when I'm trying to get dressed and he's hanging around trying to have a gawp at me it gets a bit annoying. Mel would be sat at the table at lunch and be quite open about her sex life, something else which I've never understood. Why would people be interested in my sex life? I have to admit some of the stories she told were funny, others a bit too far over the 'this should not be discussed' line but she's a character and I think that's why we listen. When the craze was in about the mile high club, they booked extra holidays just so they could have sex on a plane more often. They didn't just join it, they smashed it. She told us that they had sex in a train toilet on the way to York! Who said romance is dead? I am pretty sure that I would never get turned on in a train toilet; they're dirty smelly disgusting places to be, just like they are on an aeroplane. I like to be in bed, comfy and warm. I once had sex with Shaun in a hot tub at a friend's summer barbeque and I thought that was daring. How would I react if he sent me a picture of his willy? Would I send one back? I suppose if I didn't put my face in it I could always deny it was mine to the masses of people he may show it to. I now think about sending him a picture of a random girl from the internet, just for a laugh but even that seems a bit wrong. Three glasses of wine and a bit of horniness are turning me into a monster. I want him to come now and take me. I have not thought like this for a long time, if ever. At the end of the day he is pretty much a stranger and I would never have sex with a stranger. I remember Sally once met this guy who she had never seen before, she had only spoken to him on the telephone and whilst I enjoyed the story and the naughtiness alongside it, I would never dare. They could be a rapist or murderer. She had spoken to him on the phone at work over a few months and he had to come to town to do some training in customer relations. They had flirted on the phone and he said he was staying in a hotel and would she meet him. She did and slept with him. She said that they had initially agreed to sleep together over the phone. She was single but he was married and it was one night. They never met again although they still speak.

As if by some amazing coincidence, Sally texts saying that I missed a good night and she had only just got home. She said Dawn had told her about my mum faking her own death and understood why I hadn't gone out. Phew! I'm in the clear. Typically of Sally, she is already arranging another night out. I cannot use the same excuse to get out of this one so I agree to go. Again and very typical of her she leaves me with a hook text to get my interest. 'I have news to tell you.' I promise to go but for now I am too keen to get back to Kevin's texts.

'I wanted to kiss you tonight.' Oh my god! He wanted to kiss me. My body acknowledges this text with a tingling sensation. If someone could see me now they'd liken the sight of my grin to the cat that got the cream. I can almost feel my ears getting pushed back by my broadening smile. I rack my brains for an answer, a teasing one, but before I have spent too long thinking of one my fingers have already sent the reply.

'Why didn't you then?' I wait for the answer daring not to move as I might miss a split second in looking at his text. Two words flash up before me and it takes us to realms that I thought would be avoided.

'Your boyfriend.' I reply immediately that Tony was just a friend which isn't a lie despite us actually being on a date at the time before the developments which released me from him.

'That's nice to know. Maybe I can take you out then.' I reply that maybe he can. I have decided not to mention his girlfriend. I want to look him in the eyes as I say it. Anyone can lie in a text but lying face to face is a whole different ball game.

The texts go quiet and my head is rapidly filling with thoughts of his girlfriend coming home and he can't text anymore. It makes me sad to think that the only enjoyment I get is by text and only when she is not in. He must be a game player; there is no way on God's earth that he would want to take me out when he has a girlfriend like her. I know I must stop texting him and put it down to a bit of flirty fun. The thoughts of what he could do to me are lovely and make me feel like a woman and I am grateful to him for that. He has no idea what he has done for me in such a short space of time. I have always said that you meet people in your life for a reason. I believe Tony will become a really good friend, honest and reliable with a trust that has now formed between us that will not be broken, and that's important. I want and need to have people like Tony in my life. I believe Kevin is the one that has given me my self confidence back and made me feel that I am attractive to men and that one day I will meet someone who will confirm this. Right now I feel on top of the world that someone like Kevin has taken even the slightest bit of interest in me. Thank you, Kevin. I am still smiling although sad that I have decided to terminate my texting with Kevin and I walk through to the bedroom and drop the towel to conduct my full body cream routine.

"Bloody hell. What are you doing here? You scared the life out of me."

"I wanted to see you properly."

"Shaun, I'm not being funny, you just don't do that. You really scared me." I bend down and grab the towel to cover myself up.

"There's no need for that, I've seen it all before, Em." I still wrap myself in the towel. My heart is beating like mad and I tell him so. He shuffles across the bed and puts his hand through the gap in the towel resting it on my left side near my heart.

"I still have that effect on you."

"Like hell you do. I nearly had a heart attack." He pulls at the towel some more but harder this time pulling it away from my body and dropping it on the floor. He takes off his t-shirt and cuddles me. I am still suffering shock and don't have the strength to push him away. He pulls me close and I can feel my heart racing. He turns me so my back faces the bed and gently pushes me down so that I lie on it. I want him to stop but I don't. Kevin is not here nor will he ever be so Shaun will do. Kevin will no doubt be at home doing amazing sexual things to his girlfriend taking her to the very borders of the universe. There is no further speaking between Shaun and me, I just lie back and let him explore my body as once he used to do. Just like the last time although this setting is much comfier, he does things to me that make me balance on the edge of orgasm before teasing me making me want more, needing more and then he delivers me into the world where my head spins and my eyes flicker and my body tremors to the rhythm of love. I cannot control the noise and Shaun is left in no doubt that my needs have been fulfilled more than enough. I lie in complete satisfaction wondering if my love rival is lying on the bed she shares with Kevin feeling the same as I do right now.

Chapter Thirty-One

"Look, Em, I messed up big time, I'm really sorry for what I did. If you give me another chance we can work it out and I will make it up to you, I promise." I don't want to have this conversation at all, never mind when I am still enjoying the coming down process from orgasm. I lie in silence looking up at the ceiling wondering where he has suddenly found all this new energy. I would never describe Shaun as a selfish lover but he never lasted that long before. It's like he's found a new vigour, new techniques and at this point just like the last time I'm not remotely bothered that he probably got them from her. That was one of the best ones ever. Minutes later my body is still tingling inside. I feel as though I could probably go again. Shaun cuddles up to me and I can tell that he's done although I'm sure he could be persuaded. What is happening to me? I'm turning into a sexual monster. I really really enjoyed that and I can't think of a time when I've enjoyed it as much. Maybe I should keep Shaun as a friend with benefits. How would Lucy feel that he's cheating on her with his wife? What a strange situation but being in bed with him at this moment just feels right. It's funny how when we were together I couldn't be bothered with sex and he always had an eye on some fit girl walking past in the street and here we are in bed together having incredible sex. If it had been like this when we were together would he have strayed? Would I have wanted sex? Who knows and it's not the way to think. We split because he wanted sex with someone else and yet here he is in my bed. I do believe that life has a way of paying back when a wrong is done and although at this moment in time he is not paying for what he did, she is. She knowingly slept with another woman's husband and now he is sleeping with someone else behind her back. Is it classed as an affair if we are still married? No idea and don't care!

Jasper jumps on the bed and forces her way into a small gap between us.

"I feel like I belong here," he says. I bite my lip trying to be the better person and not drag things up all the time. This is a nice atmosphere at the moment and I want to enjoy it until of course my mouth ruins it.

"Well you belonged here last time but you couldn't keep it in your pants, could you?" He jumps up and starts getting dressed.

"I am trying to make it up to you."

"Trying to make it up to me!? You think a quickie makes up for it? Are you for real?"

"Quick? Are you joking? That lasted half an hour." I want to laugh but don't. I knew that would offend him. Always hit them where it hurts, it works every time. He stands half dressed at the foot of the bed and this time I can't help but laugh. He has his t-shirt and socks on but nothing else in between. Then another thought comes and changes to speech before I realise.

"I can see why Lucy wanted you." He huffs, puffs and turns around putting his undies and jeans on. As a woman I know how to turn a situation and I pull the covers back and the sight of me laying completely naked stops him dead.

"You know, Em, I really love you." I smile. I want to say did you think that when you were sleeping with her but my self control is good this time. I know he loves me and maybe we just fell into the rut of everyday life and became complacent. However, the facts are that he is with her and I am alone but the flirty texts with Kevin remind me that I can feel excited and I can feel wanted and attractive and I want more of this feeling. His phone beeps and he looks at it then puts it back in his pocket.

"I best go."

"Is the boss calling?" He half heartedly smiles but it is very brief. At this moment he doesn't look happy. I wonder if she still sends pictures of herself as she did when he was with me or has the novelty worn off and they go through the motions that every other couple goes through. I wonder if he sleeps in front of the TV like he did when he was living here. I wonder if he farts in front of her and wafts the cushion around like he did with me. Have they settled into the normal routine of life and the lust and passion gone or are they still sending little notes to each other and texts and pictures of body parts. I best not ask.

Standing in the garden watching Jasper sniff every plant makes me ponder my position in life. I am first and foremost a mother and just because Beth is living a long way away I don't feel any less a mother. My love for her is limitless and if she needed me I would be there like a shot. We don't speak every day because of her job but we text regularly. She doesn't bother with her dad and I'm sure he probably doesn't bother with her. The daddy daughter bond was broken when he left me; she is protective of me and I of her. I would rather be in my position than his, because my standing is driven by family and routine and normality, his is driven by sex and lust and of what could be rather than what is. On a scoring matrix of happiness, I am located between a 6 or 7 whereas I think looking at his face he would be a 3 or 4. It may be that he is good at pretending and just pretends to me that he is not happy and in reality he may just be playing a game. If that is the case I believe that I am in the driving seat of this game.

Note to self – Make him prove his loyalty.

A text from Kevin is waiting for me when I get back inside saying that he was sorry and that his battery died on his phone. I am beginning to smell a rat already. I text back saying it is fine and that I am just going to bed. His reply makes my nerve endings spark.

'I wish I was there.' There are three possibilities here.

1. His girlfriend fell asleep without giving him what he wanted.

2. He is playing with my emotions as he knows I fancy him and he is feeding his ego.

3. He really does mean it and if that's the case I wish he was here too.

Do I text that I wish he was here too or try and tease him as he does me.

'Really?'

'Really.' His reply comes straight back.

'What are you wearing xx.' My words we have jumped from nought to two kisses. I need to play this safe and go for one.

'I'm in bed x.'

'Yes I know, that's why I ask xx.' I feel as though I have the onset of the menopause as I start with the hot flushes. Surely the menopause won't start at full speed. My mind ponders whether to play the truth or tease card.

'Just a nightie x.'

'You ok for tomorrow night sweetie?' What? I read again the message. What is he on about? I then realise that Sally has texted me again. This is getting a bit confusing. By the time I have texted Sally back I am tired and have lost my willingness to tease. I don't know why she couldn't just speak to me at work. I just need to sleep now. Shaun texts saying he's thinking of me. I don't reply, instead I turn my phone off. Between them, Kevin, Shaun and Sally have completely tired me out.

Mornings have never been too much of a problem for me to get myself going. This morning however I feel more tired than I did before I went to bed. I dreamt about being stuck in a room with no door or windows and although the room was light I couldn't work out where the light was coming from. I couldn't get out nor could I work out how I got in there. I ran around in circles trying to find a weakness in the wall or a sign that there was a secret way out and then I woke up. I'm not one to analyse my dreams but imagine someone would say that it means I feel trapped in my life with no way of getting out of my situation and I'm constantly looking for a way. I would not agree with that. I feel more alive than I have done in years and I kind of like it. My phone beeps away several times when I turn it on and the notifications of texts flash on the screen. Two from Sally, one making sure I am going out tonight. I said I would therefore I will but I don't feel like I've had any time to myself and the second one is reminding me that she has news and that Dawn is going out too. There's never a dull moment when Dawn is out that's for sure and if I have to sit and listen to Sally's news which undoubtedly will be very Sally centred, it's best if someone else can share my burden. There're two texts from Shaun, one saying how good it was to see me and the other asking if he could come round again soon. I wonder if he is more careful to delete things from his phone now or if he learnt the lessons of affairs to delete everything. There'll be no naked pictures of me on his phone for her to find that's for sure. And then there are three texts from Kevin. One carries on from our conversation last night about me in my nightie but the moment has gone so it has no effect on me now. There was another sent an hour later asking if I was ignoring him, which I clearly wasn't as I was asleep and dreaming about being stuck in a room with no door.

I notice that I feel much happier and stronger than I have for a long time. Maybe I should completely break ties with Shaun and just get on with my life. Anyway, I have a day at work to do and a night with the girls to look forward to.

'Can I see you tomorrow night? xx' was the third text and I reply a quick 'yes' to Kevin before my morning shower. I'm not sure what's going on with me. I can't get a bloke for years and now I have three, although I didn't know Tony was gay at the time of dating him. After the usual checklist of shower, body cream, hair, walk Jasper, eat breakfast, it's off to work I go. I just love a good routine. As I arrive at work I am greeted by a rather excited Sally.

"I can't wait to tell you my news." I wonder why if she can't wait she just doesn't tell me now and she could save us a whole load of trouble and money in going out. Mind you it is Sally we're talking about and she never misses an opportunity to have a drama or a few drinks or even both as it seems it's going to be tonight. She has changed slightly and my tolerance of her has grown considerably as her self-importance seems to have reduced somewhat making her a much nicer person at the minute. I like this new Sally.

"I can't wait to hear it," I say through gritted teeth.

Chapter Thirty-Two

All morning my phone buzzed away in my bag. I wasn't particularly paying attention to it but I could hear it. I have a lot to get through so a quick glance to see who the calls and texts were from was all I managed to give it. All from Kevin. I suppose I like the attention from him, after all he is gorgeous but the other part of me keeps my feet on the ground as I recognise that I am the local pub football team to his Manchester United. The level of difference in the leagues between us isn't worth measuring. Just before lunchtime I text him back promising I will go on a date with him tomorrow night. God he's keen, I'll say that for him. As though he can read my mind when I am thinking what to wear he texts me asking if I think he would be overdoing it if he wore a suit. Oh I love a man in a suit. Shaun used to scrub up well on the odd times he would wear a suit. My mother used to call him James Bond when he wore one. He made out that he didn't like it when she did but secretly I think he fancied himself a bit. Maybe that would explain why he went off with Lucy, maybe I was looking a bit old and saggy for him. Mind you, I wouldn't take that as a compliment from my mother, after all she thinks Jeremy Clarkson is the most gorgeous man who ever walked the earth. Funnily enough Dawn agrees. For me it would have to be Carlos from Il Divo and by coincidence I note some similarities in looks between him and Kevin. I must pop into town and buy a new outfit for tomorrow to go with his suit.

"Where you off?"

"Hi, Sally, I'm err, just popping into town."

"Don't forget tonight. I've got some news remember."

"I won't." I'm sick of hearing about this news before I've actually heard what it is. If I had time I would text Dawn but I haven't. My phone rings again. It's Mum.

"Hi, Mum."

"I thought I'd better ring you because if I waited for you to ring me I'd be waiting until after I'm dead." Her sentence is very typical of my mother. It clearly does not make sense. She would not be waiting until after she died and if I'm being picky I wouldn't be ringing her after she had died anyway.

"How are you?" I wait as I know it is coming.

"Thought you'd forgotten about me again." There it is, she doesn't disappoint me.

"What are you going to do, Mother, fake your own death again?" I say it quietly not really wanting her to hear it.

"What's that, love, I do wish you'd speak clearly."

"I do speak clearly, Mother."

"Oh I can't hear you." The line goes dead. Not for the first time my mother puts the phone down on me. Do I care? Not today, I'm on a mission to find something nice for tomorrow.

The first dress I see is the one that I choose. It's a white floral kimono tunic type dress and I love it instantly, it's beautiful but casual. I try it on and it fits perfectly. It comes to about three inches above my knees which will make my legs visible and I think he will like it. Something else catches my eye on the way to the checkout and I feel that naughtiness coming over me again. I have not bought underwear with a bloke in mind for some time. Shaun used to like the high leg type and the ones which covered your bum, but I can't imagine that Lucy will wear anything less than the piece of string that the young ones wear these days. I saw a picture on his phone where she was posing in a thong. There was more material on a pencil than the thing that she was wearing. I can't understand how men can get turned on by one, especially Shaun as he has a thing for knickers, real knickers I mean, the sort that I have got in my hand right now. I just hope Kevin likes them if he gets the opportunity to see them and if not they're what I call sexy so at least I will like them.

I take my dress and knickers to the checkout where the young girl looks at me and then the knickers. If I could read her mind I bet she will be thinking that I'm too old for things like that and I should wear cotton pants to reflect my age. Well if she could have seen me last night getting ravaged by Shaun she would be surprised and maybe even impressed. I was pretty impressed myself. Well, I was more impressed with him.

"What?"

"Fifty-one pounds, madam."

"Oh sorry." I got caught up in my mind reading act then. God, if only she knew what I'd been thinking.

"Thank you." I smile, she smiles and I am on my way with the lovely dress and nice pants. He's a lucky man is Kevin and if he has got some cards I hope he plays them right because tomorrow night could be the start of something good, assuming his girlfriend doesn't find out. As if I could compete with her but he obviously thinks I can and all's fair in love and war. If someone had said that to me when Shaun went off with Lucy, I would have ripped their head off.

I show Sally the dress as she nearly rips the bag out of my hand, but find myself being a bit defensive when the knickers fall out.

"Ooo, look at the red silkies." I'm blushing, I know I am, it's burning through my cheeks.

"What? I just need some new ones." I am being slightly truthful, I just don't tell her the reason why I wanted new ones.

"What's he called?"

"Just because I buy a new pair of knickers does not mean that I have a new man. You're so shallow, Sally." The thing is that since I have known Sally I have only been with Shaun, I have not had any dates other than Tony which armed with my newly achieved intelligence, was not really a date, so I don't know why she thinks that. Maybe my face is easy to read. I put it down to Sally fishing for gossip and try and move the conversation on.

"What time are we meeting tonight?"

"Seven. This conversation is not over, Emmy." Maybe I will tell her but not until there is something to tell. The afternoon goes quick and a few further texts from Kevin keep me awake through a regular monthly meeting of policy and procedure changes. I feel like a party animal always going out, my social life is on overtime.

My conversation with my mother after work is rushed.

"Are you coming over tonight?"

"I can't, Mum. I'm going out with Sally and Dawn."

"Again? They see more of you than me."

"Don't be silly, Mum."

"Silly am I? Silly for wanting to see my daughter."

"I'll see you on Sunday, we'll go out for lunch." That's usually the clincher with Mum, she loves to go out for lunch.

"I might be err," she pauses. I know what she was about to say but daren't mention the dead word after last time. She changes the sentence. "I might be going out with Muriel."

"Well if you are that's fine I will pop and see you later." I am not as possessive as my mum is and am happy for her to do things, I just wish it went both ways.

"I thought I might go to fat club at the rugby club tomorrow, I think you should come with me."

"What? Are you saying I'm fat?" My mother, as usual, is full of compliments.

"Well you could lose a bit." I really have no answer for that and the words seem to struggle to be digested by my brain. I find myself grabbing hold of stomach with one hand whilst holding the phone with the other waiting for another comment to come. Then the knockout punch comes.

"You'll never find a boyfriend until you lose some weight."

Offended and upset I finish the call and stand naked in front of the mirror in my bedroom. Does a mirror lie? I think I look okay and other than the normal marks of childbirth and age there is nothing to suggest I am a little overweight. I pull my breasts up and let them go watching them fall back into place, they still have shape and do not anywhere near resemble dogs ears. I pull at my tummy, I breathe in and I breathe out and compare them both. I turn my back and look over my shoulder to see my bum. I think it all looks fine but I live with it, maybe I can't see what everyone else sees. I will ask Sally, she will tell me the truth and if I am fat she will say it. I purposely pick a skirt which clings to my bum and a top which hugs my stomach so that Sally can have a look. I am not as forward and confident as Sally who once stripped off in the toilet to show me a tattoo that she'd had on her bum. I'm not really into tattoos although some look nice on a man with muscles. Sally had dated a tattoo artist very briefly and he tattooed her bum with the word cheeky in italics saying he wanted to leave his mark on her. I thought it a very strange and possessive thing to do but she loved it. Until they split that is and she regretted letting him do it and take a picture of it which ended up on facebook. You couldn't see her face but you could see her whole bum. I suppose she should have been grateful that he didn't tag her in it but he sure left his mark. Jasper is getting depressed and I can only put it down to being left all the time. I love her but she gets a bit jealous when I go out without her. I always tell her 'Mummy's going to work.' I doubt she believes me now, even she is not stupid enough to believe that I go to work all the time unless she thinks I work by day and have a slightly less glamorous job on as night working the streets.

Sally and Dawn are already waiting at the bistro and Sally's comment that I look good relays all my concerns and I put the comments from my mother down to my mother just being my mother. I have no idea why she says things like that but I guess older people just become outspoken and offensive and I suppose at least it gives me something to look forward to in my old age. Sally's choice of food makes me think I should start being more careful in my choices as I am drawn straightaway to the burger section. My first choice of burger with Swiss cheese, jalapeños, peppers and salsa makes my mouth water but Sally shames me when she chooses a spinach salad with breadsticks so I go along with her choice. Dawn as usual doesn't care what others are having and goes straight for the herb crusted butter chicken with half rice and half chips.

"Have you had the spinach salad before?" I ask.

"No, but when you hear my news you'll know why I chose it." Oh the news: the real reason why we are all gathered here. I had forgotten, I suppose I have to play along.

"Oh what it is it? I can't wait to hear about it?" I lie of course but sound convincing. Dawn throws me a look and rolls her eyes, luckily Sally is watching me and enjoying my interest so misses it. As soon as she starts telling us the food arrives so the start gets postponed. I quite enjoy my forced second choice of spinach salad although I don't feel as full as I would have done with the burger. My mouth, however, waters at the sight of Dawn chomping on the chicken. My phone vibrates several times and I subtly read the messages from Kevin while the others eat. I can't sex text when I'm with company so my answers are very brief and straightforward.

"So I have to tell you," starts Sally. I have finished my food which cannot really be called a meal due to trading standards advertising rules, but Dawn is still throwing the remaining chips down her neck as though she has an allotted time to eat them in before they get taken back.

She swigs on her pint of lager to wash them down. Sally, who is the much more etiquette friendly of us, sips her wine. Yet again I choose to drive so sip my coke, albeit a diet one, because every bit helps in my quest to lose weight and make my mother proud of her slim daughter.

"Go on." I prompt because I am sure that she is stalling for dramatic reasons.

"Marcus and I are back together."

"Oh that's lovely," I say trying to rid myself of the tint of jealousy that's sneaked in without me realising until it was ready to come out. I know Sally has always thought herself a bit above others but going out with Moneybags Marcus makes her even more convinced of that as she can spend obscene amounts of money on things far too expensive for the likes of me. Yes I have my gemma-bags and nice clothes and more shoes than I care to think about but she has got the man as well. Not that Marcus is my sort of man but he is a man all the same. All I have is a few dates under my belt with a fat gay man who is lovely by the way and flirty texts from a man way out of my league, and my ex. Actually I quite like the flirty texts so I cannot complain; it would just be nice if someone said them to me rather than text them and then at least he could do something about it rather than leave it to my imagination and use of my own fingers.

"We had a long talk and decided to give it another go. He's taking me to Paris next weekend to make up for splitting up with me." There we go, she just has to drop things in doesn't she? I think I much prefer the single Sally. My phone buzzes. 'Can't wait for tomorrow xx.' Nor can I. I want it to come more than ever.

"I have to go soon; I'm having to get up at the crack of

Dawn tomorrow," I say. I am not lying, I have to walk Jasper, but the truth is I've just had enough of this conversation.

"Oo err, nobody's going up my crack in the morning." Dawn just makes me laugh, I love her. Always one to make a joke and make me laugh. Sometimes intentionally, sometimes not.

The rest of the night Dawn and I listen to Sally go on about what he said to her, where he will take her and what he will do to her, both sexual and non sexual. I had started to feel positive about myself but have the feeling now that life has built me up only to drop me down. I don't know why I am jealous as I have never been one to up cast things like her. On the journey home I can hear my phone buzzing like mad and when I think of having a bath and replying to Kevin's texts I start to feel excited again. Who needs trips to Paris when I can use my imagination to take myself to all sorts of places with a little help from Kevin and a few flirty texts.

Chapter Thirty-Three

Sally has constantly banged on about her and Marcus today. Normally at work I don't see a great deal of her but today it's like she's followed me around. Every time I've gone to the water machine she's there, every time I've gone to the kitchen, she's there, every time I've gone to the toilet she's been there shouting things under the cubicle door and I even decided to go for my lunch at a slightly later time and guess what? She's taken a later lunch too. Sometimes tales of people's sex lives can be quite entertaining and I've mentioned Mel and her body pictures stories and other things that people have chipped in with as part of those conversations but Sally seems to think I need to know every detail. I don't. I really don't. I do not need any ideas nor do I need to take inspiration on things to do. I am quite happy with a straightforward sex life with a few extra bits. I have to confess if I could have regular sex, something which I wasn't that bothered about when I was with Shaun, I'd be happy with that and lesson learnt, the next time I get into a proper relationship I will not ever say no to sex. I just hope that whoever the lucky man is he can fulfil my needs. I could jot down a few ideas from Shaun the other night but I think that would be a bit off putting if I tell him to do it to me like my ex did. I will just hope that I am lucky. Shaun has unlocked a beast inside me that wants sex. Flirty texts were something that I would never have taken part in before, in fact I would have found it quite disgusting but here I am having text sex with both Kevin and Shaun. I used to think that girls who talk about masturbating and using toys were just plain common but I have joined them, not that I use toys but I have joined the world of masturbation and have to admit I am getting quite good at it. I am happy that Sally has found Marcus again as she needs to be part of the social circle of rich people, it gives her others to compete with and compare with. She can't compare with Dawn and me as we don't have the attitude. We both have nice clothes and bags and furniture but neither of us would spend £10,000 decorating our living room. However, it is Sally and we accept her for how she is. Not sure where it came from because her family background was very basic and she is the only person who has achieved anything. Talking of achieving things, Beth has become the senior cabin crew member; I got a text off her in the middle of all the flirty ones last night. It brought me back to earth because I was enjoying the horny texts from Kevin and then the one from Beth kind of killed the moment but in a good way. I am so proud of her and can't wait to see her. My phone rings. I don't like answering it at work if I can help it but it's Mum so I think I'd better.

"Are you coming over tonight?"

"No I've got a date."

"With a man?"

"Of course with a man – who else would you think?"

"Well I don't know, you might have turned into one of them melons."

"Mother, the fruit you are thinking of is lemon and don't call lesbians lemons as it's offensive."

"Okay, stop being defensive, you can be whatever you want. I need you to come and look at my TV." I despair,

I really do. On so many levels my mother is just wrong.

"What's up with your TV?"

"Well if I knew that I wouldn't be ringing you, would I?"

"Well I've got plans so I don't really have time."

"Oh you get a date and forget about me. Well don't worry I'll sit here without a telly."

"Is it not working at all?"

"Yes it's working but there's something wrong with it."

"Well if it's working you won't be sat without it, will you?" I'm shouting but whispering at the same time. Is there no end to my talents?

"It's fine, you go and have your date, don't worry about me, I'm only your mother." There goes the guilt trip.

"I will call but I cannot stay."

"What about yoga?"

"What about yoga?" I throw back as a question.

"It's on tonight and you said you'd take me."

"I did not."

"Yes you did." My mother is so childlike sometimes.

"Mother." I always call her that when I mean something. It's my equivalent of a mother using the child's Sunday name when going into telling off mode, or my mother calling me Emily Jane. In fact thinking about it I know about four people called Emily (girl's of course) and every one of them has Jane as a middle name. Emily and Jane clearly go together.

"I did not say I would take you and I cannot take you. I will call in after work to sort out your working TV that isn't a working TV." She has a habit of mumbling so I can't hear what she says so I just say bye and end the call. I can feel my blood boiling. I don't know how she does it but she always manages to get it to boiling point. I take some time owing to finish earlier than normal and get to my mother's to sort out this bloody non-working working TV. After several reminders from Kevin about tonight I reach my mother's house only to find that she isn't in. I gave her my key back as she had a joiner going in to do some work so I end up sitting in the car on her drive getting angrier and angrier by the second. I make use of my time answering texts from both Kevin and Shaun. I text back slowly so as not to mix them up, I am obviously putting personal things in Shaun's texts that I cannot yet put in Kevin's. After twenty minutes my mum walks slowly up the drive.

"I didn't expect you."

"I told you I was coming after work."

"You must have finished early," she says checking her watch.

"I finished early so I could come here."

"Well you never told me, I wouldn't have gone out had I known." I cannot continue this pointless conversation and I will let nothing spoil tonight.

"Show me your TV," I say.

"Well you know what it looks like, dear." I swear to God I'm going to strangle her.

"What's wrong with it?" I turn it on and flick through the channels. The sound is good and the picture is clear.

"Here," she says flicking through the sky channels that Dad got installed. "That episode of Dallas is on there but then it's on again there," she says pointing to another channel.

"Yes," I say to confirm that it is indeed on again.

"Well I want the next episode, but that's the same one."

"The next one will be on tomorrow or next week." I flick through the schedule and search tomorrow and sure enough the next episode is on at the same time tomorrow.

"Yes, but they're doing it again tomorrow."

"Doing what again?"

"Playing the same episode."

"Where?" I ask.

"There." She points and sure enough the same episode is on.

"Mother, that is the plus one channel."

"The what channel?"

"The plus one. It plays the same thing an hour later."

"Well I want the next one."

"That's on tomorrow."

"Yes, but twice? Why do they put it on twice? I'm not senile. I can understand it first time round."

"It's not just for your benefit. If you came home late and missed it you could watch it at 8pm instead of 7pm."

"Well I won't be here at seven, I'm at line dancing."

"Exactly so you can watch it at eight."

"But it's on at seven."

"Yes but repeated an hour later on the plus one channel."

"Oh it's too technical for me."

"So you asked me to come here because Gold plus one plays the same programmes as Gold but an hour later?"

"Well I don't want it to." I give up. There is no reason

250

behind her thinking. I think it is in the title of the channel but it has quite obviously passed her by. I don't stay I have things to do and I need to get ready for my real date with a real and this time hopefully straight man. I get home slightly quicker than I would have done by sticking to the speed limit and jump straight in the shower. I have always wondered why we say we jump in the bath or shower as I have never jumped in either. I shower and lie on the towel on the bed drying off naturally. I wonder what Kevin would really think if he was standing over me now. Bearing in mind I am forty-nine, I think I look fairly okay but if he is used to looking at his girlfriend I wouldn't look fine to him. I guess some guys like older women, which he clearly does but there's still the chance that I am a challenge to him and I don't intend to make myself easy. If we end up in bed, it is because I want it to happen and not because I want to be the tick in the over 45s box. I put my new knickers on and they feel great, they're silky across my bum and make it feel tight. I look in the mirror and turn around so that I can see them from all angles. The embroidery on the front shows a flower design in a darker red which would only be appreciated close up and there are two teasing see through patches on the hip. I like them and as I touch them I can feel my body ping into life. I love feeling sexy, I love being a woman. I didn't get a matching bra but I have a relatively new one which matches it in part so I put that on. I think I look great to the point that it's a shame I have to cover up. I am no match for Lucy or Kevin's girlfriend but I would certainly turn someone's head dressed like this. Once my hair is straightened I put on my kimono style dress which fits perfectly over the top of my sexy underwear and I stand taking extra time to look at myself. Kevin texts telling me to meet him at Frankie & Benny's. I can't believe he would take me to the place where he works so I hope that's only a meeting place and he will be taking me somewhere else.

I arrive at Frankie & Benny's at the arranged time. Shaun has been texting asking if he can come and see me. I told him that I had a date and in reply to his following question it wasn't with the fat man. I think he was pissed off when he saw Tony because he still thinks of himself as a bit of a lady magnet, not sure why, and the fact that I was going out with Tony and not dropping him when he wanted to see me pissed him off. Well that's tough shit because I wasn't the one who left. Not only did he leave he destroyed my life and stamped all over my heart. I am in recovery now and am on the mend and no longer do I sit and feel sorry for myself. I am an attractive woman going on a date with Kevin, a younger man who's fit as anything. I sit in my car waiting to see him. I don't want to go in on my own as they all know him. I arrived five minutes early and now it is five past seven so I have been waiting ten minutes. A knock on my driver's window makes me jump and a noise to suit forces its way from my mouth. Kevin is there smiling. He has beautiful teeth.

"I didn't think you were coming," he says, offering his hand to help me out of my car.

"I wasn't sure whether to go in or not."

"I hope you don't mind coming here, you look absolutely gorgeous." He continued with the compliment so that I didn't have time to answer his question. Of course I don't mind going there to eat, but I would have just preferred not to go to his place of work. I will feel like I am in a gold fish bowl. They'll all be watching. He leans in to kiss my cheek. He smells nice. I'm not too bad at guessing aftershaves and this one I would guess is Jean Paul Gaultier La male, I make a note to ask him later. He opens the door and ushers me in – passing the stand where you wait to be seated. I noticed he quickly checked the book of reservations himself before guiding me to our table like the waiter that he is. I settle down onto the dark green bench seat that I have so often sat on before, the last few times to ogle him funnily enough, and there is nothing different about this time only he is closer, or he would be had he sat down with me. I can see him at the far end talking to one of the staff, a girl. Is this the sign of things to come?

Chapter Thirty-Four

As we sit down at the table I think I will get the awkward question out of the way as it is niggling me a little bit.

"Where is your girlfriend tonight?" His face loses its smile. A straight face looks back, slightly twisted at the eyebrows. He's thinking of an excuse, I can see it in his face.

"My girlfriend?"

"Your girlfriend. The girl that I've seen with you a few times. Really good looking, long dark hair."

"Oh, she's not my girlfriend, she's my sister. She's been visiting from Oxford, she's gone back home now."

"Oh, I thought she was your girlfriend."

"That's a job I'm saving for you." I blush. What a sweetie. He really is good looking and I have high hopes for this date.

"Are you all good looking in your family?" I feel nervous and try to lighten the mood.

"Yes," he says. I didn't expect such a forward reply. Maybe he's joking, so I laugh. He doesn't.

"How long has your sister been up for?"

"Just a week."

"What's she called?"

"Nicky."

"How old is she?"

"Twenty-nine."

"So is she older or younger than you?" I don't even know how old he is.

"She's younger."

"How old are you?"

"Thirty-three." Our age gap wouldn't be too bad.

"What about you?"

"I'm forty-nine." I wait for a compliment and it seems like he's realised that I'm waiting.

"You look fab, really fab." He stresses the word 'really'.

"Thank you."

A thought comes to me and it's something that I haven't ever thought before. Should I have trimmed? I really hadn't thought about what if it goes further. I push the thought out of my head. It would be wrong to sleep with someone on the first date, wouldn't it? Morally it would but how exciting would it be to get this stud in my bed after fancying him for so long.

"Back in a minute." He gets up and goes.

I sit alone watching him for what seems like an eternity, which in reality is probably a few minutes, but I feel forgotten about. I feel overdressed for Frankie & Benny's and almost cheated out of a date with us coming here. I think of the lovely place that Tony took me to, a dimly lit cosy and even romantic little place. I check my phone for the time but notice bizarrely enough Tony has texted. I feel a warmth wash over my body. I am fond of Tony and know that I have met a friend for life. His text said that he had accepted what he is and can move on with his life and that he was glad for my friendship. What a true gentleman, unlike this idiot. Fifteen minutes later he finally returns to the table but still sounds and acts like a waiter.

"Are you ready to order a drink?"

"Coke please," he disappears again returning a few

minutes later with a coke, and a pint of lager for himself.

"Are you working tonight?" I have to ask because I certainly have that impression.

"No. You look lovely by the way." He laughs at my suggestion of him working.

"Thank you. I bought this dress especially." I think of the effort that I have made for him even down to picking beautiful underwear which complements him in his black suit, white shirt and pink tie. I'm not into men wearing pink but he pulls it off perfectly. He is very good looking with his hair swept back into a quiff of a young Elvis Presley complimenting his brown eyes. If he was Italian his accent would have been seductive but in reality it's more Leeds than Lazio.

"Are you ready to order?" I wish he would switch off for one night. I choose New York chicken. He disappears. Again I see him talking to the other staff and also that girl again before returning. I like to know what other people order but because he rushed off I don't know.

"What have you ordered?"

"Sweet cured bacon steaks," he says kissing his thumb and index finger in a well rehearsed Italian waiter kind of way. He looks the part on that side of the table but he lacks quality on the dating side of it.

"I'm just going to pop to the toilet," I say getting up. I can see him eye me up and down. I'm glad because I love this dress and think it fits my body perfectly. The girl that he keeps speaking to passes me as I go towards the toilet. If looks could kill I would be dead for sure. She looks at me like I'd gone into her house on Christmas Day and pissed all over her presents. I smile and say hi but she completely ignores me. She obviously has her sights on him and views me as the enemy. Whatever happened to customer service.

Note to self – Complain to the manager about the miserable cow.

Just for my own information I check the concern that I have over the trimmed or not issue. I think it all looks fine down there so that is something less to worry about should things develop. The fact that the waitress looked at me like shit makes me want to sleep with him even more and take pictures to send to her on top of telling her in graphic detail what he has done to me. I check myself in the mirror to make sure the dress isn't tucked into my knickers and I'm ready to return. As I open the door from the toilets I see her walking away from our table.

"Who's she?" I ask.

"Danielle," he replies.

"Why is she giving me mucky looks, has something gone on between you two?" My phone beeps. It's Shaun. I ignore it.

"No," he says. He's lying, I can tell.

"I'll go and ask her then." I jump up.

"No, okay, I'll tell you." He pulls my hand and ushers me to sit back down.

"We had a fling at this lad's leaving do, that's all."

"When was that?"

"A couple of months ago. She wants to get together but I don't."

"Is this why you brought me here?" I will not be used by anyone, good looking or not.

"No, I didn't know she was working."

"Well, I actually thought you may have taken me somewhere better than the place where you work." I have lost the will to try and make this date a success so decide to speak my mind.

"I'm sorry, I don't have a lot of money and really wanted to take you out and I get it cheaper here with the discount. I do really like you, Emily." I'm not sure if I should take it as a compliment that he really likes me or as an insult that he feels that I am a cheap date. It's good that he assumes that he will be paying for me as that is what I would expect from a proper gentleman. However, I am more than happy to pay my way. This time my phone rings. It's Shaun.

"Sorry, I need to take this." I get up and go outside and answer the call.

"Hi, Shaun, what's up? I can't really speak, I'm on a date."

"Sorry, Em. I didn't want to disturb you that's why I texted first but you didn't reply." I can talk to Shaun whilst observing Kevin. I watch as he signals the girl over. They laugh together and it certainly doesn't look like the way he has portrayed things. I make a snap decision that I cannot trust him. My instincts are usually right. Kevin is a player. They touch each other on the arms and she is full of smiles. She flicks her hair and walks off and he watches her.

"Your mum rang me. She's not well. She wants me to go round because she said you're too busy. Is that okay with you?"

"She's being a bit of a drama queen, Shaun, if I'm honest, but if you want to go that's up to you, just don't play her games. Go see her but tell her you can't stay, she'll have you doing all sorts."

"Okay, I just wanted to check with you first." Are there are no depths that my mother won't sink to. I decide to ring her but she doesn't answer. She has a number display phone so she will be thinking it will add to the sense of urgency if she doesn't pick up.

"Is everything okay?"

"It's just my mother, she's not well; I'll have to go after we've eaten." I have no plans to take this man to my bed anymore. I observe the glances between him and Danielle and he is either stupid or so smitten with her he doesn't notice me seeing them. She then brings our food, putting his plate down gently whereas mine is almost slammed on the table.

"Enjoy your meal," she says quite clearly talking to him and not me.

"I think you two should get together."

"Why?"

"I have seen the way you look at her and she at you. There is more chemistry between you two than there is in the science lab at school." He smiles.

"She's not really my type."

"I think she's exactly your type, Kevin and I think you should stop using other people to make each other jealous and just sort yourselves out." I stand up.

"Where you going?"

"Thanks for a crap evening, Kevin. Please delete my number as I can't even say I'd like you as a friend." I leave him sat speechless. I think he is of the opinion that he can do whatever he wants as women will flock around him. I, however will not. I have more pride than letting myself be used as a toy in a game of which I am not a player. I feel in control. I commanded that and left him looking stupid. 1-0 to Emily. I head home and am greeted by the old faithful Jasper. I tell her all about it in the garden whilst she has a wee. The clear sky making the starts twinkle confirm that I did the right thing. No doubt Sally will want to know the full details and I will tell her the truth, no point dressing it up as anything other than a disaster. I make myself a cheese and pickle sandwich which is not as nice as the New York chicken which I ordered at Frankie & Benny's but as there is a possibility that my New York chicken contained hidden spit from Danielle's rather over the top lipsticked mouth I will enjoy my sandwich much more. Jasper stands close by tapping my leg with her head to remind me that she loves cheese and loves it even more when she gets thrown the odd bit from the ends. I stand over the television whilst flicking through the guide seeing what's on for me to watch. I laugh about the plus one channels and wonder if my mother was being serious or was it just a ploy to get me there. I wonder what she has Shaun doing for her, a series of pointless jobs whilst she tells him what a rubbish daughter I am. A couple of programmes catch my eye and along with the knowledge that there's a bottle of wine in the fridge, my night is sorted.

Kevin texts. 'Sorry for a crap night. Give me another chance and I'll prove it's you that I want.' I reply quickly. 'Which part of delete my number did you not understand?' and just to make sure the message gets across clearly I add to it. Get lost!'

Just as I am about to go upstairs, Shaun's car pulls up. I think I secretly expected it.

Chapter Thirty-Five

"Go on then, what did she want?" I ask as I open the door and leave it ajar for him to come in. He says nothing. "Shaun," I prompt again.

"Em, you look stunning."

"Thank you, now what did my mother want?"

"She was having a problem with that little heater, she said it wouldn't come on."

"And what was wrong with it?"

"She hadn't switched it on. It was plugged in and switched on at the wall but not on the little switch on the side."

"I think you were called under false pretences, she knows about that switch." I flick the kettle on and start to bring Shaun up to date on her over her newly acquired demanding ways."

"Yes, I know she's a bugger."

"What do you mean you know?"

"Err," he stutters. "I've actually been round to see her a few times, well quite regularly actually."

"Ah, I get it now, that's why she always defends you when we talk about you." I'm not sure if I am surprised really. If my dad was alive he wouldn't have kept in touch with him. Pushing aside the betrayal from my own mother I feel a bit stupid as though I've been kept in the dark and I now have in my head the thought of the two of them plotting behind my back. Luckily I haven't done a great deal since we split up because she would have told him everything anyway. Shaun and I are getting on better than we have done for a while and I guess my mother being happy is more important than anything else. She always liked him much more than Dad did, and I suppose that Dad would just have been protecting his daughter no matter who I was with. He wouldn't have liked Kevin but he would have liked Tony. Tony, apart from being gay is old school who would open doors for a lady and compliment her. Dad was just like that, always the gentleman.

"That dress is lovely, how long have you had it?"

"I bought it for my date tonight."

"Oh I'm sorry, have I ruined your date?"

"No it's fine, don't worry."

"How did it go?"

"Why do you want to know how my date went?"

"Just asking," he says shrugging his shoulders.

"I'm sure we can find other things to talk about. Where does Lucy think you are when you go to my mother's?"

"Touché," he says. I laugh. I know that by mentioning Lucy he will stop asking about me. I will not tell him the truth but I could certainly make it sound like I am in control of my own life.

"It was okay, he was nice." Shaun's head bows. I seize the opportunity. "Actually he was really fit. Thirty-three, Italian looking and really attractive." Shaun remains silent with head bowed. I continue.

"He's really keen and wants to see me again." Shaun looks gutted.

"I'm really pleased you've found someone, Em. You deserve it."

"Yes I do. Do you know how hard it is when the person you expect to spend the rest of your life with cheats on you?" He looks like a sad child with big puppy dog eyes.

"Em, if I could turn back time I would." I want so much to launch into Cher's song but I resist for fear it may lighten the moment. I need to hear this. "If I could undo what I did to you I would."

"Only because you got caught," I say. "If you hadn't been caught out you would still be going off to work and doing extra assignments just so you sleep with her and all your other models."

"Emily," he uses my Sunday name to emphasise his point. "I never slept with anyone else other than her."

"I—" He stops me.

"What I did to you is unforgivable and I cannot even begin to justify it. I lied and cheated and hurt you." He looks sincere and I can't help but listen to his words.

"You had pictures on your phone of her naked, Shaun. How can you expect me to believe it wasn't planned?"

"We were stale. There was no kissing and cuddling, I couldn't come close."

"All you ever wanted was sex. You never thought about taking me out or cooking for me." I remember my old attitude to sex and compare it to how I feel now. I feel sexually alive now, then I just couldn't be bothered. I know that I have to take some responsibility for how things turned out. I know Shaun would love to be with me now and my new found female seductiveness, mind you after the other day I think I'd like it too. Sex with Shaun feels natural and normal. He is the proverbial glove that fits so snug. The kettle clicks off and the noise from it boiling disappears into the previous minute. We stand in the kitchen together looking at each other but saying nothing. He continues to look at me.

"The date was not a good one." I need to break the awkward silence and can't think of anything else. My phone is on the work top and it buzzes making me jump. It's from Dawn. 'Just been on a date with the sergeant.' The smiley face I assume is confirmation that it went well.

We take our coffees to the living room and sit together on the sofa, he in one corner turned slightly to face me and I in the other corner turned slightly to face him. Jasper lies on the floor in the middle of us. I have never let Jasper purposely sit on the sofa although she does it when I go out I have no doubt of that because she doesn't have the inclination to remove the evidence before I get home. There was a time after he left me that I was glad of the company and would let her lie on my lap on a night just so that I could feel close to someone so I guess with the mixed messages that I have sent out she now just pleases herself.

"Why, what happened?" I laugh not knowing where to start.

"Let's just say he clarified the saying about looks not being everything."

"Well he's stupid, Em, because as I have learnt, he'll never find anyone better than you."

"You did," I reply.

"That's the whole point, Em, I messed up big time. Lucy isn't a patch on you." What a shame he had to throw away our marriage to find that out.

"Are things not going well?" I sense the answer anyway but the question is asked before I know it.

"Not really. It's not even about the sex. It's purely and simply I don't love her. I still love you." I don't know how to respond to that or even if it would be a good idea to respond at all. I still love him but I cannot forget what he did. I stand and lean across him to close the blinds. He laughs as I push my breasts into his face and feel almost cheated that he didn't attempt to touch them.

"That dress really is lovely, it makes your figure stand out." I unzip my dress and pull it off my shoulders peeling it down over my body like a skin and let it fall down onto the floor. His eyes light up at the sight of my seductive silky red knickers. He stands up.

"No touching," I say pushing him back, teasing him, "you just sit there." I turn on the TV and flick to the radio stations. Perfectly enough Meghan Trainor is singing and I mouth the words to him stating that I am going to love you like I'm gonna lose you. His face is wide, his eyes round and his mouth open transfixed on me. This is the attention that I crave, that I want and need. My pulse beats through the music to the depth of my body and I feel ready for him. I rub my hands up my tummy and despite the stretch marks that I call Beth marks he watches, loving it, wanting to join me in exploring my body inch by inch, but for now he has to sit, watch and be teased beyond the normal boundaries. He looks as though he will explode, yet I continue. I move closer to him so that his nose is nearly touching my burning flesh. I feel so in control of our sex life that I wish to god I had done it years ago. I am enjoying this just as much by teasing his whole existence. My bra straps fall down over my shoulders dangling half way down my arms making it easy to pull away. I push them close to his face then pull away before he can reach.

He tries to undress himself but I stop him. I am in

control and this will be on my terms. I let him have a quick touch as though tempting him but pull away when he tries to touch again. He is struggling to control himself but after what he did I believe he needs to learn self control. I will give him a night to remember, he will not leave my house and never think about this night. I will make sure this night is etched into his memories forever. I take his hand and lead him upstairs. I am glad I went to so much effort in my choice of clothes and knew that it would have the desired effect although at the time I didn't expect Shaun to be the one seeing the effort first hand; I rather expected it to be Kevin. Kevin wasted a perfect opportunity but I am sure that Shaun is more than happy to step in for him and to be honest so am I. If Kevin had been here I would probably have been more shy and embarrassed about doing this sort of thing but Shaun has seen me warts and all and I have no hesitation in dancing for him. I push him onto the bed and pull his jeans down slowly. He pulls me onto the bed and kisses me as though he is checking every inch is intact. Every single kiss is like an electric shock making the nerve endings jump into life. I touch him and can feel his heart beating in time with mine. Nothing is said, no words are needed, we do our talking in the best way possible that any couple can.

Light streams through the window waking us both up. We haven't moved at all and we wake up in the same position that we last remember having been in. He smiles and I return the smile.

"Morning, gorgeous," he says in the same way he did twenty years ago.

"Morning, handsome." He may not be the best looking

but he is Shaun and he's my Shaun.

"Emily, will you please take me back and give me an opportunity to make it up to you?" I think about Tony just beginning to find his way in life. I think of Sally and her rekindled romance with Moneybags Marcus, I think of Dawn finally becoming a sergeant and I think of Kevin the man who clearly isn't a patch on Shaun.

"Yes I will," I say, "and boy am I going to make you pay for it."

"I promise I will. I will never let you down again."

"Well you can start by packing your bags and getting away from her." He smiles.

"Already done, my bags are in the car. I left her days ago, she did my head in."

"Spent too much time playing with her Barbie dolls did she?" He now laughed where he would have defended her a few weeks ago.

"I am going to take you out tonight to celebrate. How about Frankie & Benny's, I know you like it there." I nearly choke on the morning air, of all the places for him to think of.

"Frankie & Benny's is perfect," I say.

Other books written by Andrew Milner

www.andrewmilnerbooks.com

Printed in Great Britain
by Amazon